EXPRESS WESTERNS presents

WHERE LEGENDS RIDE

Acclaim for our Authors:

David Whitehead:
"A dedicated Western writer . . . has a firm grasp on this genre . . . in these novels guns blaze, cowboys ride hard, and heroes still win with a measure of dignity and a code of honor. In truth, no one writes the Western series novel any better than David Whitehead!"
—Link Hullar, *Horizons West*

". . . A real corker. This is fine western action and adventure . . . certainly a treat for this western fan!"
—*Pulp Vault*

I.J. Parnham:
"I.J. Parnham's fast-paced story . . . won't fail to delight."
—*Booklist*

Gillian F. Taylor:
"Gillian Taylor's [writing is a] splendid evocation of the Old West . . . the denouement is fast and furious . . . plenty of action and character development. . . . "
—*The Portsmouth and District Post*

Lance Howard:
"Lance Howard is the Master of Westerns."
—*All About Murder Reviews*

"Howard's characters leap off the page. [They] possess interesting psychological depths."
—*The Portsmouth and District Post*

EXPRESS WESTERNS presents

WHERE LEGENDS RIDE

NEW TALES OF THE OLD WEST

EDITED BY

MATTHEW P. MAYO

EXPRESS WESTERNS

2007

www.expresswesterns.com

WHERE LEGENDS RIDE
Edited by Matthew P. Mayo
First Paperback Edition: November 2007

*Our special thanks to Robert Hale Ltd.,
publisher of the Black Horse Western series,
for keeping the spirit of the Old West alive.*

Publisher Ian Parnham
Co-edited by Nik Morton
Introduction by David Whitehead
Proofread by Gillian F. Taylor & Nik Morton
Express Westerns Logo by Nik Morton
Cover Painting by Stan Pitt
Cover Design & Back Cover Photograph by Jennifer Smith-Mayo

ISBN 978-0-6151-7581-2

Published by www.expresswesterns.com
An EXPRESS WESTERNS Publication

CONTENTS

INTRODUCTION
David Whitehead

With a few notable exceptions—no, let's make that a whole *fistful*—Western fiction has never truly received the respect and recognition it deserves, especially here in Britain. Its detractors, most of whom have never read a Western in their lives, of course, have always been quick to dismiss such fast-moving, action-packed tales as cliché-ridden "shoot-'em-ups," pulp literature of the very worst kind, and as such to be avoided at all costs.

Fortunately for those of us who know better, a number of publishers on both sides of the Atlantic remain justifiably proud of their Western lists. One such is London-based Robert Hale Limited, which regularly issues new titles every month under its "Black Horse Western" banner, and whose authors—or at least a goodly proportion of them—are showcased in the collection you are now about to read.

Hale first set up shop in 1936, and published its first Western the following year. By the 1960s the company was issuing five new Westerns every month, most of them written by a mere handful of prolific and, on the whole, pretty good writers: unsung heroes like Geoffrey John Barrett, David Bingley, Vic J. Hanson, Lauran Paine (the only American in the bunch), and Donald S. Rowland.

Between them, these men wrote close to 1,600 Westerns under something like 150 pseudonyms, from "Bart Adams" and "Rex Anders" to "Steve Yarbo" and "Roger Yorke," and though few, if any, of their books could ever be called classics, they were quite good.

For many years, Hale Westerns were issued in red cloth boards and dust jackets, but in the autumn of 1985, the line underwent something of a makeover. The dust jackets were replaced by brighter, laminated pictorial boards featuring truly fabulous artwork by such gifted artists as Prieto Muriana and the seemingly indefatigable Faba, and each new book now carried an eye-catching logo that proclaimed that this was indeed *A Black Horse Western*.

In January, 1986, the first batch of BHWs hit the shelves. They were *Rogue Mustang* by genre stalwart Max Brand, *Santa Fe* by the multiple award-winning Matt Braun, *Tumbleweed Twosome* by Jerome Gardener, *Buffalo Range* by Frank Koehler, *Texas Pay-Off* by Alvin

Ripley, *Reaching Colorado* by Frank Roderus (two-time Western Writers of America Spur Award-winner), and *Return of Amarillo* by Geoff Sadler, who would eventually go on to edit the prestigious second edition of *Twentieth-Century Western Writers* for St. James Press.

Over time, the formerly rigid writers' guidelines were relaxed, too, and Hale's stable of writers suddenly found themselves with an altogether freer rein. Once upon a time, the idea of cowboys trading shots with biplanes in the revolution-torn Mexico of 1913—and using a machine gun to do so—would have been unthinkable in the pages of a Hale Western. And yet when I wrote just such a scene in *Tanner's Guns* (1991), Hale's editors didn't even bat an eyelid.

So, what exactly *is* a Black Horse Western? Take a look at any new batch and you'll get your answer. They are cavalry stories and range-war stories, stories about lawmen and outlaws. They are gunfighter stories and stories based on real-life events, Westerns set aboard stagecoaches, riverboats, wagon-trains, and railroads. They feature bounty hunters, land-grabbers, gun runners, and Texas Rangers, and in style they range from traditional to modern and frequently an appealing mixture of the two. They may be series Westerns or stand-alones, and just like all the truly great stories, they deal with love and hate, jealousy, greed, honor, and revenge. And in that regard, the stories collected here—which, incidentally, have never appeared anywhere else—are no different. In short, there's something for everyone.

Despite what its critics may say to the contrary, the humble but oh-so-much-fun Western isn't ready for Boot Hill just yet. And the newer generation of writers represented here are determined to make sure it not only survives for a good long while to come, but that it also positively thrives.

BHWs are written, read, enjoyed and collected by aficionados all over the world, and if you're not already part of this big, happy family, then I hope you'll look upon the stories in this volume as the warmest of welcomes. I know for certain you'll enjoy them. *I* sure did.

—*David Whitehead*
Lowestoft, Suffolk,
United Kingdom
June, 2007

THE PRODIGAL
Chuck Tyrell

Born in a small town on the Great Colorado Plateau above the Mogollon Rim, Charles T. Whipple (writing as Chuck Tyrell) grew up on stories of the Hashknife Outfit, the Pleasant Valley War, Chief P'tone, and Geronimo. A student of Western history for decades, he brings the hardy people of early Arizona to life in his fiction.

Stomp Hale rode up to the RP Connected with a cloud on his face and fire in his eyes.

"Light and set, marshal," I called.

He grunted a mite as he heaved his thick body off the paint and wrapped her reins over the hitching rail. "Goldamn if you don't live a long way out, Ness Havelock."

"Come on in out of the sun," I said. "Probably scare up some coffee, if you're interested." I opened the front door and motioned Stomp in. My wife, Rita, met him halfway across the room, both hands extended. "Adam Hale. You've not been here for ages." She took Stomp's hands. "How are you, Adam? Tell me." Only Rita called Stomp by his given name.

Stomp got a half smile on his square face. "Come all the way out from Saint Johns for a cup of your fine coffee, Miz Havelock. I surely did."

"Then you sit right here at the table and I'll get you a cup." Rita led the sheriff to our walnut dining table and sat him in a high-back chair. "*Momentito*," she said, and disappeared into the kitchen.

Stomp turned his Stetson around in hard, weathered hands. He said nothing, so I let him sit. He'd talk when the time came.

Rita brought coffee and, sharp girl that she is, she could see something was bothering Stomp so she left the two of us to sort it out.

"Damn good coffee," Stomp said.

"That's what keeps me here," I said. "Good coffee and that good-looking woman."

"Was I you, I'd stick mighty close to this spread."

"Kenigan takes care of the spread," I said. "He's forgot more about raising cows than I'll ever know."

9

"Yeah, I reckon."

"Stomp?"

He looked at me.

"I got a feeling you didn't eat dust all the way from Saint Johns just to drink my wife's coffee."

Stomp's voice came out low and kinda hoarse. "Fargo stage got robbed out by Navajo Springs," he said.

I waited.

"Them owlhoots killed Denton Scrubb. Shot him right off the high seat when the stage started down into Lithodendron Wash. Got the shotgun rider, too. And that weren't enough, neither. Drummer from Albuquerque. Longtooth Alice from Crown King. Rusty Gaines, that young looie from Fort Apache. Lined up against the cut and shot dead. Damn." Stomp crumpled his Stetson in his big hands. "All dead. All robbed. And the stage's strongbox is gone."

"Mail?"

"And twenty thousand. Fletcher Comstock's payment to some outfit back east for machinery."

Stomp smoothed the crumples from his hat. "Ness. I'm asking you a favor. Ride with me."

I'd ridden with Stomp Hale before. When he was town marshal at Grant's Crossing and me close to heading down the wrong side of the Outlaw Trail. I rode into Grant's Crossing on a long-legged roan, me not yet twenty years old. I'd come south from Moab, stopping in Mexican Hat before the long, dry stretch to Navajo Springs. Dust lay thick in my throat and I had a mind to cut it with a swig of good rye whiskey, and Bartley's was the only place in Grant's Crossing where I could do that.

I got a bottle of Turley's Mill and a cloudy glass and settled in at a corner table. I'd just tossed back the first shot when Farley Dodd pushed his way through the batwings with three of his dirty boys at his back. Some said Dodd was a hard man, but I'd yet to see any of his graveyards. Still, I could see he had a head of steam on and his men scattered around the room to watch his back.

Dodd stood smack in the middle of the room and faced the bar. "Shig," he said to the bartender. "Could be you ought to stand at the south end."

Shig scuttled to the end of the bar.

"Now, I was telling you men," he said to the strongarms, "it's no good to get your six-gun out fast if you miss what you're shooting at. Observe." His hand swept to the handle of the pistol in his waistband. As he drew it, he cocked the hammer, then ticked off the trigger as the gun came level. A bottle standing amongst its fellows behind the bar exploded. Dodd returned the pistol to his waistband and repeated the maneuver, taking out the next bottle in the line. He did it again. And again.

Dodd's men weren't watching him at all. They kept their eyes on the batwing doors and their hands on the butts of their guns. Beneath the table, I eased my .44 from its holster and let it lay in my lap. Another bottle crashed with the sound of Dodd's Colt, then the sound of boots on the boardwalk outside. Dodd's face held a tight smile. His men eased their hardware like they expected trouble.

The footsteps went on by.

Dodd killed another bottle.

Stomp Hale stepped through the back door. "That'll be enough, Dodd," he said. His soft voice held a hard edge and his hands held a ten-gauge Greener.

I put my .44 on the table and cocked it. "I'm with the marshal," I said. My gun pointed at the man in the corner. Stomp's shotgun hung in the crook of his elbow, and his six-gun was stuffed in a holster that rode high behind his right hip. His eyes flicked to me for an instant, and he gave a little nod, as if to recognize my presence.

"Let's go," Stomp said to Dodd. "Your strongarms ain't gonna do you no good. The kid's got a gun on them. And you've destroyed enough property to have to spend a little time behind bars."

Dodd's head came up. "I'll pay for the damage. I always do."

"One time too many, Dodd. Come on." Stomp held out his hand for Dodd's pistol. I kept my eyes on the others with my cocked gun pointed at the dark man in the far corner.

Farley Dodd stayed behind bars in the marshal's office of Grant's Crossing for ten days. And Stomp Hale invited me to deputy for him. "Don't pay much," he said. "Six bits a day and found. You'd make more riding the line, but I like the way you hold yourself."

I took the deputy badge from Stomp and wore it for nearly a year. And all that I learned working with that straight man kept me on the right side of the Trail.

"You was the best deputy I ever had, Ness, and this time I'm gonna need more than the ordinary posseman to do the job." Stomp gulped at his coffee. "That bunch what robbed that Fargo and killed them people ain't gonna get away with it. Mark my word. Will you ride with me?"

"I'll ride," I said.

He handed me a badge, a star in a shield, embossed with the words DEPUTY U.S. MARSHAL. "Been a long time since Grant's Crossing," he said, "but making off with the stage's strongbox makes that crime a federal one. So I got jurisdiction. We'll ride them down."

After Grant's Crossing, Stomp spent a term as sheriff of Apache County, then lost to C.P. Owens. Wasn't two weeks before he was wearing a U.S. marshal's badge. J.T. Carr saw to getting Stomp that federal badge, I heard. "How long you figure to chase these owlhoots, Stomp?"

"A day. A week. A year. We'll go 'til we catch 'em."

"You sit. Have another cup of coffee. I'll rustle my stuff together and we'll ride."

Stomp nodded. He just sat there, staring into that empty coffee cup.

"Honey," I said to Rita on the way through the kitchen, "pour Stomp another cup of coffee, would you please? And have Snuffy Dagan put together vittles for five days, bedroll and slicker, too. I'll talk to Kenigan."

Rita flashed me a look with those dark Spanish eyes of hers, but she didn't balk.

I found Kenigan Zane at the calf pens helping an orphan calf bond to another mother so we wouldn't have to raise him by hand.

"The white face cows look good, Kenigan," I said.

He nodded but kept his attention on the calf.

"Stomp Hale come to ask me to ride with him for a bit. I'd be obliged if you'd watch the RP Connected while I'm gone."

He nodded again.

"May be gone a while."

"RP Connected'll be here when you get back, Ness. I'll see to it."

"I know that, Kenigan. And I appreciate it. I'll ask Rita if she wants to go over to Rancho Pilar while I'm gone, but I imagine she'll stay right here. She's that way."

"I reckon. But that's no problem. She carries her weight and she cooks almost as good as Snuffy." Kenigan grinned.

I turned to go.

"Boss?"

"Yeah."

"I know you're a hard man and better than most with that .44, but you take care. Anyone Marshal Hale's chasing's bound to want to fight it out rather than hang. *Quidarse*, as the missus would say."

I smiled. "Yeah. I'll be careful. Thanks, Kenigan."

He was already striding toward the barn. I was lucky to have the best foreman in Arizona, just as good as Dan Travis, topkick for my brother Gareth at the H Cross.

Stomp and I rode away from the RP Connected long before the sun reached zenith, me on my tough lineback dun and Stomp on a three-color paint. I had five days grub and my soogans behind the cantle and two boxes of .44 cartridges and an extra Colt in my saddlebags. "You riding that paint horse, I can see we're not going to sneak up on those owlhoots," I said.

Stomp ignored my jibe. "Sign said there was five in the gang," he said. "One leaking blood. They struck out down the country. I figure they'll go to Mogollon, then jag over to the Coronado Trail and head for Mexico."

"Going to Mogollon, it's easiest to ride around the far side of the Little Colorado, but it's quickest to go over the divide and down through Frisco."

"Speed ain't all that important right yet. Let's save the horses and go around."

We set a course for Escudilla Mountain and crossed the Little Colorado beyond Seven Mile where it wasn't much more than a healthy creek. The land settled down on a plateau that skirted the Blues and turned into the foothills of Escudilla. When we could, we let our horses out into a long lope that ate ground without costing the cayuses too much energy. On the upgrades, the horses walked and we talked. Well, I talked. Seemed Stomp had other things on his mind.

"You figure them that jumped the stage are going south, then? How bad's the one hit?" We were coming off the flanks of Escudilla and a haze from the hearth fires of Mogollon obscured the flats. The uphill breeze brought a whiff of wood smoke with it, and I imagined the muddy smell of strong coffee.

Stomp reined in his paint on a rise overlooking the town. "Yeah. Not much blood sign. But he's hurting."

"Five, you say?"

He turned a tortured face to me. "Ness. I couldn't say it back at the RP Connected. But I know who we're looking for. Ty Sinclair, Kid McGee, Frenchy Destain, the man they call the Breed . . . and my son, Nate Hale."

Me being half Cherokee, I didn't much like the word breed, and if there was one thing Stomp Hale regretted about spending his life upholding the law, it was Nate. Stomp wasn't home much, and the boy had only gentle Martha Hale to show him the right and wrong of things. He loved his ma, and hated his pa. And Stomp, knowing that he wasn't around to guide the boy most of the time, gave him more leeway than he might have otherwise. Now Martha was dead and Nate was running wild.

I took a deep breath. "Nate, eh? Somehow it doesn't surprise me. He's been looking after trouble since he was a little tyke, and now he's pushed being the prodigal a little too far. That's what I'd say."

"Gotta bring him in. Ain't no other way." Stomp clamped his mouth shut and started the paint down the hill toward Mogollon.

The town showed signs of sudden growth. A new street led off the main drag that ran north and south along Mineral Creek. A new whitewashed sign stood at the outskirts. "Welcome to Alma," it read. I looked at Stomp. "When'd Mogollon turn into Alma?"

He shrugged, and turned the paint down main in the deepening dusk. Sounds of a piano trickled up the street, telling us a saloon lay in that direction. Windows blazed with light at the intersection. A sign shaped like a Rhode Island Red hung like a lawyer's shingle. 'Red Hen—Fine Food.' The savory smells coming from the restaurant backed its claim. I couldn't help but smile. "Whoa up, Dun," I said to the lineback. "Time for coffee," I said to Stomp. "And maybe some apple pie."

When the sun goes down in high country, things cool quick. Inside the Red Hen, coal oil lamps on a wagon wheel suspended from the rafters spread warm light to every corner of the room. Eight tables hosted four straight-backed chairs each, and only one table was empty. Two cowboys and a rancher. Some miners. And a well-dressed woman in a plumed hat. Me and Stomp took the last table, although it wasn't in a corner where I like to sit.

A girl came from the kitchen with two plates of roast beef, potatoes, and gravy on her left arm and a gallon coffee pot swinging by its bail from her right fist. "You come back the minute you get that food to Doc Smithson's place, you hear?" A portly woman in a stained apron saw the girl off from the kitchen door. "They's too many customers here for you to be lollygagging around."

Stomp and I exchanged a look. "Order me apple pie, Stomp. I won't be long. I left the makings in my saddlebag." I wasn't a smoker, but that gave me a reason to step outside and watch the girl. She hightailed it across the street, balancing those plates as easy as you please. I followed just close enough to see when she went in a small frame house with a white picket fence around it. I was at my table in the Red Hen by the time the girl got back.

"More coffee?" The girl stood by our table with a coffee pot in her hand.

Stomp shoved his cup at her. "See the town's got a new name," he said.

"Captain Birney bought most of the land in town," she said. "He changed the name to Alma in remembrance of his mother, they say."

"Nice thing to do," Stomp said. "Family's all there is, come right down to it. Thanks for the coffee."

Gradually, the other customers finished and left. Stomp hunched over his coffee. "What say we pay a visit to the doc," he said quietly. He plonked a cartwheel on the table and shoved his chair back. "No telling what we'll come up with."

The girl came out to clear the table. I lifted my hat to her. "Ma'am, I'm Ness Havelock from over Saint Johns way. That was mighty fine pie."

She dimpled. "Ruby bakes the pies," she said. "I'll tell her what you said."

"Come on, Ness," Stomp called from the door.

I tipped my hat again and followed Stomp outside. The sun had long since set behind Escudilla Mountain, but wagons still moved on Alma's main street. A half-dozen horses stood hipshot at the hitching rail in front of the saloon three doors south. The tinkle of the piano was a little louder than before. Stomp set his hat on his head four square. "Where's the doc's place?"

"Just over the way." I stepped off the boardwalk and walked through the powder dust of that New Mexico street with Stomp Hale at my side. I stopped at the picket fence gate to let Stomp go first. He was the marshal. A small sign to the left of the window read, 'Walter Smithson, M.D.' Stomp knocked.

The man who came to the door stood taller than either Stomp or me, and he had a serious look in his gray eyes. "How can I help you, gentlemen?"

Stomp showed his badge. "Name's Hale. U.S. Marshal," he said. "We come from over by Navajo Springs where owlhoots robbed the Fargo stage. Killed everyone. Sign said one of them outlaws took lead. And we heard you've got a boarder. If you don't mind, we'd like to talk to your guest."

"Come in, gentlemen." The doc stepped back. "But be quiet, please. The youngster in the bedroom is near death. Peritonitis. He's been shot in the abdomen."

"Is he awake?"

The doctor shook his head. "I've sedated him with laudanum. It allows him to sleep through the pain."

"Know his name?"

"Those who brought him to me called him Kid."

"Kid McGee."

The doctor shrugged.

"Mind if I look at him?" Stomp asked.

"This way." The doc led the way to a bedroom door. "Only for a moment," he said, and opened the door.

Stomp can walk quiet for a big man, and he catfooted right up to that bed and stared down at the youngster sleeping there. After a moment he nodded and came out of the bedroom. "Kid McGee all right. How long's he got?"

"A day," the doctor said. "A week. It's hard to be sure."

"Hope you don't mind me being curious, Doc," I said. "But that boy's in no condition to eat. Why'd the Red Hen send two dinners over here?"

"Oh, they do that every day," he said. "My wife, bless her heart, is a nurse by training and her cooking leaves much to be desired. We much prefer to partake of hearty fare from the Red Hen. Why?"

I smiled. "No offense meant," I said.

Stomp took the conversation right back to the point. "Tell me, Doc. Did those what come with the Kid say anything about where they was headed?"

The doctor shook his head. "Not that I heard. One of them, a tall young man with dark curly hair, gave me two double eagles. 'Take care of the Kid, Doc,' he said. 'He promised to have a drink with us at the King's Palace.' That's all I heard."

The doctor saw us to the door.

Stomp jammed his hat back on his head, four square. "Thanks just the same, Doc. Sorry to bother you."

"Good night, gentlemen." He closed the door.

Stomp said nothing as we walked. Then, "The curly haired one. That's got to be Nate. Always did stand by his friends." It sounded like he was talking to himself.

"Stomp?"

"Guess we hit the Coronado Trail," he said.

"Stomp?"

"What?"

"You ever heard of the King's Palace?"

"No. Why?"

"It's King Fisher's place in El Paso. You ask me, those yahoos are crossing the *mal pais*. Short cut to Mexico."

Stomp heaved a sigh. "Time's come to ride hard, Ness. Let's go."

We stopped at the livery stable long enough to get two more horses on U.S. government vouchers, a long-legged bay and a hefty dappled sorrel. We trailed our own horses behind us and rode the fresh mounts. Without even stopping at the Red Hen for supper, we hit the trail south, heading into the *mal pais* badlands.

The way through the badlands is a chancy thing. There's water if you know where to look, and lava bubbles that can swallow you whole, if

17

your horse steps in the wrong place. The moon was out so we could see. We loped the horses when we could, kept them in a single-foot when we couldn't. Stomp was dead set on catching up with Nate's gang before they made El Paso.

At dawn, we stopped long enough to switch saddles, me to my dun and Stomp back to the paint. Then we brewed coffee over a hatful of fire, drank it down, killed the flames with the dregs, and rode on.

We found their first mistake in the early afternoon. A lava dome sloped in toward the trail, overlapping it by several feet. But instead of solid footing, a jagged hole gaped. I pulled up the dun and left him ground tied, the lead rope to the bay dallied around the saddle horn. I didn't dare walk out on the dome, so I got down on my hands and knees, and finally I bellied my way to the edge of the hole and looked in.

"Horse dead, Stomp," I said. "Looks like he got busted up in the fall and they put him down."

I scrambled back to the lineback for my lariat. I jerked the saddle off his back and left it on the ground, the bay tied to it. Choosing the thickest edge, I laid my saddle blanket over the lava to protect the lariat and hitched the rope around my waist with a bowline.

"Lower me easy, Stomp," I said, handing him the other end of the rope. "I want a look at that horse."

Down in the lava tube, I could see the horse had broken a front leg and cut his flank badly. I laid a hand on his hide. Cool. Grabbed a foreleg. It bent at the knee. I walked back to the edge. "You can haul me up, Stomp," I hollered.

He did.

"The cayuse's cool to the touch but not stiff yet," I said. "And now someone's riding double. No telling if the rider got hurt, either." I gave Stomp a hard look. "Think they know we're on their back trail?"

"Sooner or later, they'll know."

"They gonna hole up and bushwhack us?"

"May try."

"Damn."

"Saddle up," Stomp said. "Let's ride."

Evening saw us under an overhang in a lava rock canyon cooking bacon and saleratus biscuits over a bitty little fire. The horses had their noses in gunny sack nosebags chomping on the last of their oat ration. The only water we had was in our canteens.

"Still a far sight to the Rio Grande," Stomp said. "Any water twixt here and there?"

"Some. If you know where to look. Closest is Eagle Nest tanks. Twenty miles, I'd say."

"Make it by morning?" Stomp folded some bacon in a biscuit and shoved it in his mouth.

"More likely by noon. Still got some almighty rough country to cross." I joined him in chewing on biscuit and bacon. Tasted right good. Washed down with a swig of canteen water.

Stomp rummaged around in his saddlebags and came up with a sack of cartridges. "Think I'll take a couple of minutes with the short gun," he said, and walked away from the fire. I heard him fire and reload his .44 five times. A man needs to practice to keep his shots accurate. And Stomp Hale was nothing if not accurate.

"Get yourself forty winks," Stomp said as he sat down to clean his Colt. "I'll wake you when the moon comes up. We'll leave then."

I'd no more than shut my eyes than Stomp was shaking me. A full moon showed over the edge of the canyon. We saddled the livery horses and hit the trail, riding at a steady pace until a bullet stopped us about an hour after sunrise.

With the report of the rifle Stomp went off the sorrel like he'd been shot. But the way he rolled for cover said no bullet had found him. I slipped off the bay, stripping my .44-40 from its scabbard as I went. A bullet ate a piece off the rock I ducked behind. The bay and my lineback dun hightailed it back down the trail with Stomp's horses in close pursuit. After a minute, I let out a whistle. If I was lucky, the dun would hear me and stop.

"Stomp."

He turned, and I tossed my Winchester to him. "Keep that shooter busy," I said and backed down the trail after the horses. I was lucky. The dun stood by a cluster of rocks looking at me, the other horses nearby. The Winchester crashed and a bullet whined away up the canyon. Stomp provided the cover I'd asked for. I dug a pair of moccasins from my saddlebags, ditched my hat, and tied a brown bandana around my head. Growing up in the Indian Nations with a Texas Ranger pa and a Cherokee ma gave me more than a little chance to learn how to injun around. If that shooter was kept occupied, he'd soon find my Colt against the back of his neck.

I pulled my .44 from its holster and checked the loads and the action. I added a sixth cartridge to the cylinder, replaced the gun, and pulled the loop over the hammer to hold the Colt secure in its place.

Suddenly more Cherokee than white man, I made my way up the side of the hill. Every once in a while, Stomp would let loose with the Winchester to help the shooter on the canyon side keep focused down hill. I topped out a good quarter of a mile north of whoever was shooting at us and catfooted along the rim, keeping back far enough so I wouldn't be skylined.

I found the man settled down in a nest of boulders, and I injuned up behind him on my quiet moccasins. Took me nigh half an hour to go the last few feet, but finally I was where I could almost reach out and touch him.

"Reckon you'd better lay down the rifle and raise up your hands," I said, and cocked my .44 for emphasis. The shooter froze. I laid the muzzle of my Colt against his neck and plucked the pistol from the *buscadero* rig on his hip. "Let go the rifle," I told him. "It's all over."

He did, and I gathered up the long gun. "Stomp!" I hollered. "We're coming down." I prodded the shooter with my Colt, "Now, if you'll just clasp your hands back of your neck, we'll go down and talk to the marshal."

We had Frenchy Destain tied to the livery bay, and faced three men down the trail. They'd hit us when we least expected it, Frenchy said, and then be free to head into Mexico. "Killing you two won't mean much," he said. "We already done in them on the stage. Made us a haul, too. More money'n you ever saw." The Frenchman couldn't help bragging a bit.

Stomp rode his paint out front with the sorrel on a lead, sitting his saddle like he wore his hat, four square. I came up behind and Frenchy brought up the rear, not wanting to realize that his ride was a one-way trip to a hanging noose.

We rode with rifles across our saddle bows and restless eyes scanning the countryside. Scrub oak and *piñons* eked out a hardscrabble living among the rocks and a single red-tailed hawk soared above the canyon walls. Any other time the beauty would have been breathtaking. Right now a body wondered where the next bullet would come from.

When it came the bullet only made a spurt of dust in the trail ahead of Stomp's paint. A puff of smoke marked the shooter's position. I piled off the far side of my lineback. He was a good horse, but I wanted him stopping any bullets, not me. Stomp just sat there, rifle in his hands.

"Pa?"

"I hear you, son. Put that rifle down and come on in. Don't make me have to come and get you."

"You can't do it, Pa. We got you dead to rights. If you want to live, let Frenchy go, throw your hardware on the ground, and back off down the trail."

"Guess that shows you who's boss, old man," Frenchy sneered.

"Pa? You hear me? Throw down the guns!"

Stomp heaved a sigh, then tossed his saddle gun off to the side of the trail. "Ness," he said. I knew what he meant. I tossed my rifle and Colt over next to his guns.

"Don't forget Frenchy's gun," Nate called. Stomp threw it out.

"Okay. Back off."

Stomp backed the paint. I led the lineback. We stopped where we could still see the guns, and waited.

Frenchy let out a shout. "Come on, Nate. I'm tied to this goddamn saddle."

Stomp climbed off the paint. "Give me that Colt in your saddle bag, Ness." He spoke just above a whisper.

"Now Stomp. There's four of them and only one of you."

"That's my son out there. Give me the gun!"

I handed Stomp the .44.

"Cartridges." He held his hand out.

I broke open a box of .44s and gave him a handful.

The outlaws must have tied their horses some distance away, because they came for the guns on foot. They'd gathered the firearms up, laughing like they didn't have a care in the world. Stomp loaded the empty cylinder in the .44 and, holding the six-gun alongside his leg, he started walking up the trail. Nate and his boys didn't seem to notice.

"Nathaniel Hale, you put those guns aside and give yourself up!" Stomp roared. "You done wrong and you gotta pay."

The dark man they call Breed got off the first shot. The bullet kicked up dust a good ten feet in front of Stomp. He calmly raised the .44 and fired it as his right foot came down. The Breed flung his arms wide and crumpled.

Frenchy dived for his gun, which still lay on the ground where Stomp had thrown it. Both Nate and Ty Sinclair fired at Stomp at the same time. But it's a hard thing to do, hit a moving target with a short gun, takes a heap of practice.

Stomp kept marching straight at them. "Nate, don't make me shoot you," he called.

Nate laughed and triggered off another round.

Stomp staggered. Then kept on walking. He raised the .44 again, triggering it as his right foot hit the ground. The bullet hit the hard pan six inches in front of Frenchy Destain's nose and ricocheted up to tear a jagged chunk from his forehead. Frenchy slumped and lay still. Stomp kept walking, but a dark stain showed along his left side.

Sinclair fired. Nate fired. Stomp went down. But the .44 came up, roared, and Ty Sinclair collapsed like a poleaxed steer.

Stomp struggled to his feet. "Let go the gun, son," he said.

Nate shook his head. "No, Pa. I can't let you take me back." He thumbed back the hammer of his six-gun and shot Stomp dead center.

Stomp fell backwards, spreadeagled across the trail.

Slowly, Nate walked over to look down at his father's face. "Never was any way I could please you, Pa. No way at all."

Stomp's big left hand moved, lifted, and grabbed a hold on Nate's trouser leg. "Stop it now, Nate. Or you'll be running all your life."

"You're dead, old man, and just don't know it." Nate kicked his leg free.

The .44 in Stomp's right hand seemed to rise of its own accord. It fired up into Nate's body, then fell away into the dirt of the trail.

"Oh shit oh shit oh shit." Nate dropped to his knees then slowly toppled over, his body falling across his father's legs.

I carried Stomp Hale and his son home so they could lie next to Martha at Grant's Crossing. Fletcher Comstock's money I turned over to Sheriff Owens in Saint Johns, but I kept the badges. Two weeks after we buried Stomp, U.S. Marshal M.K. Meade rode up to the house at the RP Connected.

"Heard about Stomp Hale and his boy," Meade said over coffee.

"Not happy that all I could do was watch."

"Stomp was a good lawman, Havelock. It was him who always said there's no way to stop a man who knows he's in the right and just keeps on moving."

I went to the roll-top desk in the corner and from one of the pigeon holes I pulled the badges me and Stomp had worn. "Marshal Meade," I said. "You'll be wanting these." I held out the badges on the palm of my hand.

Meade took them and slipped the deputy badge into a vest pocket. The marshal's badge he juggled in his hand. "This is a growing country, Ness. And it needs good men to keep it headed in the right direction. What do you say? Why not make Stomp proud and wear this badge for him? We need a good marshal in northern Arizona and I figure you fit the bill."

Rita came in with a plate of donuts. "Marshal Meade, Snuffy Dugan, our cook, makes the best bear sign in Apache County. Would you like some?"

The marshal's smile was answer enough.

"Honey," I said. "Marshal Meade wants me to wear Stomp's badge. What do you think?"

She looked me straight in the eye. "Johannes Havelock," she said, "as always, you'll do what's right."

EASIER THAN WORKING
Gillian F. Taylor

Gillian F. Taylor grew up in Norfolk, England, playing with cowboy toys. She moved to Sheffield to attend university, and stayed there to be a writer. Her latest Black Horse Western, Two-Gun Trouble, *is her eleventh book. She lives with two cats and an ever-expanding collection of pony books. Visit her online at: www.gillian-f-taylor.co.uk.*

"In a cavern, in a canyon, excavating for a mine, dwelt a miner, forty-niner, and his daughter, Clementine."

Tomcat Billy's pleasant tenor was joined for the chorus by Irish's tuneless baritone.

"Oh my darling, oh my darling, oh my darling Clementine. Thou are lost and gone forever. Dreadful sorry, Clementine."

More than once, Irish had said of himself, "Sure an' I can't carry a tune in a bucket." But out here on the Nebraska prairie there was no one but the wildlife and his friend to hear him. Tomcat grinned at him, enjoying the fun of singing together without worrying about the quality of the singing. As their horses jogged through the stirrup-high grasses, they completed the rest of the song.

The horses slowed to a walk as they headed to the top of one of the rolling crests of the prairie. Tomcat gazed out at the swaying sea of grass and wildflowers, feeling the warmth of the sun on his wiry body.

"This sure beats working for a living, don't it?" he drawled, in his thick Tennessee accent.

Irish chuckled. "Elliot might be a humorless bastard, but sure an' he's got some brains." He reached behind his saddle and patted one of the full saddlebags with his massive hand. The bag made a muffled chinking sound. "Eight hundred dollars each!"

"Setting a lil' fire under the floor of the bank so's folks'd think the place was burning was real smart," Tomcat agreed. "They all done run out, and we snuck in and took the money. Never even had to point a gun at no one."

"And we ain't seen a trace of pursuit since we left Lincoln," Irish said. "I wonder how Black Elliott and Joe be getting on?"

Tomcat snorted. "I don't care too hard about them, 'specially Curley Joe. He's too damn quick tempered." He shook his head, dismissing thoughts of their partners-in-crime. "Now, I wonder what the women in Laramie are like?" he said, his green eyes sparkling.

"Same as the women in any other cowtown," Irish replied.

Tomcat nodded at this wisdom. "You're surely right, pal. But they ain't had the pleasure of my company yet." He thought for a moment, then his face brightened. "Say! With eight hundred dollars each, we could really get to someplace new. Once we've done some celebrating in Laramie, how about getting on the train and going to someplace like . . . San Francisco!"

Irish stared at him, taken aback by such a grand idea. "I never saw the ocean," he said.

"They say California's hot even in the winter," Tomcat said, alive with enthusiasm.

Irish was much bigger than short, wiry Tomcat, less quick in his movements and with ideas. His deliberation balanced Tomcat's impulsiveness, while Tomcat's energy led Irish in directions he'd never consider on his own. Tomcat didn't plead his idea, but waited for Irish to consider it at his own pace.

"I'd like to see the ocean," Irish said decidedly.

"Then by hell and highwater, we'll do it!" Tomcat exclaimed.

They reached the top of the slope and reined in to let their horses rest, gazing over the new landscape revealed below. The open prairie stretched out to the horizon, now fading from green into its late-summer tawny-gold. A wandering line of darker green were trees marking the course of a river. Only the tops of the trees were visible, the river itself was down in the flat-bottomed groove it had worn for itself in the untouched land.

Incongruous in this wild setting was a single canvas-covered wagon. It stood maybe a mile or so from the nearest point of the river, motionless amidst the rippling grasses. A thin plume of smoke twirling in the air marked the camp fire.

"Now they're after stopping early today," Irish remarked.

"Good, they might have some coffee on," Tomcat drawled. He nudged his brown mare into a walk. "Let's go be sociable."

When they got closer to the wagon, they saw that it dipped down to the right rear corner. The wheel was lying in the grass, with the corner of the wagon propped up on a barrel. A single, heavyset bay horse grazed nearby on a picket rope. Tomcat and Irish rode slowly towards the wagon, approaching openly. A woman stood by the fire, a pistol in her hands, watching them carefully. Tomcat caught a glimpse of children's faces in the gloom under the canvas wagon cover. He halted his horse at a polite distance from the little camp.

"Howdy, ma'am," he drawled, raising his soft, cloth cap. "We was just passing by. Kin we be of any assistance to you?"

Irish had politely tipped his hat too, both of them careful to keep their hands in plain view.

The woman looked from one to the other. Her hands were clenched tight on the revolver, though she kept it pointed at the ground. Apart from his green cat-eyes, there was nothing remarkable in Tomcat Billy's looks, but his smile and enthusiasm for life gave him natural charm. Irish was tall, powerful, and rather oxlike on first impression. In spite of his threatening size, he had a mild face that suggested a placid nature.

After long moments of thinking, the woman sighed and relaxed. "You're welcome here," she said quietly. "An' I'd be plumb grateful for some help right about now."

Tomcat and Irish dismounted and led their horses closer to the fire. The children began to creep out onto the seat of the wagon.

"I'm Tomcat Billy, this here's Irish." Tomcat gestured at himself and his friend in turn.

"Mrs. Edison." She made a belated effort to tidy herself, tucking a stray lock of light brown hair beneath her bonnet.

The limp cotton bonnet hadn't been too effective in protecting her skin from the sun and wind of the prairie. Her plain face was prematurely aged and dried, wholly unremarkable until she smiled shyly and revealed beautiful white teeth. Mrs. Edison wore a faded pink calico dress, with the remains of cream lace still showing at the end of one sleeve. Any other trimmings had been sacrificed to the hard journey across the wilderness.

"I guess you broke an axle?" Irish said, looking along the tilted wagon.

Mrs. Edison nodded. "Mr. Edison saw it was cracked yesterday. He fixed rope around it, to hold it until we could reach some timber, but it gave out this morning." She turned and gazed towards the treetops visible about a mile away. Her face grew tense but her mild voice remained calm. "He took one of the horses and went to cut a tree to make a new axle. I was expecting him back for dinner at noon, but he still hasn't returned."

It was now moving into late afternoon. Tomcat reckoned that Mr. Edison was nearly four hours overdue.

"I daren't leave the children alone," Mrs. Edison added, still looking in the direction she'd last seen her husband.

"We'll go look for him, ma'am," Irish offered immediately.

Mrs. Edison closed her eyes for a moment. "I'd be so grateful," she said softly.

"We'll be as quick as we can," Tomcat promised.

He shot a quick glance at Irish, then the two of them had turned their horses and sent them towards the river at a steady lope. They'd almost reached the line of trees before either of them spoke.

"Brave woman," Irish said.

"Reckon she'll have to be," Tomcat replied soberly.

At the top of the bluff, they cast about for a bit before Irish found the crack in the cliffs that led to the river bottoms. The recent prints of a shod horse were clear in the reddish earth, heading down, but not up again. Tomcat led the way, bracing his moccasined feet in the wooden stirrups as his horse cautiously made its way down the steep slope. Cliffs of banded earth rose around them as they descended through the crack in the bluffs. The sun's heat radiated from the stone walls. Grass on top of the bluffs waved in the breeze, but there was no wind in the gap that Tomcat and Irish followed.

The cliffs abruptly gave way to the open, level ground of the river bottoms. It was fresher and greener down here, below the prairie, the grass heavily patched with woodland. A cluster of pronghorn antelope on the other side of the river stared at the new arrivals for a moment, before bounding away at high speed, the patch of white hair on their rumps flashing alarm in the sunlight. Tomcat leaned sideways in his saddle, searching for more tracks.

"Ah! He done headed this way." Tomcat turned his horse upstream, toward a thick cluster of trees.

As they rode into the shade of oak and hickory, a horse somewhere up ahead whinnied. Irish's roan lifted its head and replied. They let the horses find one another, bending low in the saddles to avoid branches as the horses pushed their way through the undergrowth. When they found the wagon-horse, they found Jacob Edison. The meek horse was harnessed to a roughly-hewn log that had jammed between two trees, trapping the horse in the woods. Edison lay a short distance away, where he'd fallen from the horse's back. The lower part of his left leg was wrapped in a blood-soaked bandage torn from his shirt.

Tomcat jumped from his saddle and hurried to Edison, while Irish went to the wagon horse. Edison's face was white under his prairie tan, and his lips were pale. It only took a few moments for Tomcat to be sure that Edison was dead. He looked the dead man over carefully, seeing the dried blood on his work-hardened hands. Carefully, Tomcat unwrapped the crude bandage and examined the deeply sliced wound. He glanced at Irish, who was unfastening the traces that hooked the wagon horse to the log.

"I guess he done had a slip with the axe," Tomcat drawled. "Tried to get back to the wagon but bled out first."

"Sure an' he must have done it trimming branches off the log, after he cut it down," Irish replied, looking at the slender hickory trunk that the horse had been pulling. He sighed. "We'd better be taking him back to his family."

Tomcat was gently rewrapping the bandage with agile hands. "I never made no axle before, but I guess we got to make one now."

"Better find the axe," Irish said practically.

With Jacob Edison wrapped in one of Tomcat's blankets and tied across the back of the wagon horse, they returned to the wagon. The log for the axle dragged through the long grass at the end of the funeral procession. Mrs. Edison stood straight, watching them approach, her youngest daughter in her arms and the other two children clustered around her. When they reached the wagon, Tomcat dismounted and took off his soft cap.

"I'm real sorry, ma'am."

The children stared at the wagon horse with wide, anxious eyes.

Mrs. Edison kept all expression from her tired face as she looked at Tomcat. "What was it?"

"He had an accident with the axe," Tomcat told her quietly. "Got his leg."

He didn't need to explain more to this range-wise woman.

Mrs. Edison heaved a long sigh and hitched the toddler higher up on her hip. "Thank you for helping us out. At least now I know. . . . "

There was a silence before Irish spoke.

"If you want to be seeing to your husband, we'll be digging a grave."

"Yes, thank you." Emotions were pushed aside by the need to deal with the practical. Mrs. Edison glanced about at the sweep of the prairie. "Anywhere here would do, I guess. There's a shovel fixed to the side of the wagon." She handed the toddler to the oldest child, a girl of about nine. "Nettie, you mind Patty behind the wagon. Duke, I need you to dip water from the barrel into the washtub."

The children scattered to do as they were told as the adults prepared for the burial.

Digging the grave was hard work. The dense roots of the prairie grasses matted the sod and were difficult to cut through. Irish and Tomcat spelled one another at the work, cursing under their breath as they hacked through the tangled mass of roots. They quit when the hole was a little over three feet deep. Tomcat looked regretfully at the blisters on his hands.

"Anyone who sets out to try farming this land is either as dumb as a shovel or got more grit to them than a farmer's got hay."

Irish held out his own sore palms. "Now I surely remember why I quit earning an honest living. Stealing's easier."

Tomcat looked across at the battered, weather-worn wagon, and the bereaved family around it. "Yeah. I guess so."

There was nothing fancy about Jacob Edison's funeral. His widow took off her apron, and wore a black shawl over her calico dress. Tomcat and Irish washed and tidied themselves, and wore their usual clothes, as did the children. Mrs. Edison offered her *Book of Common Prayer* to the two men, asking if one of them would read the service.

"I'm sure sorry, ma'am," Tomcat said, glancing at his friend. "Neither of us kin read too good. It wouldn't sound so smart, coming from us."

Irish nodded agreement.

So Mrs. Edison read the service for her husband, with her three moist-eyed children and two strangers at the graveside. When the two older children had solemnly tossed handfuls of dirt onto the blanket-wrapped shape in the grave, Mrs. Edison closed the book and held it against her chest. She stared into the grave for a few moments, then looked at Tomcat and Irish.

"Supper will be ready when you've filled it in."

With her children around her, she turned away to see to the needs of the living.

Tomcat woke suddenly during the night. He lay silent and motionless in his bedroll, listening to the night noises to discover what had disturbed him. The most obvious sound was Irish snoring in his own bedroll on the other side of the banked-up campfire. A coyote wailed in the far distance, but the steady tearing sound of a horse grazing reassured Tomcat that there were no predators close to the camp. As he absorbed the usual night noises of the prairie, he realized that the out-of-place sound was human in origin.

Propping himself up on one elbow, he turned to look at the wagon where Mrs. Edison and the children were sleeping. The sound that had disturbed him was soft, steady weeping. Tomcat listened to the grief for a few moments then settled down again, pulling his cap over his ears to muffle the noise, not wishing to overhear private sorrow.

The next morning, Mrs. Edison appeared calm and in control of herself as she tended to her children and cooked breakfast.

"We can be fixing you a new axle today," Irish said, accepting a bowl of cornmeal mush. "But it won't be a proper job, for sure. Where was you heading to?"

"We were going to Fort Hartstuff. It's being built on the North Loup," Mrs. Edison replied, supervising Patty as the toddler spooned up mush. "Mr. Edison was aiming to get carpenter work building the fort, then we were going to settle on a homestead."

"What will you do now?" Tomcat asked.

"Fort Hartstuff is only about a week's travel from here," Mrs. Edison replied. "A friend of Mr. Edison is already there, he wrote us and suggested we come out. He'll help us get settled, I'm sure. I can get work taking in laundry, sewing, or baking. The men at the fort will need someone to do those things for them. Once I've got a grubstake, I can find a nice section of land, hire some help, and set up a homestead, just like we planned."

Tomcat felt a fresh wave of admiration for this ordinary, remarkable woman. He glanced at Irish, and saw the same opinion in his friend's eyes.

"We'll escort you to the fort, make sure you-all get there safe," he drawled.

Ordinarily, both of them would have stayed well away from the military, or anything resembling the forces of law and order, but he couldn't help responding to Mrs. Edison's steadfast courage.

She showed them her rare and lovely smile. "Thank you, gentlemen."

Shaping a new axle was no easy task. Fortunately, Mr. Edison had owned a good set of tools, and kept them in excellent condition. The first thing Irish did was to find the wagon jack, and use it along with a flour barrel to support the wagon while the wheels were off. They didn't have the skills or equipment to transfer the metal fittings of the original axle to the new one, but the metal was carefully packed into the wagon to be re-used when a proper repair could be made. Tomcat and Irish both had sore hands from the previous day's grave-digging, but they persevered with hatchet, saw, and plane, shaping the hickory log into a new axle.

Mindful of the children, only the occasional curse escaped them, followed by a blushing apology to Mrs. Edison. Mid-morning she brought them ginger water and cornmeal patties spread with rosemary-infused lard. Both men drank deeply from the stone jar before starting on the food.

"Thank you, ma'am. That ginger water's real good on a hot day," Tomcat told her.

"It doesn't chill the stomach like plain water does," Mrs. Edison said, stoppering the bottle and putting it in the shade of the wagon. She watched them eat the patties for a few moments.

"Let me see your hands," she said to Irish.

He held out one massive hand towards her. She looked at the reddened skin and blisters.

"I've got some salve that will soothe them," she said. "I'll apply that and put bandages on. You'll both be more comfortable."

"Sure, an' you're mighty kind, ma'am," Irish rumbled.

She tilted her head back to look him in the face. "I can never repay what I owe you two. You will always be in my prayers."

"We ain't good men, but we couldn't be calling ourselves any kind of men if we left you settin' here alone on the prairie," Irish answered awkwardly.

"God's will sent you here in my time of need," Mrs. Edison replied with quiet certainty. "I'll get the salve and bandages."

Time passed as Tomcat and Irish worked on the wagon. By trial and error they fitted together a new axle assembly, crawling around under the propped-up wagon to fix it in place. Not only did they have to fasten the axle assembly to the wagon box, they had to fit it to the rest of the undercarriage, the reach and hounds that connected the two axle assemblies. With that done to the best of their ability, they had to reattach the wheels and thoroughly grease the hubs.

The day seemed to get hotter and hotter as they heaved the first iron-banded wheel into place. Tomcat leaned against it, feeling sweat run down his face, as Irish wrestled with the hub, screwing it into place. He felt an increasing sense of urgency to get the wagon fixed, without knowing why.

Little Duke appeared and sat on the grass, watching them as they struggled.

"Will you get it done before it rains?" he asked.

"Rain?" Tomcat asked incredulously.

"There's a black cloud over there," Duke said, pointing away from the wagon to the north-west.

Tomcat and Irish both looked to see what he meant. Sure enough, black clouds were billowing up on the horizon, but it wasn't rain. Under the cloud was an ominous orange glow, and Tomcat realized that he'd been smelling smoke in the wind for some time. Now his attention was off the wagon, he noticed movement across the prairie, jack rabbits, snakes, prairie hens, even a mule deer, all racing away from the fire to the creek bottoms.

"Duke, ask your momma to come talk to us right away."

The little boy leapt to his feet and hurried off.

Irish stared towards the fire. "Sure an' the wind's blowing it this way. You reckon we got time to finish fixing the wagon?"

"We got to try," Tomcat answered determinedly. "This wheel's about on. We only need it to hold together long enough to get to the bottoms."

Mrs. Edison came running around the corner of the wagon, holding her long skirt up to move faster. Irish went on fastening the hub while Tomcat laid out rapid plans.

"Harness the wagon horses, then saddle up our horses; leave our saddlebags in the wagon, and pack a few of your things onto the horses. Put Nettie and Duke on my horse, you and the baby take the other. I'll come give you a leg-up when you're ready. You and the children head for the creek bottoms without waiting for us. If we don't get the wheels on in time, we'll ride the wagon horses. Got that?"

Mrs. Edison nodded, turned, and hurried away without wasting time with questions.

"This one's fixed," Irish said, stepping back from the wheel.

"Good."

They hurried around to the far side of the wagon, away from the approaching fire, and picked up the second wheel. Between them they hoisted it into place on the end of the axle. Tomcat braced himself against it as Irish picked up the hub and began attaching it. Specks of ash floated in the air, settling on their sweaty skin. They could hear the fire now, the eerie roar of the flames, the crackling of vegetation as it burned. Tomcat glanced over to where Mrs. Edison was strapping satchels onto the horse's saddles.

"Can you hold this yourself?" he asked.

Irish just nodded, strands of sweat-darkened blond hair plastered to his face as his sore hands wrestled the hub into place.

Tomcat sprinted across the grass, feeling his eyes starting to sting with the smoke in the air. He smiled at Nettie, who was holding the reins of his brown mare.

"You-all's gonna love riding Sarah," he said, bending to take hold of the little girl. "She's a swell horse, and she'll look after you."

He swung Nettie up into the saddle with a whoop, making a game of it. She smiled in response, though her eyes were anxious.

"Up goes the little man." Tomcat boosted Duke up to sit in front of his sister. He passed the reins to Nettie. "Now, you-all hold on tight to the saddle and follow your momma."

With a quick slap on his horse's neck, Tomcat turned to help Mrs. Edison. He legged her into the saddle of Irish's roan, then lifted up Patty, the toddler. Mrs. Edison swiftly tied a shawl around herself and her small daughter to hold Patty safely in her lap. As she tied the knots, she looked down at Tomcat, holding the reins of the restless horse.

"Everything on the wagon is just goods. It can all be replaced. Lives can't," she said.

Tomcat grinned recklessly at her. "Tomcat Billy's got plenty of lives left. You get yourself and your children to those creek bottoms." He handed her the reins and sent the horse away with a slap. Just as soon as he saw that both horses were moving in the right direction he turned back toward the wagon and the fire.

He went first to the wagon horses, spending a few moments to soothe them, and to check that the wagon brake was on. Irish was still working on the wheel hub, grimacing and cursing freely now as smoke and sweat found their way into the raw spots on his hands. Ash was thick in the hot, breathless air now. Twists of flame broke loose from the fire and rushed ahead on the wind, coming down to blaze ahead of the crackling wall that approached them. Tomcat guessed that the fire was moving as fast as a horse could run. It was terrifying and yet beautiful in its fierce glory.

Wind-borne sparks were already coming close to the wagon. Tomcat dipped the wooden bucket into the water barrel strapped to the side of the wagon, enjoying the tepid splash of water on his hands, and started hurling water onto the canvas wagon cover. There wasn't enough water to soak the whole thing properly, but he dampened what he could. By this time, the roaring of the fire was all he could hear. His breath was coming in short snatches; there didn't seem to be any air to breathe. Tomcat looked over his shoulder at the fire, then dropped the bucket into the empty barrel and sprinted around the back of the wagon.

"We gotta go!"

Irish looked up, his blue eyes startlingly pale in his sooty, sweaty face. He nodded once, his hands still moving as he smeared thick grease onto the hub. Tomcat ducked under the wagon and collapsed the wagon jack. The massive wagon bed settled onto the wheels, creaking as Tomcat scurried out from beneath it.

"No time!" he yelled, his voice cracking with smoke-dryness, as Irish reached for the flour barrel that had also been used to prop the wagon up. Still clutching the wagon-jack, Tomcat agilely climbed over the wagon tail-gate and inside. A few moments later, Irish appeared on the seat at the front. As soon as Irish released the brake, the horses sprang into a gallop.

Tomcat held his breath as the wagon jolted forwards. He could see the onrushing fire through the puckered opening in the canvas cover. They had a head start on it, but only just. They gambled everything on their repair work being good enough to hold the wagon together as they sped over the prairie.

At first Tomcat's attention was concentrated on the creaking and rattling of the wagon as it bounced over the rough ground. He couldn't tell what might be the goods fastened on and around the wagon rattling together, and what might be the sound of their repair job breaking. Then a more pungent smell of burning made him look up. A spark had set the canvas wagon-bonnet smoldering. Tomcat hastily stripped off his sweat-soaked shirt and used it to beat out the glowing spot.

As the wagon continued its hell-for-leather run, Tomcat balanced nimbly in the swaying wagon bed, beating out sparks as they landed on the canvas. The air inside the wagon was stifling but Tomcat kept going. With every jolt and bump there was the fear of the wagon breaking, stranding them in front of the racing fire. There was no time to give into the fear though. Tomcat staggered back and forth, gasping for breath, flailing his increasingly ragged shirt against the rain of sparks.

"Tomcat! Brake!"

It took a few moments for the meaning of the yell to sink into his fuzzy brain. When it did, Tomcat dropped his tattered shirt and stumbled forward to the driving seat. Irish had his hands full with the reins, trying to control the panic-stricken team as they approached the narrow gap that led to the river bottom. Tomcat climbed alongside his friend, hanging on grimly when a bump threatened to throw him off the wagon. Clinging to the front wagon-bow with one hand, he put the other one on the long brake lever.

"Ready!"

The horses bolted on, showing no inclination to slow as the ground sloped downwards. Irish braced his feet and hauled on the reins, calling, "Whoa," in his deepest tones.

Tomcat pulled on the brake as wagon and horses entered the crack in the cliffs. The horses crouched, sliding as the weight of the wagon pressed against the breeching of their harness. One horse tossed its head, whinnying in fear. Loose items shifted inside the wagon and a small box came flying out, catching Irish on the shoulder and bouncing off the rump of the near-side horse. Wagon and horses skidded down the steep slope together.

Down and down they went, the horses struggling to keep their feet as the wagon closed on them. The near-side horse stumbled, but Irish's firm hand on the reins kept its head up. The horse plunged, snorting, and found its feet again before the wagon could overrun it. Flames roared above and to either side as the fire swept to the edge of the bluffs. It stopped there, reaching into the sky, unable to follow down the bare earth of the crack in the cliffs. Tomcat bit his tongue as the wagon jolted over a rock, but the ground was beginning to level out.

They burst out into the green freshness of the river bottoms. There was smoke in the air, but the fire was above and behind, trapped at the top of the bluffs. The horses began to slow to Irish's soothing tones. He played with the reins, getting them to drop back to a lope, then to a trot. Tomcat released the brake as the horses responded, and looked about to find Mrs. Edison and her children. His eyes stung with smoke and he was as sweaty as the wagon horses, but his teeth showed white in his dirty face as he smiled.

A childish whoop told him that the wagon had been seen. Irish turned the team towards the sound, and lifted his hat to wave it at the family waiting eagerly for them.

"You should put your shirt on," he told Tomcat.

Tomcat glanced down at himself and grinned. "I guess that would be the proper thing to do. We mustn't forgit our company manners now. Mrs. Edison might start to thinking we're not gentlemen after all." He turned and scrambled into the back of the wagon in search of his tattered shirt.

Nine days later, Tomcat and Irish were on their own again. Once more they let their horses run for the sheer pleasure of it, exulting in the freedom of the prairies. Only when they settled back to a walk, breathless and contented, did they talk.

"Sure and Duke would have enjoyed that," Irish said.

Tomcat nodded. "Nettie, too, if her momma would have let her." He thought for a moment. "I'm gonna miss them kids, but it's sure nice not to be responsible for a family no more. I don't know how folks like Mrs. Edison can do it."

"Case of 'have to'," Irish answered simply.

"That woman's sure got a lot of grit," Tomcat said admiringly. "She's worth a dozen of the likes of us."

"You're plumb right there; she's a worker. For sure, I don't care if I never get another blister again." Irish held out one beefy hand, still red and tender on the palm.

Tomcat grinned, green eyes sparkling. "I reckon we really done earned our vacation. Soon as we hit town, I'm gonna be whoopin' it up for sure."

Irish nodded slowly. "Sure. I don't know about going all the way out to California though. Sure an' it might cost more than we reckoned. We gotta think about making the money last."

Tomcat looked at him in surprise, then started to chuckle. "Irish, did you leave some of your money hidden in Mrs. Edison's wagon, to help her buy that homestead?"

Irish was so startled he inadvertently snatched on his horse's reins, causing the roan to throw up its head in protest. "Why—did you find it there?"

Tomcat shook his head, still laughing. "That's exactly what I done. I left her half my money, figgered she'd use it better than I would."

"I left her half mine! Sure an' she's got eight hundred dollars sitting in her wagon, and we just got the eight hundred between us now." Irish began to laugh too.

"I bet we can get to California and back with eight hundred dollars," Tomcat said. "And if we need more, hell, we know how to steal it."

Irish nodded. "It sure beats working for a living."

A TIME TO LIVE
Jack Giles

Born in North Finchley, London, England, Ray Foster (writing as Jack Giles) maintains a lifelong interest in Western books and movies. Married and with six children and thirteen grandchildren, Ray is hard at work on his ninth Western novel.

Billy Gentle was, by far, the tallest child in the class. Five foot ten and with a stocky build he dominated everything and everybody—and he made sure that folks saw him coming. He liked it when he was noticed. Even better when they did what they were told, when they were told. If he wanted to play baseball, then every kid, boys and girls, had to join in.

At one time he was one of the kindest and more thoughtful children in the class. But back then his father was a simple farmer and not the local figurehead he had become.

Time changed Billy's father. That and the drought of '86 when the cattlemen noticed that the farmers were taking what little water there was to irrigate their land. The cattlemen tried to drive the farmers out but Al Gentle was a tough man who fought for what was his. He was instrumental in banding the small community together to take a tough stance against the ranchers. There were deaths on both sides. Despite this, it was acknowledged that neither side was prepared to back down. The townsfolk made it plain that they would stay neutral even though opinion was that the cattlemen were in the right. Even slow and aged Sheriff Matt Brogan took the unusual step of not allowing guns within the town's limits.

It was the winter that brought hostilities to an end. Though both the cattlemen and the farmers were affected by the heavy blizzards and deep snow, it was the cattlemen who suffered the most. Their herds were depleted and investors, mostly European, pulled out because of the losses. All of this happened while the farmers went back to their plowed fields and sowed new crops.

Among the farmers, Al Gentle was hailed as the man who stood up to the cattlemen and brought them to their knees. He was regarded as a hero and he believed it, too. Soon the hard-working farmer became a braggart and a bully who took his anger out on those who chose not to back him in that fight.

There were many who thought that Al Gentle had grown too big for his boots, though they didn't dare say so out loud. They grew to like the power the fight gave them. The farmers became so unified that when they came to town even Sheriff Brogan found something to attend to that would get him out of the way.

And so, because of his father, young Billy thought he could do as he liked since no one would dare touch him. That's what he believed when, just for the hell of it, he tugged Molly Shelby's pigtail and made the small, shy girl shriek out in pain.

"That's enough," the new schoolteacher barked, his eyes going straight to the perpetrator. "Get yourself down here, Billy Gentle."

Billy just grinned. An insolent grin that said that he was ready to accept whatever challenges the teacher had to offer. He had already driven off the two previous teachers in the last few months.

This one, he considered, was nothing. The schoolteacher, John Gant, was five foot eight, slim, and on the wrong side of forty. Nothing more than a lightweight with graying hair who looked as though one punch would lay him out. Billy thought he could deal with this problem without dragging his father into it.

"You can't touch me," Billy announced, as he swaggered down the aisle between the desks.

He grinned at his cronies as he passed them. He was that confident that there would be only one winner in this contest and that pretty soon this teacher would go the way of the others.

The whole class was suddenly transfixed as Gant, tired of Billy Gentle's attitude, moved to intercept the boy. He caught the youth off balance, grabbed him by the collar, and half dragged Billy to the front.

"You can't do that," Billy blustered, straightening his shirt, and hopping from foot to foot in anger at this sudden humiliation.

"Just did," the schoolteacher pointed out. "And now, you are going to discover that I will not have disruption in my classroom."

Bunching his fist, Billy took a wild swipe that was meant to connect with Gant's jaw. Except that Gant saw it coming and sidestepped with unexpected agility. Billy stumbled against the schoolmaster's desk where, half sprawled across the scattered books, he felt a searing pain across his backside. Screaming out, he tried to scrabble clear but not before a second lash brought tears to his eyes. Sobbing with humiliation he tried to crawl to the door—but found his path blocked.

"Now get back to your desk," Gant ordered, pointing the cane, the instrument of Billy's discomfort, at the boy. "The school day hasn't finished yet."

There was something about Gant's tone that told Billy that he had no choice but to do as he was told.

"My pa'll have something to say 'bout this," Billy spluttered in tearful defiance as he backed up the aisle toward his desk.

"I'm not going anywhere," Gant assured him. "He wants to find me, he knows where to come."

As he sat down rather gingerly, Billy looked around at the class. The other children were regarding John Gant with respect and offering their full attention. For the first time Billy wondered about the wisdom of telling his pa about what had happened to him. But common sense was not one of Billy's strong points.

"Heard you had a bit of action today," Doc Calloway mentioned over dinner that evening.

"Just handed out a touch of discipline," John Gant mentioned firmly to the young, chubby doctor who had obliged him by providing lodgings. "Boy needed to know who was in charge. Isn't that why you and the Town Council hired me?"

For a moment Calloway looked perplexed. "I don't know what you mean."

Gant leaned forward, closing the distance between them. "When I came West I came with the intention of teaching school," Gant pointed out, almost reminiscing. "And you—" he stabbed a finger at the white-faced doctor, "you know what happened next. So, when you interviewed me, you saw a means to an end."

Slowly, the doctor got up from the table and went to the fireplace where he retrieved a pipe from the mantelpiece. He took his time tamping fresh tobacco into the bowl from a leather pouch. Reaching down he lifted a spill from a fluted container, touched it to a burning log and put the flame to the tobacco. He savored the smoke for a moment before turning back to Gant.

"Yes, you're right," Calloway conceded, tossing the spill into the fire. "I mean straight off I recognized you—but not the name."

Gant held up his hand to silence the other man.

"Who I was is not the issue," the schoolteacher assured him. "I took the job here in good faith. It's the things that I heard around town that bothered me. Things that neither you nor anyone on that Town Council ever bothered to mention. Makes me think that you needed a town tamer more than you needed a teacher."

"Don't blame them," Calloway hastened to say. "Not one of them knows that you're Marshal John Gantwell."

"Ex-marshal," Gant explained, just managing to stop himself from thumping his fist on the table. "Those days are done. I want to do what I was trained to do. And that is to teach. Not fight a war you people are too scared to deal with."

"I didn't know what else to do," Calloway confessed. "We're not getting any backup from the cattle company and those damn farmers are doing what they damn well please."

Gant leaned back in his chair with a smile almost forming on his face as he shook his head in disbelief.

"Cattlemen have enough problems of their own," Gant pointed out. "I don't blame them if your mess means nothing to them. And as for letting the farmers do as they please, well, isn't that your fault? People only get away with things if you allow it to happen."

"And you?" Calloway almost pleaded. "What will you do?"

"Exactly what you pay me to do," Gant replied, rising from the table, tired of the conversation. "Teach."

"So you won't help?" Calloway asked scathingly, surprised at his own bravado. "The great John Gantwell backing down from a fight."

"Not my fight," Gant replied, leaving the room.

Alone in his room John Gant stood at the window and wondered what he had gone and got himself involved with. The opening and the closing of the front door beneath him disturbed his thoughts. He watched the doctor walk down the street and disappear from view.

At least he wasn't heading for the saloon, thought Gant. But he was probably going to talk to Vern Ellis, the head of the Town Council, to air his grievances. Maybe come the morning Gant wouldn't have a job and then he could move on.

He wished it were that simple. But he knew he had started something and he would have to see it through, no matter the consequences. It was fair comment that he felt he was hired under false pretenses, though he still set events in motion. He was the one who had listened to the town gossip and drew all the right conclusions. With that knowledge he could have quit and just walked away. Instead, he walked into trouble with his eyes wide open and, from what he heard, Gentle would make sure that it was his fight.

Nor was he sure what had driven him on. Maybe it was the challenge, but he could not quite admit to it.

Gant moved away from the window and crossed to the bed. He set down a small brown valise and flipped back the clasps. He opened it wide and pulled out a cloth-wrapped bundle and gently he lifted the folds to reveal an ivory-handled Colt that rested snugly inside a well-oiled brown leather holster.

Drawing the gun, he held it for a moment, feeling the familiarity of its weight. Then, almost reluctantly, he slid it back into the holster. He felt sorry for Al Gentle—the farmer had no idea of the man he was about to face.

The following morning John Gant came down to breakfast dressed as usual in gray trousers and vest with a crisp white shirt. He sat at the table where he waited for the housekeeper to serve up his bacon and eggs.

"I spoke to Vern Ellis last night," Calloway mentioned, now that they were alone. "If you want to rescind the contract, we'll not raise any objections."

"Really?" Gant said with reluctance, preferring to eat his breakfast rather than get involved with a conversation. "Well, you can forget that. I was hired to do a job and I intend to see it through."

"But—," Calloway protested.

"I came here to teach," Gant said, forcefully. "And that is what I intend to do."

Having made his intentions clear, John Gant managed to eat his breakfast in silence.

Returning to his room, he put on his gun belt, ensuring that the holster was comfortable against his left hip, before donning a gray three-quarter-length jacket. Turning to the full mirror set in the

42

wardrobe door, he studied his appearance and allowed a slight smile to touch his thin lips.

Setting a gray derby on his head, he opened the door and left his room. For a long, thoughtful moment he stood at the top of the stairs before coming to a decision.

"Now it begins," he sighed.

As usual Fred Olson, the oldest member of the farming community, drove the buckboard loaded with children up to the schoolyard. Glancing back he noticed that his subdued charges were reluctant to climb down and join the other children. And when they did they kept their distance, for there was no Billy Gentle present to dictate things.

Almost as an afterthought Fred looked at the schoolmaster. Slowly he nodded because he saw from the other's stance that today things were going to be different.

"Be back at three," Fred confirmed, much to the consternation of the farm children, who exchanged confused glances before looking to Fred to supply answers. But the old man was more concerned with turning the buckboard around and heading back up the main street.

Then the tall, bearded Al Gentle rode into town flanked by Billy and four farmers riding abreast behind them. Grim-faced men with only one thought on their minds and that was a determination to see that justice was done. Almost as though it was prearranged, the group of four pulled their mounts over to the saloon.

Al and Billy covered the short distance to the schoolyard. As they dismounted, one of the farmers took a coil of rope from his saddle horn and another came up with a bullwhip. Both men exchanged grins and turned to walk down the street when they found their way barred.

Sheriff Matt Brogan stood there with a shotgun leveled at their bellies.

"Don't think you fellas are goin' no place," he said, steadying the shotgun.

"Don't you have someplace else to be?" the bullwhip carrier sneered.

"Guess you didn't hear right," came another voice, forcing all four farmers to turn and find the bartender, also armed with a shotgun, flanking them.

"What the hell—?" Bullwhip protested, his eyes swiveling around as he saw the storekeeper, Vern Ellis, powering up the street with a rifle held across his chest.

"Folks have had enough!" Ellis roared.

"We thought it was about time Al Gentle fought his own battles," Doc Calloway said from behind the storekeeper. "Without you lot backing him up."

Bit by bit the main street filled with angry and armed citizens who forcibly disarmed the protesting quartet of farmers and marched them into the saloon.

Al Gentle rode into the schoolyard just as the schoolmaster ushered the children into class.

"You!" Al bellowed as he climbed out of the saddle.

Gant turned around and held up his hand. "Whatever you've got to say can wait," Gant stated, without the nervous quaver that Gentle had expected. "Let me settle the children first. You wouldn't want any of them to get hurt, would you?"

Against his nature, Al Gentle found himself nodding in assent. He cast a confused glance at his son before deciding that he was the one who was supposed to be in command here. Indignantly, he bore down on the classroom entrance only to find himself backing away as John Gant emerged. Gentle's eyes had dropped to the gun belt that the schoolmaster was wearing. It didn't take him long to fathom that he was facing a man who knew how to handle a gun.

"Now, Mister Gentle, was there something you wanted to discuss with me?" Gant asked in a businesslike manner.

"You hit my boy," Gentle barked, trying to hold his ground. "Nobody does that to my boy."

"He was being disruptive," Gant informed him. "I had no choice but to inflict punishment. What did you expect me to do? Let him get away with it?"

"Not my boy, mister. You don't lay a hand on him," Gentle protested. "Bet you wouldn't have done that to one of them town children."

"Any child who asks for chastisement will receive it," Gant assured him.

"Why don't I believe you?" Gentle sneered. "We've had to fight for everything we've got."

"Fight? For what?" Gant asked. "The way I see it, when the cattlemen needed water it was you who kept it for yourselves. You think you beat them? Mother Nature did that, not you. And what help have you offered them? None. You throw your weight around like you're somebody, but you're nobody, Gentle. Just a loud-mouthed braggart. And your boy follows your example."

"Who the hell—?" Gentle roared, turning around and intending to summon help.

Instead he found himself alone, faced with the prospect of dealing with the situation on his own. Angered by his predicament he slammed his hand down and grasped the butt of his pistol.

"Pa!" a distraught Billy Gentle yelled out.

Al Gentle stared down at the pistol aimed at his belly. He hadn't seen the schoolteacher move but the gun seemed to appear in his hand. Nor did he do anything to stop Gant from relieving him of his own firearm.

"So those damn cattlemen have brought in a hired gun," Gentle spat.

Gant shook his head. "I was hired by the community to do a specific job. Not just the cattlemen but by the people of this town—including you. But what happens next is going to be down to you and you alone."

"To me?" Gentle asked.

"What happens next," Gant prompted. "Whether we fight to satisfy your pride or I get on with the job of getting your boy an education."

"Pa, you can't let him get away with what he done to me," Billy protested, pointing at the schoolteacher and looking at his father.

Intuitively, Gentle was almost prepared to throw a punch at the man who stood in front of him. Yet that action was curtailed the moment the thought appeared in his mind. Only seconds before he faced death at the hands of the only man who dared to stand up to him—and then who allowed him to live.

"Figure I can," Al Gentle conceded. "Now you get yourself in that classroom, boy. And don't cause this man no problems."

"But—"

"Dammit, do as you're told!" Gentle barked, glaring at his son.

45

Grudgingly, Billy Gentle did as his father told him.

"One thing," Gentle wondered aloud. "You could've killed me back then. Can't figure why you didn't."

"And it would have proved what, exactly?" Gant replied.

Gentle watched his son, head bowed, enter the schoolhouse. Nodding, he caught the meaning behind Gant's words.

He watched as Gant unbuckled his gun belt and held it loosely in his left hand. "Will I be needing this again?" Gant demanded of the farmer.

Gentle shook his head. "Figure I learned my lesson."

Gant smiled. "That's why I'm here. To teach."

PRETTY POLLY
Duane Spurlock

Duane is a writer, editor, and illustrator residing in Kentucky, where he and his wife and their children garden, draw, and tell stories to one another. He maintains a website devoted to the popular fiction magazines of the first half of the 20th century, www.pulprack.com.

"Oh, Lord, Mr. Bear, please don't kill me!"

The man pleading for his life hung upside down, tied at his ankles with his own rope, which was thrown over a tree limb and hitched to the saddle horn of his horse.

The man he addressed—the man who'd strung him up in this manner—stood with his revolver drawn. He said, "You think I might kill you?"

"Oh, yes sir, but I beg you don't."

"You know who I am?"

"Oh, Lord, yes sir, you're Grizzly Bear, a terrible desperado, and please don't kill me!"

A smile almost lit Bear's face. Griswold Bear—whose nickname newspaper editors disputed should be Grisly or Grizzly—was indeed a terrible man and had been notably so since he rode out of Missouri with Bloody Bill Anderson. With the war's end, his demeanor and behavior hadn't grown milder, and his head now carried a bounty as a result. His ruthlessness and gregarious meanness—not the ursine-pelt coat he frequently wore—gave rise to the nickname, which was recognized throughout the West. Bear's appearance certainly enhanced that recognition: His long hair flew untamed about his head, and the care he lavished on his moustache—a shrub of frightening proportions—made up for the lack of attention he gave his wild locks, for each day he waxed it into points that suggested his knobby face was armed with tusks.

"What about your pard, here? You beggin' for him, too?"

Another man hung beside the first. Unlike his verbose companion, the second man remained silent and goggle-eyed. He had soiled his trousers, which may have contributed to his expression and lack of speech, and certainly accounted for Bear standing a good three yards from his upended captives.

"Oh, yes sir, Beaman is a good feller and don't deserve to die neither."

The former guerilla had surprised these two and another cowboy on a lonely stretch of road leading to the village of Wicket. It was the evening of payday, and the three were sharped up in boiled shirts and clean britches, so Bear anticipated finding pocketfuls of cash. The third member of the party had been playing possum, and had scrambled up and ridden away while Bear was trussing his companions. The robber was angry at first, and wanted to shoot somebody outright, but instead he called out after the escaping rider, "You tell 'em I'm on my way to Wicket!" He felt better, knowing that the worry of his impending arrival would probably put the townsfolk into a state of knock-kneed terror, so they would likely submit to anything he wanted. On the other hand, Bear would now be short one pocket's worth of money.

He said, "Let me tell you boys, I've been the victim of lies all my life. Them righteous folks with their starched shirts have laid frightening crimes at my feet for years. Maybe I was a bit wild in my youth, but I'm an older and wiser man now, and I've calmed down terrible much, even though I yet ride the owlhoot trail. But in the eyes of the law I still shoulder the burden of great guilt for crimes I ain't never even thought of.

"So I tell you, what if you just give me all your money and I'll cut you down? How's that sound?"

"Oh, yes sir, Mr. Bear, yes sir."

The silent Beaman nodded. He pulled a chamois-wrapped packet from within his shirt. His talkative partner directed Bear to a pocket in one of his saddlebags.

Once Bear had the coins clinking in his palm, he smiled and said, "That's just fine, boys. Thanks so very much."

Then he raised his sidearm and put a bullet through the brainpans of both prisoners.

True to his word, Bear cut them down before he rode off.

Sheriff Billy Shoat surveyed the landscape of his contentment and was dismayed by the measure. Most mornings by this time he would be standing in the dusty street before the sole hardware and mercantile store in Wicket enjoying a cup of coffee, just as he did now. Quite contented, most mornings. And on this day he had expected to be even more content than usual, because he'd planned to leave town a few days to visit at the home of an old friend. And this friend happened to live two counties away, so Shoat would be far from the concerns of sheriffing and he would while away the time playing cards and drinking fine barn whiskey.

However, on this particular morning, the joy for his trip had been stolen from him.

Before dawn Shoat had been awakened by a drover who worked for the Bar D. The kid looked like he'd tangled with a mountain lion handy with a barbed wire lariat, and claimed he'd escaped from Grizzly Bear, who'd hollered out he was on his way to Wicket.

So the sheriff was up and around before he'd intended, had stuffed down his eggs, biscuits, gravy, and side meat in a hurry, and now stood in the dirt with fiery belches percolating in his belly.

Sheriff Shoat wasn't so much worried about Bear's arrival as peeved by the upset of his plans. He'd handled rough cases before. When he first arrived at Wicket the village was wide open to lawless folks. Shoat had ridden in, mood already foul thanks to a wen on his backside, and the surly responses he'd gotten to his greetings and questions only irritated him further. After shooting three sour and stinking fellows who had laughingly belittled him and his mule while simultaneously committing a crime against sensitive eyes and noses in broad daylight—and in the middle of the main street—Shoat went on a minor rampage. He ran out of town the primary bullies who instigated and promoted most of Wicket's sins, and put the fear of God and Samuel Colt into the rest of the ruffians.

By the time the tumult was settled, Shoat found he'd been named town sheriff.

He'd never been a sheriff before. It sounded like a way to earn a little cash, make sure his belly got full with only a little effort. So he thought he'd try it out.

The new sheriff's initial public act was to order the closest thing to a local doctor sobered up for tending to the first three men Shoat had shot. After sufficient healing the three were to build a public outhouse near the livery. At the ribbon cutting Shoat commented, "That'll prevent any more such nasty displays."

Shoat's next act was to have the sobered doctor ease his backside's pain.

Wicket had remained much calmer since the sheriff's installation, but Shoat kept a wary eye open. Occasionally knotheads still drifted into town to stir up a ruckus. The sheriff's job had been easier since he hired as deputy a fellow who arrived only about a month ago. He was mostly a quiet sort and sometimes prodding him into action was similar to lighting a wet fuse. But once his tinder caught the new deputy could be an awful terror. If a wandering rascal strayed out of the bounds Shoat's whims considered appropriate for the day, the sheriff could rely on the deputy to set the offender straight.

Deputy aside, today Shoat had to contend with a terrible hellion who'd sent plenty of men to meet their Maker. And he had to do it before lunch, as well.

He grimaced as his belly grumbled. Shoat realized his tendency to act rashly when irritated wouldn't help him today, so he tried ignoring the tussle in his gut. He had to keep a level head to deal with Bear.

Thought of the outlaw made the sheriff look up. Beyond the end of what passed for a main street in Wicket came a rider leading two saddled horses. Shoat waited where he stood, swirled the remains of his coffee in its tin cup. Eventually the rider stopped before the sheriff. Sure enough, he was wearing a bear-fur coat.

Shoat tried not to scrunch up his nose. *He for sure smells like a bear's backside*, he thought.

He opened deliberations. "You must be Griswold Bear."

The rider sneered in answer. "Who're you?"

"Sheriff of Wicket."

"Sheriff? There weren't no sheriff last time I came through here."

"Town's trying to keep up with the times. Truth is, I'm glad you're here."

Bear's eyes twitched before he quickly hid his confusion. "Oh yeah?"

Shoat nodded. "You can help me out. I got to go over to another county a few days. But I hate to leave things here untended. I figured I could put the town in your hands to keep the rabble down. Who's gonna cross Grizzly Bear, right?"

He waited only a moment for an answer, then continued. "The pay ain't much, so don't expect to get rich while I'm gone. But there's two full meals a day that'll stretch your belly to horizons of contentment it's never known." Shoat held down a belch and felt the trapped fire behind his breast bone. "And even better, there's Pretty Polly."

"What?"

"Pretty Polly shares her charms with one man and one man only. The sheriff of Wicket."

"You got a whore just for bein' a lawman?"

"Now that's a trashy thing for a smelly owlhoot to say! She ain't no whore, she's what you might call a civil servant servin' the public good. Only she don't service the public. She serves the sheriff." Shoat sighed and looked skyward. "Your own mammy couldn't make a quilt to wrap around you so nice. Your purtiest cousin couldn't sweet talk you so fine."

"I ain't no sheriff!"

"You can be. All you gotta do is wear this badge while I'm out of town. Then you're the sheriff. While I'm gone. When I'm back, you can move on with a bag of vittles, the money you earned, and no regrets."

"Who says I won't shoot you down when you come back, and I'll just stay sheriff?"

"When I get back you'll either be bored to tears or the citizens of Wicket will be irritating you like fleas with all their little worries and demands."

Bear showed him a smirk exaggerated by the fangs of his moustache. "Maybe I'll just perforate that big breakfast behind your shirt right now, and you won't be worrying no more about going or coming back."

Shoat shrugged. He tipped out the dregs of his coffee. "You can. But who talks to you straight like another man instead of an animal? Who's offered you something on the up and up without trying to save his own hide? Who's the last person to make you an offer without peeing down his leg? I figure you can do whatever you want, but why do what you always do—raise hell and run again? I'm making you a square offer. It's up to you what you want to make of it."

Bear made a face—like something bitter was wrestling in his mouth.

Bear stood down from his horse in front of a log structure that sat nearly in the middle of Wicket. He'd been here before. Back then a rough board nailed beside the door had the word DRINKS burnt into it with a running iron. That sign was still there, but now a larger one, painted by a surer hand, accompanied it over the door: Blue Dick's Saloon. This designation came from the proprietor, Dick Hoots, who'd gained a more colorful appellation from patrons who saw his face while he was throttled by Baxter Birdwhistle, a muleskinner of prodigious strength and appetite for whiskey, after an argument about Birdwhistle's currency. The saloonkeeper lived to carry the burden of his new name and hire an itinerant sign painter when Sheriff Shoat arrived and buffaloed Birdwhistle with a whack behind the ear using his sidearm. As Hoots was unable to respond to anyone while his throat healed, there was no way to escape his evermore being Blue Dick Hoots, short of leaving town.

This history was beyond the ken of Griswold Bear as he pushed open the door. Shoat had sent him here, saying he had a few traps to gather before leaving town, and encouraged Bear to try out the role of the town's temporary caretaker. He'd said, "You gotta be enthusiastic about calling out Polly. She's generous, but she's gotta know she's wanted and appreciated. Don't hold back. Why, I'm sure you won't."

As Bear's boots thumped the floorboards, he saw a bartender, a big fellow on the drinkers' side of the bar, and two men slumped over a table as if in prayer for their empty glasses. He also spied a door at the back of the room, past the bar, which probably led to Pretty Polly's domain.

The customer at the bar held Bear's attention longest. He was at least six feet tall, but the way he hunkered over the rough-sawn planks of the bar and held onto a bottle suggested he was clinging to one or both to stay upright. His clothes were trailworn. Bear couldn't decide which looked more battered, his out-of-fashion beaver-fur hat or his face. The fellow wasn't wearing a gun, the two worshippers at the table appeared in no shape to use the ones hanging from their cartridge belts, and the bartender looked barely awake, so Bear detected no threats to his person.

He cleared his throat, recalling Shoat's words, then lifted up his voice. "I'm here to see Pretty Polly! Pretty Po-LLEEEEEE!"

The prayerful table sitters perked up. The bartender turned his head, doglike, and watched Bear. The big ugly customer didn't move, didn't even take his gaze off his bottle.

Bear continued. "Pretty Polly! I hear you got eyes like blue diamonds. I hear you got a mouth will make a man weak in the knees."

The men at the table stirred enough to move their chairs and watch Bear's performance. The big man at the bar shook his head and stood a little straighter.

"Pretty Po-LLEEEEEE! I'm here for you, darlin'!"

While Bear watched the back door for Polly's entrance, the big man started walking for the front door, which stood behind Bear. As the latter stepped aside for the customer to pass, the big man's left arm whipped out and backhanded Bear. The outlaw staggered and his attacker then buried his left fist in Bear's gut. Bear snapped forward and expelled a bellow, whereupon the big man uncoiled an uppercut with his right, which laid out the former guerrilla straight as garden string.

The only thing that kept moving was the dust raised by the ruckus. Less than a minute later Sheriff Shoat strode through the door.

"I heard— What's happened here?"

The big man, whose expression had changed not a whit during the entire violent episode, turned his sad face toward the lawman. "He was makin' fun of me, Sheriff." The bar's other occupants—those who were upright—nodded agreement.

Shoat looked down at Bear, then stepped back, as though startled. "Great jumping frijole farts! This here is a wanted man. In fact, I've seen a reward tagged to his name—Grizzly Bear!" He shook the big man's hand. "Congratulations, Deputy Polycarp! You've fed our mutual money box."

A wan smile lit the deputy's face.

Sheriff Shoat's mood was much improved by the time he rode out that day. Judge Bean might have a pet bear, but Wicket had caught an authentic wild Grizzly—top that!

Shoat planned to wire the governor from the next town about Griswold Bear's capture. When the law man returned to Wicket he expected to have his share of the reward waiting for him, and Bear would no longer be housed by the stable, shackled in the public privy.

The sheriff grinned. He'd jailed—perhaps privvied was more accurate (maybe his next public order would get a jail built)—a Fearsome Desperado. He had a binge of gambling and drinking ahead of him. He was soon to be in receipt of cash that would replace what he was sure to lose at cards the next few days and he had justified his hiring of a deputy over the timorous objections of Wicket's citizens.

Before his arrival in Wicket Deputy Polycarp must have followed a terrible knockabout livelihood, which gave him that face like a mule-kicked bucket. But Shoat appreciated his loyalty and didn't give a hoot about his looks. And when he thought of the reward money for Griswold Bear the sheriff could consider the deputy's sad, battered face only as sweet, and its owner as Pretty Polly.

THE BALLAD OF JESSE BARNETT
Lance Howard

*Writing as Lance Howard, Howard Hopkins has penned twenty-eight
Black Horse Westerns, his most recent being* Haunted Pass *(August,
2007). He's also written pulp adventure stories for recent anthologies
such as* The Spider Chronicles *(with John Jakes). A musician, he lives
in Maine, USA, and performs in a quartet at local nursing homes.
Visit his website at www.howardhopkins.com.*

Please don't hit her again. . . .
Sometimes thunder didn't crash solely from a rain-bloated sky.
Sometimes it crashed as a fist shattered bone. Sometimes it echoed
from the helpless feeling a mother experienced when a force beyond
her control overwhelmed her life, threatened her child.

Sometimes it took that crash of emotional thunder to awaken her to
the fact that should she tolerate her husband's cruelty even a day
longer then the one thing she held most precious in her life might be
torn away from her forever.

Her husband had never hit the child before. Jesse Barnett always
told herself, lied to herself, that Justin, twelve years her senior, would
never cross that line. She'd convinced herself of a passel of lies over
the past eight years. Too many. Perhaps the worst of which was the
notion that her eight-year-old daughter, Jessalina, would actually
benefit from a loveless marriage held together by fear.

A laugh trickled from her lips; she wasn't quite certain whether it
was sane.

Buttery light from a low-turned lantern mixed with shadow and fell
in a marbled pattern across her features and auburn hair. Her normally
pretty face with its high cheekbones and soft, full lips was set in grim
lines as she sat in the overstuffed chair in the parlor of the tumble-
down homestead she and Justin owned on the outskirts of Angel Pass.

Parlor. Another lie. She liked to call the shoddy room a parlor
because it made her feel somehow better about the roof that leaked
with each rain and the roaches and mice that scurried across the
disintegrating floorboards. Fancy ladies had parlors. Fancy ladies had

husbands who loved and cherished them. Husbands who didn't raise their fists in anger.

The room held sparse furnishings—a collapsing sofa, a rickety table, scattered pieces of cloth from which she fashioned dresses for some of the women in town. Lord knew, someone had to bring in money for food.

Instead of drink.

Mostly the room just held a peculiar scent, a sickly aroma only she could smell. The musky stench of failure. Her failure.

Ten minutes ago Jesse had dragged the chair across the room to a position a few feet in front of the door. She'd chosen this chair because her ma had given it to her before her pa had killed her with a single blow to the head.

And because she could hide a loaded Peacemaker in the cushion.

Please, Justin, don't hit her. Don't—

Shut the hell up, woman! The child needs punishin' fer what she done. Stealin's a goddamn sin.

Tears shimmered in Jesse's washed-out blue eyes and her hand drifted to the locket at her neck. The locket, a tarnished silver heart, rested on the collar of her faded blue gingham dress. She pried open the locket, though her eyes remained focused on the door. One side held the likeness of Justin, the other, Jessalina. Balls of muscles knotted on her jaw and her throat tightened with choked-back fury. Using a fingernail, she gouged Justin's likeness from the locket, then snapped it shut.

A fragile smile played on her lips.

I loved you once, Justin. I loved you like you were the sun in the morning and the song of the whippoorwill.

Why couldn't he have loved her the same way? Why couldn't he have cared enough to stop spending his evenings in town, in the saloon? Drinking. Doing unclean things with those *women* when the only way he cared to touch his wife was with a fist.

He hadn't been that way in the beginning. She wasn't sure exactly what caused the change to come over him, when it started. Things like that . . . well, sometimes they came on slow like. By the time a body noticed 'em. . . .

56

She wasn't sure either how she'd become so used to his nightly tirades, how she'd come to accept violence as a normal part of affection. Somewhere along the way everything had blurred, washed from black and white to gray.

Her hand drifted to a blemish running along her jaw, the ghost of a bruise. He rarely put marks on her face. He retained enough control, even drunk, to make certain when he hurt her it was in places unlikely to bring questions from curious townsfolk.

But he'd slipped up a few nights ago. He had been getting worse over the past months, though she continued to lie to herself, assured herself that things would get better, that he really didn't mean to hurt her.

His steak was not cooked the way he liked it. His trousers were mis-sewn. His breakfast was cold again, despite the fact he'd been too hungover to eat when she made it.

Nothing he could be blamed for. It was her fault. It was *her* fault.

How many times had he blamed her? How many more had she blamed herself?

As many as it took to believe the lie their marriage had become.

Until he'd struck their child and all her self-imposed rationalizations came crashing down like the thunder of Revelation the preacher talked about each Sunday.

Even still she had nearly blamed herself for the fact Jessalina had stolen an apple from a shop on her way home from school. Mr. Perkins had been kind enough not to charge them for the apple, but he had mentioned the incident to Justin, thinking it would do some good, sober him to the notion his family was going without while he wasted away the evening with whiskey.

Mr. Perkins knew, somehow, gave her looks of pity that made her avert her eyes in shame. Others cast those looks her way as well—the general store owner, the ladies who bought her dresses, the marshal. Everybody knew, she reckoned.

Everybody except poor deluded Jesse Barnett.

Mr. Perkins had used poor judgment, telling her husband about Jessalina's moment of weakness. He had likely never considered that a man who hit his wife might also strike his child.

She couldn't fault him for that. She was guilty of the same sin. But whereas with the shop owner it had been an error in judgment, for a

57

mother it was an act of reprehension. More so because her moment of clarity had not occurred when Justin struck the girl, but the instant Jesse told their daughter it was her fault for angering her pa, her fault for asking to be hurt.

A great sob shuddered Jesse's small frame and she put her face in her hands. Tears ran through her trembling fingers, the bile of emotion.

"I'm sorry, Jess. . . . " she muttered. "So very sorry. . . . "

Her daughter. Her precious daughter. And she'd nearly thrown her away, shackled her to the life she herself now lived. The life her own mother suffered and bequeathed to her like a legacy from the Devil.

She'd lain awake the entire night. It showed in the dark pouches beneath her eyes and the sallow complexion of her skin. Lain awake and begged a God above she'd never had much use for, for His forgiveness and the strength to do what she'd spent the moments just before dawn planning.

After Justin left for town, Jesse had taken her daughter to a friend's for the evening, a friend she knew would gladly provide for the child until Jesse's sister in St. Louis came for her. A short time later she'd visited the marshal. She told him everything, every callous mistreatment, every mean-spirited word, every heartless cruelty Justin visited upon her over their years of marriage. He listened, never interrupting, until she finished an hour later. Then he confirmed her conviction that he had suspected the truth all along. Marshal Thompkins had always been extra kind to her and Jessalina, much to Justin's jealous disapproval. She believed in her heart, had Justin not been around, the lawman would have courted her.

He'd offered to arrest Justin, see to it he never touched her or her daughter again. She refused to press charges, at least until tonight. She asked the marshal to remain outside the homestead at the hour Justin normally wandered back from town, then give her five minutes after he entered to tell him she was leaving the marriage and taking Jessalina with her. She told the marshal she owed Justin that much. What did one more lie matter?

The marshal hadn't been easily swayed and perhaps that was because she was the pitiful liar she knew herself to be, or perhaps because he worried over her safety after the things she had told him about Justin. It didn't matter.

For she wasn't leaving Justin. At least, she wasn't leaving him alive.

The sound of hoofbeats reached her ears and dread skewered her belly.

In her mind's eye she could see him half hanging from the saddle, drooling, his eyes wild with whiskey-fortified rage at nothing in particular. She watched him in terror from the window enough times for the image to be permanently burned into her mind. Tonight would be no different.

The hoofbeats drew closer and her dread strengthened. Nausea came next, sickness brought on by night after night of conditioning, facing the Devil.

She didn't have much time left, and with that thought her hands began to tremble.

How many times had she envisioned killing him? Watching him die with the same terror reflected in his eyes she'd experienced each night of her adult life? Why was she suddenly so frightened now that the moment of truth, of justice, was near?

She had to go through with it. It was too late to back out, now. The cycle stopped tonight. Or never.

"You shouldn't have hurt her. . . . " Jesse whispered. "I shouldn't have let you make me blame her."

She prayed God would forgive her for that. And for murdering him.

The hoofbeats stopped and her heart started to thunder.

Bootfalls. Like gunshots. Each punching into her composure.

The door flew open and he stood there on the threshold. A devil of a man in a stained bibshirt and soiled trousers.

A stench reached her nostrils: perfume mixed with whiskey. He'd been with another whore. That should have made putting a bullet in his black heart easier, but fear mocked her, told her she was wrong, told her she was still at fault for every sorry deed he'd ever imposed upon her.

"What the goddamn hell ya doin'?" he asked, voice as thunderous as his fists.

"I'm sorry," she said. Damn, her voice shook. She had hoped she could recite his list of crimes firmly, tell him exactly in ice-coated words why she was murdering him.

"You're always sorry." He didn't bother to ask why she felt the need to apologize, and that little surprised her. "Get the hell out of that chair and fix me some supper."

"No." There. The first time. She'd told him "no" for the first time and it felt . . . terrifying.

"What the hell did you say?" His tone said he hadn't heard her right, or that perhaps she had taken leave of her senses.

"I said 'no.' You won't be needin' dinner tonight."

"The hell I won't! What the goddamn hell's gotten into you, woman? You know better than to backtalk me."

She drew a shuddering breath, struggling to keep her composure. "I did know better, Justin. I swear I did. I just couldn't admit it to myself. But now I can. Now I know I don't deserve that way you treated me. Neither does Jessalina. And for what you've done to me and to her, I aim to kill you."

She didn't expect him to laugh at that, but he did. Maybe he was more drunk than she'd thought.

"You plumb lost your wits?" He took another step into the room, swinging the door shut behind him.

"Reckon not. Reckon I finally found them." Her lower lip quivered. Sweat trickled from beneath her arms.

Anger. No . . . rage. That's what flashed in his eyes. He wasn't that drunk tonight. That had been a mistake on her part to assume. He laughed because he was mocking her, telling her she did not have the backbone to act against him. Never had, never would. Because she was too weak, too much the creature of lies he had made her.

"Why, Justin?" she asked. "What made you hurt me? What made you want to hurt your daughter?"

His rage-filled gaze flicked to a small room off the parlor to the left, Jessalina's room, and a wave of ice water washed over her heart. It assured her she had made the right choice, sending Jess away, deciding to finally stand up to him, and to her suffering.

He lunged, teeth clenched, fingers balling into a fist.

The blow crashed into her jaw, stifling any gasp she might have made at his sudden attack. Blackness stormed across her mind, blackness filled with thunder, but it only lasted for a moment. She'd gotten used to his blows, could take a lot. Pain splintered through her teeth; the gunmetal flavor of her own blood filled her mouth. He grabbed both arms of the chair and shoved his face close to hers. Whiskey assailed her senses.

"You ruined it all for me, Jesse. You went and got yourself with child and ruined everything. You made me marry you. My life wasn't supposed to be a struggle, you stupid whore. Wasn't supposed to have another mouth to feed. You reckon I should just let you get away with that?"

Her eyes narrowed, the words stinging, though she knew she should not have let them. "You said you loved me, Justin. You told me you wanted a family. How can you blame me for giving you what you wanted?"

Something crossed his eyes then, something dark and lost and she saw now the reason behind his rage: his own failings, his own weakness—for drink, for whores, for whatever reason he'd never become the man he expected himself to be. Somewhere, somehow, he had lost his way and the trail back was hidden to him. There was only a coward's knowledge that a man wasn't strong enough to admit his own shortcomings, his own mistakes, and accept them.

He was going to strike her again. She saw it like a grinning skull in his eyes. She always did. And she'd always let him.

But not this time.

Guided by a strength she never believed she possessed, she jammed her hand into the cushion. When it came free, she clenched the Peacemaker in bone-white fingers and swung it with all her might.

Thunder again. Crashing as steel slammed into bone. His jaw fractured. She heard the snap. He staggered back and she was suddenly on her feet.

She swung again, before he could gather himself, hitting him in the temple, the very rage that had filled his eyes now swelling in her own veins.

He collapsed to his knees.

With a final blow blood sprayed from his nose. He went over backward and onto his side, whimpering.

It was the last thing she expected from him. Defiance, fury, spite— those she would have thought likely, but not this.

"Please, don't kill me. . . . " he said, the rage gone from his eyes, replaced with something else: fear. She knew its face only too well.

She aimed the Peacemaker at his forehead. She'd imagined how his brains would spatter the floor, how his body would spasm in death, and how she would laugh and laugh and then cry before they took her away to hang her. One squeeze of the trigger, one bullet, and everything would be over. Jess would be safe.

Her hand began to shake harder. Tears trickled from the corners of his pleading eyes. Then a wave of horror washed over her at the sight of the way he cowered before her, the blood on his face, the terror in his gaze. She had thought it would be satisfying to see it in him, but it wasn't. It brought a surge of bile into her throat and disgust to her soul, because for a spell she had been no better than the man now helpless before her. She had let her own rage intoxicate her. Everything she had despised in him had, for a few moments, thrived in her, and it was something she never wanted to feel again.

"Dammit, no!" She lowered the gun, her entire body shuddering now. "I wanted you dead, Justin. Truly, I did, and that hurts me maybe as much as your fists ever did, that I could feel such hate for a person I once cared for. But I won't be like you. I won't let you take the last thing I got left and if I kill you I'll lose Jess and any chance at helping her see wrong from right, the way I never did."

"Jesse?" a voice came from behind her and she turned to see the marshal standing in the doorway. She hadn't heard him open the door.

She smiled her fragile smile. "I got something back tonight, Marshal." She went to the lawman, handed him the gun, and looked into his eyes.

"What did you get back, Jesse?"

"My honesty. Won't have to lie to myself or anyone else no more. And I reckon I got a duty to my daughter to see to it she never makes the same mistakes I did, neither."

She stepped past the marshal, out into the night, wrapping her arms about herself. For the briefest of moments she turned her head to look back into the house, at her cowering husband, wondering why being free felt nearly as frightening as being chained to a life she despised. Then she walked toward town, praying she'd be able to undo some of the damage she might have done to Jessalina. . . .

BUBBLES
Ross Morton

Nik Morton served in the Royal Navy. Now he's an editor living in Spain with his wife, Jen. He has sold many short stories, articles, and illustrations. This year his first Black Horse Western, Death at Bethesda Falls, *was published. He writes for English periodicals in Spain and for UK's* Portsmouth & District Post.

Last night's storm had swollen the river and it seemed to be rising by the minute as they herded the longhorns into the fast-running shoals. "Keep movin', movin'!" Josh Mason barked. He was a big-boned young man and, though he'd lost a lot of puppy fat, he was still overweight. Guiding his whickering horse among the steers, he boldly continued to chivvy along the fearful critters with shouts and whistles. On the other side of the broad wedge of beef on the hoof his best pal, Scott Finley, also persuaded the cattle to keep moving.

Fording the river now was dangerous, but Boss Fairweather and his foreman, Stratton, had been adamant; they couldn't risk wasting the time to wait for the water to subside or even to skirt around the river. To mitigate disaster, they forded obliquely down stream, hopeful that the action of the water against the steers would assist them in getting across. Yet with every faltering step the animals took there was the strong possibility of one or more of them losing their footing.

Josh was tired after spending several hours helping to quell a stampede when the critters were spooked by forked lightning that made night into day. Otherwise he might have noticed the cut cinch on his saddle caused by a horn during the rain-drenched melee last night. Now the strain proved too much for it and the cinch broke when Josh was midway across.

Without warning saddle and rider slid sideways. Josh's shoulder hit a side of beef and then he plunged into the water with an almighty splash.

There was only a cluster of bubbles in the roiling water where Josh had been. Nothing else. Not even a gloved hand thrust through the surface.

"Bub!" Scott exclaimed, using a truncated version of Josh's nickname.

Boss Fairweather and his foreman turned in their saddles and stared, alarmed, then settled back to their work and hastened to get the steers to the other side before they all panicked and were lost.

"Damn you to hell, Bub!" Scott growled. He didn't hesitate but gently guided his mount through the loosely packed bodies of the steers. He knew there was no point in watching the diminishing number of bubbles, waiting for Josh to appear. Unbuckling his gun belt, he snagged it on the pommel, gulped in a big breath, and dove in after Josh.

Luckily he had plenty of practice and though the river was running fast and visibility was poor, his questing fingers found his friend's leather vest. He closed his hand around the material and, fearing that the water in his boots would drag him down and his lungs would burst, he gave a tremendous kick and pushed himself upward with all his might, hauling Josh with him to the surface.

In a welter of splashing water and bubbles, they burst into air that was hardly fresh, since a dense miasma of cattle-odor hovered over the river's surface. Barely conscious, Josh spluttered and struggled in Scott's grip.

It wasn't easy, since he had to restrain his friend's panicky gyrating arms, but Scott finally heaved Josh to the opposite bank. Fortunately their horses were well-trained and obediently followed. Scott collapsed in the mud, gasping for breath. Lying alongside him, Josh disgorged his breakfast and a fair portion of muddy river water.

Scott got no thanks from Josh and he hadn't expected any. Just the usual: "Why'd you pull me out, Scott? I near swum to the surface!"

That got a few laughs from the watching cowpokes and then, in high dudgeon, Josh dragged his horse away.

Once the cattle were back on dry land, Scott and Josh 'Bubbles' Mason trawled the river-bed with weighted lariats and after half an hour Scott snagged something. An air-pocket must have been caught in the saddle-bags and a clutch of bubbles burst on the surface.

"It's 'bout time you learnt to swim, Bub!" Scott remonstrated as he waded into the river. With nifty ropework he pulled his friend's saddle out.

"Chrissakes, you know I damn well try, Scott!"

"Yeah, if tryin' was all there was to it, you'd swim like a fish!" Scott dumped the saddle in the mud and stalked away to dry off.

Josh Mason's life seemed beset with bubbles so much that he ended up with that sobriquet. 'Bubbles' was an ill-fitting nickname as he was more morose than bubbly by nature, yet the moniker stuck.

Scott and Josh were kids together on their neighboring Nebraska Territory farms just south of the small township of Stiller's Lookout. They spent many a long, hot, late-summer day stealing Mr. Johansson's apples and ogling the Fitzpatrick sisters, whose legs seemed so long that they fair went up to heaven. In contrast, they also had simple fun blowing bubbles with sticks and soap and skylarking in one of the creeks off the Platte.

While Scott was a good swimmer, Josh never mastered the skill. He tried, but he just tended to sink. As Scott remarked more than once to those who witnessed Josh's doomed attempts, "You'd likely reckon that with Josh being so round—rotund, some polite folk call it—he'd just float like a ball." But for some obscure scientific reason he just sank. He spluttered and wind-milled his arms and hands in a fearful frenzy but still managed to sink. And always left behind lots of bubbles on the surface.

Scott soon lost count of the number of times he fished Josh out of the deep part of the creek, but he reckoned it was at least a hundred.

"What you go an' do that for, Scott?" Josh exclaimed when he got his breath back, bubbles of saliva flecking his lips, the water sluicing off of his dungarees. "I was *that* near to learnin' to swim!"

Scott's tone was close to exasperation as he replied, "One of these days, Bub, I won't be here to save your hide. Then you'll be sorry!"

"*You'll* save *me*?" Josh laughed and softly punched his friend's shoulder. "Yeh, all right, if you say so!"

As usual, Scott let it go. Pride could be something awful, especially when you were young. Fortunately, their friendship was rock solid and in the scheme of things Scott reckoned that these disagreements amounted to squat.

They'd grown up together, both the same age, though Scott sometimes pointed out that he was two months older than Josh, since he was born in December '44.

The Mason ranch was next to the Finley spread. As far as Scott was concerned, "Ranch is a high-falutin' word for what amounts to a dirt-farm." Both homes were constructed of sod since there wasn't much in the way of trees to fell nearby. But, Scott's ma kept telling him, "It's all ours, son."

On a good day he could stand on the stoop, shield his eyes from the sun, and still not see the limits of their land. Scott's pa had enjoyed some luck in the rush of '49, by all accounts, and used the money wisely. He always reckoned it was his dedication to the family Bible that ensured his good fortune.

Pa was a big man, six two in his socks, which surprised Scott. He reckoned that his pa should've built the roof of their home higher. Pa had to walk from room to room stoop-shouldered. "Penance," he called it, which didn't sit right with Scott, since it seemed self-inflicted. But religious study was not his strong suit at the Stiller school, so he let his pa's comment go.

Maybe that was why Pa don't spend much time with Ma in our house, he thought. They'd see him at food times and then he'd go off to bed early. Ma would linger a while, repeating chores, as if reluctant to retire. Then Pa'd bawl, "You comin' to bed, Eunice? I'm waitin'. You surely try the Lord's patience!"

The rest of his pa's life seemed to be spent down at the township or out on the farm, "Sowing my seed in both places, son," he would say, chuckling to himself. "One day you'll understand."

Scott never understood his pa but he knew that the old man worked hard on the land and sometimes the land was just plain cussed and denied Pa its bounty.

When the spring and summer storms started, the thunderheads a magnificent if frightening sight, Scott's pa used to turn strange and at those times he was almost as devastating as the frequent tornadoes they witnessed scourging the land. Pa raged and hit out, breaking crockery and upturning furniture, behaving like a demented animal. Ma just put up with it, saying he went like that if the weather was unforgiving. "I'd knowed it afore I wed the man, son, so I can cope," she told Scott, but that didn't make it any less scary.

Pa was strict and used his belt on both Scott and his wife to enforce his will, quoting the Bible when he was inclined. Scott tried hard to give him no cause to be displeased and performed all of his allocated chores without complaint—and made a point of being regularly seen saying his prayers. He never told his pa about "Bubbles" and him ogling the Fitzpatrick girls, though.

Scott was glad when every other month or so his father took himself off for some days to visit Stiller's Lookout. On those nights he could hear Ma sobbing in her bedroom. He lay there, wanting to comfort her but not knowing how, and he always felt guilty the next morning when he realized that she'd still been crying when he fell asleep. At the time he didn't know whether she was crying because she missed Pa or for some other reason.

Josh didn't fare any better with his father, who was a drunk. And by the time Josh was able to help out with the chores the old man made it plain that he had no respect for his wife or his farm. "Some kind of maggot must have burrowed into his brain and disturbed his humor," Josh told Scott once. Many a time Scott noticed Josh's bruises and bit back any comment.

It was no surprise to either of them when they both thought about running away from home. They had just turned fifteen and were lying in the straw in the Mason barn's loft.

"I feel sorry for Ma, leavin' her," Josh said.

"Yeah, me too," Scott agreed. "My ma's shed enough tears on account of Pa already, but I don't reckon I can take much more of this dirt-farm life, Bub."

"Me neither. We ain't cut out to be cornhuskers."

"And I'm sick of his Bible thumpin'."

"I hate Pa punchin' Ma, but I can't fight him—yet." It was true enough. Though Josh was big and round, he was more flab than muscle and no match for his brutish father.

"If we're serious about goin', we need to get provisioned up," Scott mused. "A change of clothes and other necessaries."

"We'll need six-guns, Scott. For our protection—and to hunt for food, mostly."

"Yeah, I've put aside a few dollars in savings. What about you, Bub?"

"I can afford a gun. But what about transport? Do we walk everywhere?"

Scott chuckled. "I've been thinkin' on that, Bub, and I have an idea where we can get us some money *and* horses."

Eyes widening at the prospect, Josh said, "It sounds to me we've gone and decided."

Scott nodded and stood up, a serious cast to his young features. He brushed straw from his trousers. "Bub, it's time we stopped playin' at adventure and went and found some for real."

Josh jumped up, grinning from ear to ear. "By God, Scott, let's do it!"

Laden down with spare overshirts, undershirts, cotton and wool drawers, socks, spare shoes, belt knife, and whetstone, they slunk away from their homes and met up under the light of the moon. Later the next day, at Three Crossings on the Sweetwater River, they lied about their ages to Mr. Slocum, the division superintendent who conducted their interviews.

Slocum had hired Scott but now eyed Josh with some misgivings. "I reckon you're too heavy, son. We're after riders who're about 125 pounds."

Scowling, Josh clambered into the corral and mounted a horse already saddled in the enclosure for tryouts. "I can ride better'n the next man!" Josh said and proceeded to prove his point with ease.

"Okay," Slocum said, coughing on the dust raised by Josh's antics. "You're hired."

For $50 a month plus board and keep they signed the pledge of honesty, loyalty, and sobriety, and joined the Pony Express.

Besides riding superior horse flesh, they proudly used the special lightweight, stripped-down saddle over which was draped the leather *mochila*, complete with its four padlocked *cantinas* or pouches. With the hard riding and long hours came an unexpected bonus—young women seemed to take a shine to riders of the Pony Express. While Scott was fortunate to find a young lady to introduce him to the heady experience of physical love, Josh remained overweight, unattractive, and uninitiated.

One of the relay riders working with them was a fourteen-year-old by the name of William Cody; he was a mite full of himself, Josh thought. The days riding to Red Buttes on the North Platte were tough, and after some months Josh actually lost weight. It was as if those many hours in the saddle were preparing them for future employment and vocation, but they had no inkling what. They dodged Indians with mounts that could easily out-distance the grass-fed Indian ponies and got the mail through without fail.

But they'd also seen the telegraph poles being erected. The transcontinental telegraph was completed that year and Scott knew it was only a matter of time before the Pony Express bit the dust. The months passed and they moved from post to post until they were the last Express riders to arrive in San Francisco in the fall of 1861. Newspapers read: 'You have served us well!' But such praise didn't put food in their bellies and they found themselves without a job.

They lingered for a week, regaling folks about their exploits—and Scott made a few more female conquests—but that soon palled and Nebraska seemed to call them back. Scott fancied going home to see how his ma was faring, but Josh didn't want to face down his pa yet. So they got work on the overland stage coach between Atchison and Denver and spent a couple of years eating dust and shaking their bones to hell and back.

When the papers were full of the news about the Homestead Act—which didn't apply to them, since they were not yet twenty-one—it looked like Nebraska would be crawling with homesteaders in a matter of months.

"Too many people, if you ask me," Scott said.

"Yeah," Josh agreed. "They'll swamp the place."

So they quit and joined the Union Pacific work gang. Hard labor built up their young muscles as they helped the iron horse go west. It was damned grueling work and the pay was lousy, but they had good companions and felt they were actually making history.

When the Chinese workers were brought in for lower pay, Scott and Josh decided to quit. Unlike many of their work-mates, they'd been sensible and had banked most of their wages while some of their pals had gambled their money away each payday. Josh and Scott had plans for the future that didn't entail returning to their farming roots.

"I've had my fill of scrabbling in the dirt," Josh said.

"Aye," Scott agreed. "I want to make my mark."

They lived frugally and pay from small jobs kept them going. For almost a year they were in the Army—but Sheridan's claim that by killing the buffalo they would kill the Indians stuck in their craw.

Scott remarked, "Them prairie Indians are bein' hounded to hell and it ain't fair."

"It's only a matter of time," Josh said. "Poor devils."

"I want no part of that, Bub." So they up and left.

In '67, the same year that their territory became a state of the Union, they joined Goodnight and Loving's first cattle drive to Abilene. What a place. It was obvious to both of them that Abilene was a town growing before their very eyes. Their Nebraskan capital Lancaster was renamed Lincoln in honor of the late President, God bless him, which made them proud, but they had no wish to return yet. They stuck with driving cattle.

With his saddle dried out and repaired, Josh continued with the cattle drive to Abilene. They found that the place had changed a lot since their first visit. Josh finally built up enough courage to frequent Miss Dora Boston's Parlour House, which was referred to by many as the House of Ill Repute.

"Never seen nobody ill in there," Josh remarked afterwards. "Lots of smiles, though." He too wore an uncharacteristic smile as wide as the Colorado for a whole week and Scott never knew if it was the champagne—bubbly, they called it—or the pretty, half-dressed strumpet who kicked him out after two days.

"You know, Bub," Scott observed. "You ain't half as cussed as you used to be, since you took up with Miss Rosie Lil."

Josh threw his hat at his friend. "Every time, Scott, she bursts my bubble!"

But by then his nickname wasn't going to change.

As usual, they banked some of the cattle drive earnings and blew the rest in the town, playing poker or just boozing. When that money had gone, the pair moseyed on to Wyoming, landing up there just at the time when it was announced that the women of that State would have the vote.

"Seems fair to me," Josh said.

Scott shrugged. "Women don't have the power, Bub. Look at our mothers. They're drudges for unappreciative men!"

"Well maybe if they could vote they could change things," Josh suggested.

"Maybe."

That conversation spawned an idea that had been brewing over the years. They up and left the next day and, with mixed feelings, went home.

In the nine years that Scott had been away, his pa had aged. Part of the reason was the grave out back. Ma had died two years gone. Guilt pummeled Scott's chest as he felt sure that the old man had driven her to an early death. If he'd stayed, maybe she'd still be alive, he thought. He wanted to use the man's own belt on him, but he didn't have the heart. He walked out, surprised to see that the familiar view of their land was blurred. Wiping the unmanly tears away, he saddled his horse and rode over to the Mason ranch.

When he got there Josh was dunking his pa in the horse-trough and there were bubbles floating to the turbulent surface. His ma was trying to drag Josh free, but she might as well have attempted moving a mountain.

Scott pulled out his six-gun and fired it into the dirt a few feet away from the trough. Mrs. Mason shrieked.

Josh desisted from near-drowning his pa and stood back, his clothes dark with splashed water. "What you go an' do that for, Scott?"

"I'm saving your hide, Bub, that's what!"

"*My* hide?" He gestured at his gulping, gasping, sorry excuse of a father. "He was near done for and serves him right! You saved *him*, not me!"

"I've no hankering to see you strung up for his murder, Bub. Maybe if you leave him be, your pa will now behave himself." Scott shrugged. "But whether he does or don't, he sure as hell ain't worth dying for."

Josh nodded, seeing the sense in that. He turned to his mother. "Me and Scott are going away again, Ma. But if I hear he's gone back to his old ways, I swear I'll return and next time he'll breathe his last!"

His pa weakly moved a hand and spat out green-tinged water. "I'll try, son. . . . "

Josh's ma crushed him to her, the top of her head barely reaching his chest. For a fleeting moment Scott was envious of his friend. "Be careful, son," she sobbed, and let go.

They took up buffalo hunting for a few months and again met William Cody, who was now quite the dandy compared to the rest of the crew. But it was dispiriting work and their hearts weren't in it. They kept remembering Sheridan's prediction.

"If they're lucky, they'll have ten years," Scott observed, sadly. "Then there'll be no buffalo left. Leastways not enough to support the Indians."

Footloose and fancy free, they wandered down to Los Angeles but didn't stay too long and got out during the nasty citywide anti-Chinese riots. They returned briefly to San Francisco where they marveled at the newfangled cable cars. That was followed by a short stay in Deadwood. They caught the Black Hills gold fever and bubbles again figured in their lives.

Bubbles mingled with the lustre of gold in Josh's pan. They shared their stake and used the money to buy a small cattle ranch in New Mexico. This wasn't like cow-punching. They owned the beef and hired men to work the long, hard hours.

They met an Englishman by the name of Tunstall and before they knew it they were caught up in the Lincoln County Range War. It was a bloody affair and Billy the Kid was bred out of that mess. Sickened by the blood-letting and bad feeling, Scott and Josh decided to sell up. They were lucky and managed to buy a cattle ranch up north, shortly after the death of McSween, and not long before the Kid's Regulators were branded as outlaws.

The world was changing. Billy the Kid was shot down and the fight at the OK Corral in Tombstone created controversy over lawmen taking the law into their own hands. Scott couldn't believe it when he heard that the Texas Panhandle cowboys went on strike for higher wages.

"You either sign on for the wages they offer or you find another job!" growled Josh.

"If they try that on us, Bub, they'll get short shrift!"

Neither of them had to face a demand for higher wages and they prospered on their ranches for three good years. Then, in the winter of '86, terrible blizzards decimated their cattle on the northern range and within months it seemed as though the beef bonanza was at an end.

"Our financial bubble's burst," Josh said somberly. Scott went on a two-week drunk but found he was only poorer at the end of it.

Reluctantly—they were in their forties and their bones were starting to ache—they joined the Buffalo Bill Wild West Show. Although it wasn't their idea of proper work, they stayed with it for three years and yet amassed little in the way of savings.

"I can't stick Cody another day," grumbled Josh.

"He's headin' for a fall," Scott said, his tone sympathetic. "The poor idiot's a soft touch for any sob story that comes around—except from his poor workers!"

"Let's git," Josh said.

South of the border beckoned. Those were the days, south of the Rio Grande where they found the living easy and the women generous.

Unfortunately, Pancho Villa didn't take kindly to gringos in his territory. One night they were rudely awakened and advised to flee the pueblo. Their women stood by, watching in tears to see them go.

Without horses, they couldn't get far. Villa had a couple of half-breed trackers and wanted to find and punish them to serve as an example to any other *Americanos* who ventured on his land.

With only the clothes and boots they stood up in, and with a single pistol between them, they ran for their lives under a bright, full moon. Finally, they could run no further as they had to cross the river—there was no ford or bridge for miles.

"I can't swim!" Josh said. "I'll fight them off so you can get away."

Scott shook his head. "We're pals, Bub. I haven't let you drown yet, have I?"

He shook his head, eyes full of fear. "No, Scott. I won't be the cause of your demise."

"If'n that's the way you want it, then. . . . " Scott said, turning away, and then abruptly swung around with a balled fist and hit Josh with all he had. Josh was felled like a tree trunk, his big body slithering down the muddy bank. Massaging bruised knuckles, Scott hastily checked that his friend was still breathing, fearful lest he'd hit him too hard. He was surprised at himself. His hand sure did hurt.

Straining with the weight of him, Scott dragged Josh into the river and grabbed two reeds. Slicing them with his Bowie-knife, he whittled an air-hole in each. Scott stuck one reed in Josh's mouth and one in his own and sank under the water, pulling his friend after him. Slowly, Scott felt his way round the reed bed, heading down river, all the time keeping the reed in his friend's mouth.

Scott peered up from time to time as he moved silently through the reeds. There were wavering images on the river bank. Horses,

73

moccasins, boots. A couple of bubbles escaped from Josh's nostrils, but luckily nobody noticed and they escaped.

Broke again. The Black Hills beckoned, but they desisted. "When we're really in need, then it'll be time," Scott said.

"Yeah," Josh said. "And I believe in rainbows!"

Scott shrugged. "We agreed. While we're still young, we'd try to make our way. That gold can wait."

Those years were filled with gun smoke, whiskey, posses, and gunfights. For a time Scott was a sheriff and Josh his deputy, and a while after that they returned to the Wild West Show, though this time they were clown cowpokes.

The century turned and found Scott sitting in on a poker game with Josh behind him. When it happened, neither could quite believe Scott's luck. "Jeezus, Bub, this is the best game I've been in!"

"Yeah," Josh said. "You've just gone and won shares in an oil well!"

The loser, whose stake was in the recent find at Spindletop, Texas, was not overly pleased. "I don't reckon you played fair, mister." He pulled out a derringer. "Keep the money, but I want them shares back!"

Bystanders shuffled away. Whispers drifted over. "This ain't Deadwood!"

"Only card sharps carry derringers!"

With pulse racing and heart pounding, Scott raised his hands. "Take it easy, mister."

"Don't tell me what to do! Just give me my shares!"

"They ain't your shares," Josh explained reasonably, leaning over the table and scooping the winnings towards Scott. "You gambled them and lost."

A few voices tended to agree with Josh but the bodies belonging to them stayed well back.

"Who the hell are you?" the loser demanded. "My goddamned conscience?"

"I aim to see fair play, mister," Josh said levelly. "And my partner here won good and square. Put down your weapon and we'll say no more about this."

"Go to hell!" Aiming at Scott, the man fired.

Scott had never seen his friend move so fast. Josh jumped in front of him, landing full onto the table, sending cards and chips and shares every which way. The table collapsed under him as one big hand wrestled free the weapon while the other formed a fist and pounded into the man's surprised face.

The bad loser jack-knifed backward, unconscious.

Scott knelt by his friend's side. Bright blood bubbled out of Josh's chest.

"I reckon I saved your hide this time, Scott," he said, forcing his mouth into an unfamiliar smile.

"Your lung, it's punctured," Scott breathed, mortified.

"Bubbling, is it?"

"Yeah. . . . "

"Then, partner, you'd better get me to a sawbones pretty darn fast."

Sticking his finger into the small hole, Scott stopped the bright red blood from flowing out. The doctor was able to siphon off the blood from Josh's punctured lung and sew it up. His lung never fully recovered, though, and he wheezed from time to time with any exertion. But the more he encountered problems, the more his sense of humor seemed to grow.

Josh took four months to recover and their money flowed in as quickly as the oil spewed out of their new oil well. Josh's luck was really in, it seemed, as he somehow discovered an effervescent personality of his own, probably due to the sweet chemistry of Jane Whitehead, a pretty redheaded restaurant owner who brought food to him in the infirmary. She was a looker, he thought, and he dived into her dark brown eyes, never wanting to surface. If he was destined to drown, this is where he wanted it to happen. When he was fit, he married Jane and at the ceremony Scott opined that his pal was well and truly sunk now.

Scott and Josh went their separate ways after the marriage. Twelve months later, Scott found himself being hounded by a young female journalist wanting to write about his exploits. "You some kind of female Mark Twain?" he demanded.

"Nope," she said. "I'm Gillian Parnham Bridges. An original, not some dad-blamed copy!" She was opinionated, sassy, and had long auburn hair and flashing hazel eyes.

"I must admit I've led a long and interesting life," he said.

"So I hear," she replied. "That's why I want to tell the public about you."

"I reckon it might take a lifetime in the telling."

"Whose lifetime?"

"Ours," he said, grinning.

"Is that the kind of proposition I've been waiting for, do you reckon?" she asked.

"It's the best you'll get this side of Sunday," he suggested.

"Okay, Scott Finley. I accept." She eyed him carefully. "Are you sure you know what you're taking on?"

Scott grinned again. "No, and that's part of the fun, ain't it?"

"Maybe it is," she said. "Maybe it is." She pulled out her notepad. "Now, where were you born?"

"Is this for the marriage certificate?"

"Nope, that's your department. I'm starting on your life, buster. So pay heed to my questions, will you?"

Well into his fifties, Scott fancied settling down with Gillian, but she wanted to live and work in New York, which she reckoned was the center of the universe. Reluctantly, Scott agreed and they were married and bought an apartment in Manhattan. Although he didn't feel comfortable in the big city with the huddled masses of people, he endured it and wrote to his friend Bubbles on a weekly basis. Josh and Jane ran a small restaurant and made a go of it, opening similar establishments in neighboring towns. Every few months Scott and Josh took the train and met up in some outlandish place and got drunk, just the two of them. By now, Scott had two children and Josh had three.

When they were in their sixties, they missed out on the last land rush to Oklahoma in 1911. "I'm considerin' land down Florida way," Josh explained, slumped over the bar one evening.

"Okay, your luck's held so far, Bub," Scott said. "Let's mosey down and take a look."

Against Gillian's advice, Scott threw in his financial lot with Josh and they speculated on land in Florida. "Bide your time, folks, this land means riches beyond your wildest dreams," the real estate agent had promised.

In 1913 they both watched Buffalo Bill's last show before it closed down, burdened by debt. "Poor bastard," Scott said. "The leeches have bled him dry."

"Yeah, it's a shame. Sure, he was overblown and over the top but hell, he brought some color and magic into the hum-drum lives of ordinary folk."

"It seems like the end of everything we knew," Scott said.

"Yeah, nobody has time for the old stories anymore."

Four years later, the four of them attended William Cody's funeral in Denver, which was a bit like a circus, according to Scott. That wasn't the only funeral they went to. Both Scott and Josh lost a son each in the Great War.

Within the next decade, Josh took to chewing the newfangled bubble-gum and blowing bubbles that burst all over his mouth. He almost choked on the stuff several times, laughing so much. "Bubbles'll be the death of me!" he laughed while his wife Jane looked on, amused.

When Josh was eighty-one, the Florida speculative-building bubble burst. That hurt their family financially and Gillian was on the verge of divorcing Scott. "We'll manage, darling," he promised and, to her surprise, he found money from somewhere without incurring any debt and they coped.

Barely three years later, worse was to come with the Wall Street Crash. That was the mother of all burst financial bubbles. At the age of eighty-four Josh and Scott left their family homes and spent a weekend camping and fishing in the Black Hills. Their long-suffering wives let them go. By now both Jane and Gillian had an inkling that these male bonding jaunts coincided with periods of financial difficulty.

Making sure that nobody was nearby, Scott and Josh took turns at the spade work and, after a few hours of sweat and toil, they dug up the last of the gold they'd hidden. Surveying their cache, wiping sweat off his brow, Scott straightened his back. "It sure kept us goin' over the years, Bub."

"Leastways we didn't squander it all at once. It's seen us and our families through the bad times."

"Yeah, it has that, Bub."

Life improved for both families and they were able to take advantage of the recovery period. Scott had five grandchildren and Josh seven and they had the most fun watching the youngsters blowing bubbles with liquid soap. It brought back memories—so many memories that seemed so delicate now, so gossamer thin, that they could be popped into non-existence, as if they had never happened.

As the industries of the United States flexed their muscles, the various Finley and Mason family businesses built on success; they learned to spread their risk and prospered.

Gray and bent under the heavy weight of years, Josh sat on the veranda in Scott's back yard. "You know, Scott," he wheezed, "living on one lung has been hard."

"Yeah, Bub, so you keep remindin' me without fail at this time of year. It kinda stopped you learnin' to swim. I always reckon that's why you got in the way of that slug. Just so you'd have an excuse."

Chuckling, Josh said, "We've had some good times, eh?"

"Yeah, we've ridden one hell of a ride." Of all their adventures, those far-too-brief months riding with the Pony Express stood out, a time when youth convinced them that anything was possible, when life seemed everlasting.

Josh sighed and coughed, his overstrained lung rebelling. "I reckon we're near the end, partner."

Scott started, brought back to the bone-aching present. "Nah, we'll both see out a hundred years, you'll see."

Josh, however, was prophetic. On the Day of Infamy, when Pearl Harbor was attacked, Josh died in his bed in New York City. He'd taken ill with pneumonia and was surrounded by his family for his last moments. The doctor reckoned an air-bubble killed him when a nurse didn't perform an injection properly.

"Hell, it seems a shame, even if he was ninety-six," Scott mumbled at the bedside.

Scott had agreed the arrangements with Josh's family. And as he stood there in the rain, wondering how long he had before he shuffled off this mortal coil, Scott smiled at the epitaph on his friend's headstone:

Josh 'BUBBLES' Mason
Born February 7, 1845–Died December 7, 1941
All bubbles burst eventually. He lasted longer than most.

ONCE UPON A TIME IN MIRAGE
I.J. Parnham

Cow-puncher, train butch, Mississippi gambler, gunslinger . . . are just some of the many jobs Ian Parnham hasn't had while he's been living in the misty glens and castle-strewn moors of the northeast of Scotland. But he has written fifteen Black Horse Westerns and four Avalon Westerns. You can visit him at www.ijparnham.co.uk.

Tucker Crowley was asleep when the new prisoner was brought in. He slipped his head out from under his blanket to see Sheriff McAllen throw the prisoner to the floor where he slid on his side against the other cot.

The prisoner gathered his breath then leapt to his feet and hurled himself at the cell door, but McAllen had already slammed it shut, locked it, and stepped back. Still, the prisoner grabbed the bars and rattled them.

"Save your strength," McAllen said, sneering. "You'll need it."

"I've still got plenty to take you on," the prisoner shouted, then launched a gob of spit that splattered over McAllen's shoulder and dripped down onto his star.

With the back of his hand McAllen cleaned his star.

"I'll be having another word with you about that later," he said, then backed away to the door to the cells. The door slammed, keys rattled.

"McAllen ain't right about much," Tucker said, now wide awake, "but he was there. You'll get to spend a lot of time angry in here if you don't calm down."

The prisoner considered his bleak surroundings: two cells, barred on three sides with a stone back wall, two snoring whiskey-hounds in the other cell.

"I guess you're right," he said, then flopped down onto the free cot.

Tucker appraised his new companion, seeing the reason for his anger. Bloody scrapes coated his knuckles, a split lip had dirtied his teeth, and an ugly bruise darkened his cheek.

"McAllen give you a hard time?"

"Not as hard a time as I gave him." The prisoner uttered a rueful laugh, which Tucker returned. They exchanged names, Tucker learning that he shared a cell with Durango Jones.

"And what did you do to get thrown in here?" Tucker asked.

"What's it to you?" Durango snarled, his brief friendly mood ending in a moment.

"Hey," Tucker said, raising his hands. "I was just making conversation. We ain't exactly got much of anything to do in here but talk."

"No point me wasting my breath on that. I don't intend to be in here for long." Durango cast a significant look at the small grill in the back wall through which the rays of the low moon shone.

"I wish you luck with your dreams, then. I spent my first month in here plotting to escape until I realized it's impossible, and after tonight it won't matter." Tucker settled down with his head resting on his hands. He'd given Durango an opportunity to talk, but if he didn't take up the offer he could just resume his interrupted sleep.

"Why?" Durango asked. "What's happening tomorrow?"

Tucker smiled. "I get shipped off to Denver. Ten years."

"What you do to get that?"

"What didn't I do?" Tucker swung his legs down to the floor and leaned forward. He lowered his voice. "The things I've done, I could have got hung ten times over, but they only got me for horse thieving."

"So what else did you do?"

Tucker pondered on whether to answer honestly. He'd killed his first man at sixteen, spent the next ten years chasing the easy dollar, and he wasn't sure how many men he'd killed in that pursuit. But with his companion being so cagey about himself he didn't feel inclined to spill his guts just yet.

"You've got to be careful what you say in here. The rats have ears, if you know what I mean." Tucker lay back down. "So you first. What did you do to get thrown in here?"

Durango sighed. He got to his feet and covered the three paces to the back wall then jumped up to look out through the grill. Having completed the tour of the cell, he threw himself back on his cot and matched Tucker's posture.

"It's a long story."

"I've got the time to listen, provided you finish by tomorrow."

Durango cleared his throat, but didn't speak while he considered whether to reveal his crime. Then he grunted as if he'd made a decision and started talking. His voice was low and melodic, and contained just enough detail to let Tucker close his eyes and imagine that the world outside his small cell did still exist. . . .

Walker Beck beckoned me to enter the hide-walled shack. As he'd promised, he was alone. He sat at a table, his hands resting on its top.

"So," he said, "you got the money?"

"I have," I said, "but only if you have Mance Ryker."

"I know where he is." Walker leaned back in his chair. "Why do you want him?"

I'd answered this question many times and never saw a reason to hide my purpose.

"My name is Durango Jones. Three years ago Mance Ryker killed my brother."

Walker spread his hands in a benevolent gesture. "Then you can have him when I have the money."

It always came to this, the moment when I learnt whether I'd get real information that would get me closer to Mance, or whether I'd just have to kill another double-dealer.

I reached into my jacket with my left hand, then stopped.

"Prove yourself. Tell me something about Mance Ryker that only someone who knows him would know."

Walker's beady eyes took in my right hand dangling beside my holster and my hidden left hand that may or may not be holding a concealed weapon.

He smiled. "All right. You're not the only man offering money for Mance Ryker."

I was considering this information, which was new to me, when Walker's gaze flicked over my shoulder in a nervous betrayal of his true intent.

I nodded, as if I wanted to hear more, making Walker relax, then ripped my gun from its holster, turning at the hip as my left hand shot out from my jacket. I blasted lead through the hide wall where Walker had looked. An agonized screech sounded at the same moment as I saw the hole in the wall through which the shot man had watched me. Then I swung back.

81

Walker was scrambling for his own gun, but before it cleared leather I kicked the table up into his face, tumbling him backwards from his chair. He landed on his back, shook himself, but by then I'd vaulted the table and had thrust my gun up under his chin so firmly I doubted he could open his mouth wide enough to answer my question.

"I ain't offering money for Mance Ryker no more," I muttered, "just your life. Talk!"

"You've made a big mistake," Walker bleated through gritted teeth. "You just shot a deputy sheriff, Lorne Wright. The law are looking for Mance, too. They're paying good money for information on anyone asking about him."

"Being a wanted man don't worry me. Now talk!"

"You didn't get my meaning." Walker snorted a hollow laugh, enjoying himself for probably the last time. "Lorne ain't the only lawman interested in Mance."

Walker's gaze again flicked past me, hinting that something was still amiss. This time I noticed it too late.

"Release him," a stern voice said behind me.

I heard footfalls as a man, presumably another lawman, settled his stance. Walker was right. I'd made a mistake, and a bad one. I weighed up my chances of taking on a man who must have a gun aimed at my back, then threw Walker to the floor.

I straightened, raised my right hand, and let the gun fall. . . .

"And that's how you ended up in here," Tucker said. "Well, at least you got to dig a hole in a lawman."

Durango's eyes flared, registering his irritation at having his story interrupted.

"I hadn't finished," he said. "I told you it was a long story, and that ain't how I ended up in here."

"You mean the lawman didn't arrest you?"

Durango laughed. "He tried, except I really did have a second gun, which I'd have told you about if you'd have kept your mouth shut, along with the fact this happened six months ago and over the state line in Newton."

"So you got away."

"Yup. I killed the other deputy and made Walker regret double-crossing me so much in the end he begged me to kill him, and I obliged. But not before he told me what I wanted to know about Mance Ryker. And it was good information, even if it came with another price."

"What price?"

"I'll tell you," Durango said, waggling a reproachful finger at Tucker, "provided you keep quiet."

I stood outside Jim Crest's mercantile with a foot raised and pressed flat to the wall while smoking, providing an impression of someone wasting away the day. I tipped my hat to the few people who passed by so as not to alarm anyone. After all, I didn't want to appear as if I was about to rob the town bank.

I'd had to do plenty of questionable things since I made it my life's mission to track down and kill the man who'd shot up my brother. This was the worst. The people I had to kill before were either aiming to kill me or stood between me and my mission, but this time I was deliberately setting out to break the law.

Walker's information had led me to Tex Cody and his motley collection of bandits. Mance Ryker rode with these men, Walker claimed. It had taken me four months to find them and another month to get close enough to observe them, but by then Mance had moved on. So I worked my way into Tex's confidence and found he was willing to talk about Mance, but only after he'd tested me.

Today I would prove I was a man he could trust.

Tex was on the opposite side of the road also acting nonchalantly. He occasionally caught my eye with secret signals that kept me informed of progress. Not that I needed that information when his bandits rode into town.

Seven men drew up outside the bank and filed inside. I pushed away from the wall, as did Tex, to await developments. It didn't take long. Two men hurried out with saddlebags thrown over their shoulders. They took up flanking positions beside the door, roving their guns back and forth taking in the almost deserted road, while the other men backed out with their guns aimed inside in case of trouble. Not that there was any. Tex planned the raid carefully and his men carried it out so far with surprising speed and without firing a single shot.

Then I noticed something, or to be more precise I noticed the absence of something. I was unfamiliar with this town, but very few people were about, almost as if. . . .

I paced down the road towards the bank, while across the road Tex darted glances at me, wondering why I wasn't following orders. He soon saw the reason for my concern. A line of lawmen rose up from behind the top of the false-fronted saloon facing the bank and fired as one. Their sustained gunfire cut down four of the bandits before they were even able to work out where the shooting was coming from.

Even seeing that they'd ridden into a trap didn't help them. Two men took cover behind their horses and fired up at the saloon, but gunfire blasted at them from the sides as other hidden lawmen made themselves known. Both men went wheeling to the boardwalk.

I couldn't help them, not that I'd care to risk myself when Tex could tell me everything I needed to know about Mance Ryker. I kept my gun holstered and turned on my heel, aiming to hurry past my horse and so give the impression I wasn't involved and was just getting away from the gunfire, but Tex surprised me with his loyalty. He broke into a run to charge across the road towards the only surviving man.

He reached him just as the man got a slug in the back that drove him to his knees. Tex slid to a halt beside him and held him up for a moment, but I'd misunderstood his actions. He wasn't being brave to the point of being foolhardy. He whipped the saddlebag from the dying man's shoulder, let him drop to the ground, then ran away from the bank.

I kept walking at a hurried pace as Tex hightailed it past me. He reached his horse, moved to mount it, but then the lawmen on the saloon roof must have decided he wasn't an opportunistic passerby but a bandit after all. A volley of gunshots peppered around him. Most missed, but then redness burst from his side, kicking him to the ground, his outstretched hand dragging the saddlebag from his mount. He lay sprawled and still until the last gunshot echo died. Then he clawed his way to his knees.

I didn't want to abandon five months' worth of effort in my quest to find Mance Ryker. So I took my horse and meandered out into the road. When my casual stroll happened to pass Tex the lawmen were checking on their targets openly as if they didn't expect trouble.

"Can you ride?" I asked Tex.

"Just get me up there," Tex said, his determined utterance being the only words that would save him.

I helped the wounded Tex up on to his horse. Then I mounted up and we galloped out of town. When I'd passed the last building I looked back. The lawmen had seen our flight and were hurrying to their horses. . . .

"So that's how you came to be in here," Tucker said, then gave a low whistle. "That's rough on you. They'll treat you as if you were a bank raider even if you only helped Tex."

"They would," Durango said, his tone irritated, "if that were the reason why I'm in here."

Tucker snorted. "You mean they didn't catch you?"

"Nope, but you'd have found that out if you hadn't interrupted me again."

"Hey," Tucker said, raising his hands, "when you said this was a long story, I didn't expect it to be this long."

"People have said I talk too much."

"You do." Tucker sighed. "But I'm not complaining. So what are you in here for?"

"I'm getting to that, if you'll let me." Durango took a deep breath before he continued, letting Tucker provide an encouraging grunt. "It was long into the night before we rested up. Those lawmen were dogged and I was sure they were still out there looking for us, but I had no choice but to stop a while. Tex was in a bad way."

I kicked Tex's side to see if he still lived, receiving in response a wheezing groan before he forced out his tortured words. "Help me."

"I will," I said, "when you tell me what I want to know."

"Mance Ryker must have tipped off the lawmen so I'll talk, but I don't know much. Harlow does though. Help me and I'll tell you about him."

I narrowed my eyes. My voice took on a world-weary tone that I didn't need to feign. "And who's Harlow?"

Tex told me, so I helped him, although I didn't waste time by burying him afterwards. Apparently this Harlow was waiting in hiding for Tex with fresh horses. Then the group would scatter to confuse any pursuit.

When I arrived at the waiting point, four men were sitting around a guarded fire arguing about whether they'd been duped. I took no chances and stayed in the shadows. I hurled an empty saddlebag into the centre of their camp.

All four men leapt to their feet, their guns drawn, and taking in the compass points as they tried to work out where I was.

"Who's there?" I knew that was Harlow from Tex's description.

"I'm Durango Jones, but you don't know me. I only just joined Tex."

"Where's Tex?"

"He ain't coming. We walked into a trap. I was the only one who escaped."

"Mighty convenient that the one man I don't know just happens to get away."

"Maybe, but I'm the one who's here and you've got to deal with me now. I've got five thousand dollars, but I don't want the money. I only joined Tex to get information on a double-crossing varmint called Mance Ryker."

"I know Mance." Harlow cast a significant glance at the other men, obviously issuing them with a silent order. "Come out into the open and we'll discuss a deal."

"Later, and whether you trust me or not, know that this is the truth: The lawmen who got Tex are still on my tail. They'll be here soon. You'd better move on."

Harlow grunted with irritation then gestured to the other men who didn't need any encouragement to hurry to their horses.

"We'll meet up in Mirage," he shouted, "and discuss the money."

"And Mance Ryker," I said, but it was to myself. By then Harlow was out of sight and I was slipping through the shadows to my own horse.

Out on the plains the low moon highlighted glimpses of the approaching riders as the persistent lawmen closed. . . .

"And so," Tucker said after Durango paused for several seconds, "that's how you got to be in here?"

"Nope. The lawmen didn't search for me when they had those four in their sights, not that they got close, apparently. I came to Mirage to wait for Harlow."

"But the lawmen found you first?"

"They didn't. I was always one step ahead of them. I disposed of the evidence by hiding the five thousand under the roots of this old hanging tree out of town. You know it?"

"Yeah."

"Then I holed up here for a week waiting for Harlow to show." Durango rubbed his jaw and smiled ruefully. "But tonight I got bored waiting, got into a poker game, and lost a hundred dollars to a man with more cards up his sleeve than were in his hand. I shot him, so Sheriff McAllen threw me in here."

Tucker considered Durango's answer to the question he'd asked some time ago.

"So the reason you're in here has nothing to do with your quest to find Mance Ryker, Walker, those deputy sheriffs, Tex Cody's bandits, the bank raid, Harlow, and all the rest?"

"Nope."

"Then why didn't you just say you shot a man in a poker game?"

Durango shrugged. "It passed the time while I was waiting to get out of here."

Tucker laughed. "You, my friend, are going nowhere."

"Well, either you're right, or those rats with ears are real noisy tonight." Durango cocked his head to one side and cupped an ear to show he was listening. Then he rolled off his cot and slid beneath it. He curled into a ball and dragged the blanket over himself.

"What the . . . ?" Tucker murmured. Then he heard the sounds Durango had heard. Someone was moving around outside, then came a tapping, then the crack of a struck match.

Tucker didn't need any more warnings. He pushed himself off the cot, taking the blanket with him, and dived beneath the cot. He'd just got the blanket over his head when the blast shook the cell. Stones peppered his body, the force throwing him into the cell bars where he lay, his ears ringing. Dust swirled around him, but strong moonlight shone through it and he realized that dynamite had bored a hole in the back wall.

"Durango," a voice urged from outside. "Get out!"

"Harlow?" Tucker asked.

"Yeah, who else? Now quit wasting time."

Disorientated and coughing, Tucker crawled across the floor with his hands questing before him until he located Durango. The blast had also thrown him into the bars and his head pressed tightly against one. He was breathing, but he didn't stir when Tucker shook him. Outside, Harlow again urged Durango to move.

Then Tucker's mind caught up with the sudden change of circumstance. The key facts whirled through his thoughts: ten years in Denver, $5,000 hidden under the hanging tree, a savior who'd never seen the man he'd come to save. . . .

"I'm coming," Tucker said. He patted Durango's shoulder before he left. "You really do talk too much, friend."

Then he hurried for the hole. Harlow didn't question his identity, merely hurrying him to a horse. Then they galloped out of town like the Devil himself was on their tails, or at least a determined lawman.

Harlow had only one man with him, but he used a variation of the plan Durango had mentioned. When their horses tired, they rode into a dry wash where two men were waiting. They holed up while these men rode out, giving the lawman recharged quarries to chase.

Even so, Harlow took no chances and dawn was lighting the eastern horizon when Tucker led him to the hanging tree.

Like Durango, Tucker had been in stand-off situations such as the one he now faced. The numerous duped and often nameless dead men in his past could all testify to the fact he knew how to get what he wanted. So in a confident frame of mind he drew his horse to a halt before the hanging tree and faced his saviors.

"Obliged for what you did," he said, "but now it's time for us to part."

"Fine with me," Harlow said. "Show me to the five thousand, and I'll show you to Mance Ryker."

"The deal's changed. I ain't interested in him no more. I'll keep half the money and Mance can go to hell."

"You're a man who's tracked Mance for three years because he killed your brother." Harlow narrowed his eyes. "What you really planning?"

Durango hadn't mentioned that he'd told Harlow why he was after Mance, but then again Tucker was thankful he'd not told him every detail of his long tale.

"Believe what you will, but know this: You'll never find the money, so you've got no choice." Tucker leaned forward in the saddle to deliver the element of his deal that would define how this stand-off would develop. "Now give me a gun. Then we'll go to the money together and divide it up somewhere where we can all watch each other."

Harlow stared into his eyes, sizing him up, then grunted a low command to the other man. This man moved his horse to draw alongside Tucker. While looking at Harlow, Tucker held out a hand for a gun, but instead he received a solid blow to the back of the head, knocking him forward, and a shove in the side that tipped him from his horse.

Tucker lay stunned then tried to rise but the men were all over him. They pinned him down, bound his hands behind his back, then dragged him to his feet to receive a pummeling.

Fierce, steady blows knocked him back and forth between the men. With no way to defend himself, Tucker had no choice but to endure and to console himself with the thought that he knew where the money was and that they wouldn't beat that information out of him.

But they asked no questions.

A blow to the head must have knocked him out briefly because he came to sitting on his horse. His hands were still tied behind his back and Harlow, also mounted, faced him. The other man was at his side, brandishing a long stick.

"Whipping me won't make me talk," Tucker said, eyeing the stick.

"He ain't going to whip you," Harlow said, "just your horse."

Tucker was about to demand an explanation when his horse took a spooked pace forward and a rope tightened around his neck. He gulped, feeling the rope burn his neck, then looked up. It was as he'd feared. They'd looped a noose around his neck to frighten him into talking. One slap and the horse would bolt, suspending him from the old hanging tree.

Despite his predicament, Tucker was impressed by Harlow's ruse. He sighed, accepting Harlow had bettered him, but now looking forward to his freedom, even if he couldn't enjoy it with a share of the money.

"All right. Perhaps I am prepared to offer a better deal. Let me go and you can keep the whole five thousand."

"But," Harlow said slowly, "there is no five thousand dollars."

"There is. It's near here. Durango. . . . I know where it is." Tucker knew he was babbling but icy fear clawed at his heart. "I'll give it to you, Harlow."

"I'm not Harlow."

Tucker flinched, rasping his neck against the rope.

"Then who are you?"

Harlow took several seconds to reply, looking Tucker over and drinking in the fear that was now consuming him.

"My name is Durango Jones," he intoned, as if he'd said these words many times. "Three years ago Mance Ryker killed my brother."

"But you can't be. I'm. . . . This other man is. . . . " Tucker silenced when he received a shake of the head.

"He isn't. I'm the real Durango Jones. The man at your side is Lorne Wright. Walker Beck and Tex Cody are the other men who helped you get away."

"I . . . I don't know what's happening here. Lorne's the deputy sheriff who got shot up back in that shack and Walker died there, too. Tex leads a bandit gang, and Harlow's a member. I don't understand!"

"There were no deputy sheriffs, no bandit gang, no bank raid, no nothing. That was just a story told by a man I hired because he's good at telling stories. Did you enjoy it?"

Tucker gulped, pressing his throat against the rope. "I did, I guess."

"Then it served its purpose."

"Does that mean there was no Mance Ryker either?" Tucker asked, still unwilling to accept the story he'd been told had never happened.

"He does exist, and he did shoot my brother, but he's known by another name."

Tucker winced as sudden understanding came to him. Over the last ten years he'd killed many men in his quest for the easy dollar and he hadn't always asked their names, but this time he asked the obvious question. "What name?"

"You know." Durango gestured and Lorne whipped the stick. The horse bolted.

THE MAN WHO TRACKED A RIVER
Derek Rutherford

*Derek Rutherford hails from the wild west of England—
Gloucestershire, to be precise. He's the author of two Black Horse
Westerns:* Vengeance At Tyburn Ridge *and* Yellow Town. *In his spare
time he plays and teaches rock 'n' roll guitar, rides large motorcycles,
and catches not-quite-so-large fish.*

The day Rufus Franklin shot dead Estelle Williams and headed west,
Sam Penn was standing beside the Black River watching the thaw
water carry broken trees, dead cows, and even a whole log cabin
somewhere to the south. It crossed his mind that there might have been
someone still in the cabin, that he should have waded into the water
and tried to get a rope around a beam. He could have lashed the other
end of the rope to a tree and let the flow bring the cabin into the bank.

But even as the idea formed it was too late. The river was running
high and fast. So he got to thinking instead of how that might be a fine
way to travel, like being in a boat but with a roof and a cot and a stove.
Hell, you could make it all the way to Texas and neither the sunshine
nor the rain would bother you.

He watched the cabin until it drifted out of sight around a long
bend. Moments later he heard gunshots from the direction of town and
instinctively knew they weren't right. Not that gunfire ever was right,
but there had been plenty of times in the last half-dozen years when it
hadn't been exactly wrong. Drunken cowboys whooping it up and
having fun, fathers teaching their boys to shoot, Jack down at the livery
sometimes having to put an injured horse out of its misery.

But not this time.

This time the sound of the gunshots carried with it some
knowledge, something that made the hairs on his neck rise. He turned
to face the town as if that might help explain away the almost
supernatural fear he suddenly felt. Then he called himself a damn fool.
It was simply his understanding of the place and the people in it that
gave him this knowledge. There were no boys of shooting age in town,
no drunken trail hands, and Jack only ever needed a single merciful
bullet for his lame horses.

Sam paused, listened a while longer, sensing there was more to come. Sure enough, there was another gunshot. Then nothing.

Despite the mid-morning sunshine, he shivered. Gunshots and broken homes floating away. There surely was something in the air.

He eased himself onto his horse and made to press his heels into her flanks, but paused.

"It ain't my job anymore," he said aloud.

But the echoes of the gunfire, combined with the years of responsibility, caused his heels to turn in, seemingly of their own accord, and he found himself heading back to town.

Sheriff Jackson Lloyd already had a posse formed. There were half a dozen cowboys riding tight circles outside Lloyd's office, horses snorting and kicking up mud, riders cursing and spitting. Estelle Williams' husband, Monroe—who was short of an eye and an arm on account of some bad dynamite when he was working on the railroad twenty years before—was standing on the plank-walk with a gun in his hand telling the sheriff to bring Franklin back alive and let him take care of the bastard.

"You got it," Lloyd said, and then turned and watched Sam ride slowly up.

"What's going on?" Sam asked.

"Your old partner, Rufus Franklin," Lloyd said. "The son of a bitch shot Estelle dead, took the money from their register, and lit out." He stared hard at Sam, a cold accusation in his eyes as if somehow it was Sam's fault that Rufus had gone bad. "We're just about to bring him back. I guess you won't wanna come."

Sam said nothing.

"We're gonna hang him up by his thumbs," Monroe Williams said. "For starters."

"Why'd he do it?" Sam asked.

"Because he was drunk and broke and Estelle said enough was enough. A line of credit can only go so far." Monroe's voice wavered. "Sonofabitch."

"I can't believe you never went with them," Maria said later.

He wasn't sure if the tone in her voice was accusation or relief.

"They won't catch him," he said.

She studied him for a few seconds and he knew that she understood what he was thinking as clearly as if he had spoken aloud.

"Then you could have gone," she said. "It wouldn't have mattered."

The only other person who had ever understood him this well, who could second-guess his words and thoughts, was Rufus Franklin. Well, with Roof it hadn't really been about words, it had been about actions, about working in harmony, about being there for one another and saving each other's lives on more than a few occasions.

"This way I still got a choice," Sam said.

She continued to study him, her green eyes boring deep inside him. He wondered if she could see his feelings for her in there. He presumed so. He figured he knew how she felt so it stood to reason the reverse was true, too. It was something she'd never questioned him about. Not overtly, anyway. There had been the odd time when the oil lamps and the moon had been low and the boundaries between landlady and lodger had got dangerously blurred. But he'd always pulled back. And he often wondered if she knew—or tried to guess—why.

"You're going to go after him?" she asked. "On your own?"

This time she couldn't read the answer in his expression because he didn't know himself what that answer was.

"They don't want me as their sheriff anymore," he said.

"I think most people would disagree."

"Then why did they vote me out?"

"Is that why you're not going after Rufus?"

He shook his head.

"Are you bitter about it?" she asked.

"I was. Not any more though."

"Then why mention it?"

"Just weighing up the pros and cons."

"The biggest con being that he was your best friend and partner for twenty years."

He looked at her and said nothing.

"And the biggest pro being that you're a good man and if anyone can bring him home, you can. Maybe you're the only one who can."

He sighed. She was right about him being the only guy that could bring Rufus back, and she was almost right that the main reason for his hesitancy in doing so was because they'd been friends and partners for so long.

Almost right.

Rufus had gone where the whiskey was. Sam knew that. It wasn't a case of trying to follow tracks in the mud and the dust. It was simply a case of getting inside his buddy's head. After killing Estelle, Roof's instincts kicked in and he'd gone west, apparently headed for the mountains where a man could get lost forever. And, maybe while the alcohol still raged in his blood, getting lost in the wilderness would have genuinely been his plan. But it wouldn't have taken him long to see things more clearly.

It probably wasn't past midday before he'd started thinking about the few bottles he had in his saddlebags and what he was going to do when they were empty. He'd know that the posse would continue to search for him hour after hour, day after day, and simply assume that their not finding him was down to him being hid out good and proper. Hell, Roof knew as well as Sam did that none of them could track a man worth a damn. So they'd spend a week out there searching for him and all the while he'd be heading someplace else.

And that someplace else was where the whiskey was.

There was nothing out west. Not for two or three weeks, maybe more. South was a different matter. He'd follow the river. There were trading posts and ferries, and a week away there was North Landing. Whiskey, whiskey, and more whiskey. Head south and it was whiskey city. And whiskey was all that mattered to Rufus these days.

"You sure you won't join me?" Rufus asked him every time they met. He would sit in Lapo's saloon with a bottle and a single glass in front of him and, when he saw Sam, he'd signal to Lapo to bring another glass over. Sam was the only man that Roof ever offered to share his whiskey with. But Sam always declined. It was a little ritual they never gave up on.

"You're still sticking to your guns?" Roof would say.

"Uh-huh."

"You're a better man than me."

"Just different, Roof. That's all. Just different."

"We all handle things the best we can, huh?"

"Yeah."

"You still think about it?"

"Every day."

Then Rufus would pour a good shot and down it in one. It was his way of hiding from the demons. Sam chose to face them head on, to revel in the pain, to accept it like it was the punishment he deserved and had always escaped. It was why he had never married Maria. It was why he had served the town for so long. It was why he rarely smiled.

Most days he figured that Roof had made a far better choice than he had done.

This day, he headed south, tracking the river, wondering what the hell he was going to do when he caught up with his partner.

He saw the empty bottle at dawn, two days out. He'd just started to get the first rogue thoughts appearing that maybe he'd read his buddy wrong, that maybe Roof really had lit out for the wilderness. And then there it was, casually tossed into the buffalo grass, glinting like something valuable in the low sun.

He wondered: How many bottles can one man carry? Three or four? Half a dozen? It didn't really matter. The river was starting to widen and by the end of the day he'd reach Crawford's Ferry. Crawford had a small store alongside the river. Roof could have picked up more whiskey there for sure, maybe some jerky, too, and feed for his horse, if he was thinking that clearly.

Just an hour later and Sam realized he wasn't going to have to ride as far as Crawford. Rufus was just up ahead of him.

He couldn't see his old partner, but he knew he was there. He knew by the way his heart had suddenly started racing, the way the hairs on his neck had prickled, the way all of his senses had suddenly sprung to life as if the one that controlled them all—the sixth sense—had sent out an order to bear arms. He could smell the rushing river water, maybe slowing just a little now as the thaw tailed off, a clean cold smell. He could taste the grass and the sycamore blossom, and hear the chirping of insects in the fresh morning air, and the rustle of riverside trees in the breeze. All senses working as one. A body tuned into the natural world and the dangers that lay ahead.

All of this happened at an unconscious level. At a conscious level what he saw told him all he needed to know. The washed away log cabin lay beached on the outside bank of a long slow bend. It had ended its current journey upright, wedged amongst a handful of giant rocks at the river's edge. The cabin was so perfectly positioned that it almost looked as if it had been built there. The river had even backed away from it a little, as if it had done its construction work and moved on.

Another discarded whiskey bottle lay on the ground outside the cabin's door, tossed onto the drying mud, as if a man had been too tired or too drunk to throw it an extra ten feet into the cleansing river.

Sam stopped. Listened. Tasted the air. If a man allowed himself to be open to such things, he could smell the truth. Roof must have come by this cabin late last night, seen it with as much amazement and incredulity as Sam had done when it first floated by him. But where he had wondered what it would be like to ride a house all the way to Texas, Roof would have pondered on whether or not the previous owner had any whiskey inside.

Somewhere a horse snorted, maybe sensing Sam's own mount.

He stopped, dropped to the ground, looped the reins around a low sycamore branch. And then he started to work toward the cabin, his eyes scouring every inch of the ground in front of him. He thought back to their army days and the skill, instinct, and pure natural ability that had kept Rufus alive when so many had died. Even in his wildest drunks Roof had always maintained such instincts. He might have been utterly amazed at the sight of a home washed up on the riverbank, offering shelter and maybe even food and drink, but he was still a man on the run for murder, and until totally inebriated he would have no doubt taken whatever steps he thought necessary to protect himself.

In the war, when they were overnighting away from the main troop—and sometimes even when they weren't—Rufus would tie out a tripwire that was cleverly linked to several sticks wedged in the ground on which swung old sardine cans filled with lead shot. "It ain't much," he used to say. "But I'm a light sleeper and it's enough." Sam couldn't remember a single occasion when anyone ever tripped that wire but it didn't stop Roof setting it religiously.

And he'd done so again now. Low across the ground in front of the cabin, one stick wedged behind a boulder against which the water lapped, another beneath the cabin window, a sardine can in the branches of a tree, with hard ground beneath.

"Damn right, it ain't much," Sam whispered, wondering if these weren't the very same tins Roof had used way back then, and whether or not the warning system would actually work. He was half tempted to kick the wire just to find out. But in the end he stepped over it and quietly walked up to the cabin door.

He touched the door. The cabin had been washed up on a slight angle and gravity swung the door open.

Rufus was inside, sitting down, watching the door.

There was a bottle of whiskey nestled in his crotch, and a revolver on the floor. His eyes and cheeks were dark and sunken, his jaw lined with stubble. He blinked once or twice and Sam wondered if he'd sat there like that all night, not really sleeping, just looking at the back of the door.

"I've been waiting for you," Rufus said, his voice heavy with fatigue. "Started to wonder if I'd read you wrong all these years. See you avoided the wire. Figured you'd remember."

"Wouldn't want to let you down," Sam said.

"You never did so far."

"There's always a first time."

"Meaning what? Meaning I let you down?"

"Uh-huh." Sam nodded slowly.

Red blotches blazed through the stubble on Rufus's cheeks. His eyes looked older and his shoulders more slumped than Sam remembered. And it had only been two days. Maybe killing a defenseless old lady did that to a man.

"I didn't know what I was doing, Sam." He lifted the whiskey bottle just an inch. It seemed to be as much of a shrug as he could muster. "If I could go back in time."

"But you can't, can you?"

"You always handled it better than me."

Sam could smell the pure mountain water rushing by outside. At the cabin doorway that smell battled against the stink of alcohol and sweat and regret that rose in almost visible waves from his old partner.

"We ain't here to talk about that," Sam said. "We talked that out long ago."

"We talked, but we never got it out. That's why I ain't ever stopped drinking. And why you never started again."

97

"I've come to take you back, Roof."

"I know."

They looked at one another. It seemed to Sam that Rufus had shrunk yet further in just the minute he'd been there. He thought Roof might have put up quite a fight, but now he realized there was no strength left in the man.

"Well?"

"I ain't coming," Rufus said.

"You mean, you ain't coming voluntarily."

"I mean I ain't coming. I know I did wrong, and I know I should face up to it. But I spent twenty years not facing up to it. The same as you did. And I ain't about to start now."

"I can take you home."

Rufus shook his head. "No. You only think you can."

"Don't make me try."

Now Rufus smiled. "You want a drink, partner? Just one? I mean, we ain't ever going to be in this situation again."

Sam said nothing.

"You know, after all we've been through," Rufus continued. "This is it. This is the last time we're gonna see each other."

Rufus lifted the bottle of whiskey and drank.

Sam drew his gun.

After Rufus finished laughing and wiped the spittle from his lips, he said, "You ain't gonna shoot me. I saved your life. More'n once."

"I think we're even on that score."

"Exactly. You ain't gonna kill a man who saved your life and you ain't gonna kill a man when you already risked your own life to save his."

Sam said nothing again. What could he say? Roof was right.

Rufus took another drink. He started to cough.

"I could take you back," Sam said. "You ain't in no fit state to put up a fight."

"No. Well, maybe you could. But you won't."

"I won't?"

"No."

"Why not, Roof?" Sam had to ask the question even though he already knew what the answer was going to be.

"Because I know stuff, pardner. Because I know what happened."

So there it was. After all these years. All the years when they'd agreed that what had happened would always remain a secret, that it would never be spoken of again. No matter how drunk or how tortured either of them was, no matter what else was happening in their lives, the one thing they knew—just like they'd always been there for each other back in the old days—was that neither would ever speak of that time.

But here it was. First murder, and now betrayal. Or at least the threat of betrayal.

Sam shook his head slowly.

"I know what you're thinking," Rufus said. "But what else have I got left to fight you with?" Sam noticed a line of whiskey running through the gray and white stubble on Roof's chin. There was a tightness and a yellow sheen to his old friend's skin. His teeth, the few that remained, were dark.

"It was the Devil that made us do it, wasn't it, Sam?" There was a different tone to his voice now, some regret, some sentimentality, some sense of an approaching end.

"It was the whiskey," Sam said quietly, hating to see his old partner this way. Knowing that the despair that had brought Rufus to this point could have done—could still do—exactly the same to him.

"It was the Devil that made us drink," Rufus said. "We were kids, Sam. It was the war. War makes everything different."

Sam slipped his gun quietly back into his holster.

They'd been young men then. Men with fear and adrenaline and revenge and, of course, whiskey running in equal measures through their veins. They'd seen colleagues blown apart, maimed, blinded. Friends who stood shoulder to shoulder with them at Johnsonville and Shiloh and were now gone. They'd been away from their farms for the first time and weren't sure that the world beyond those homesteads wasn't all like this—full of terror and horror, screams and bloodlust, and the incredible feeling of simply being alive. Most of all they'd never realized just how badly they wanted to kill Yankees. When you saw your best friends lying in the dirt with their insides spilling out and their mothers' names fading from whitening lips, all you wanted to do was kill, kill, and kill some more. And when you couldn't kill, when the damn Yankees had turned tail and refused to fight, all you had left was whiskey with which to deaden those urges and the echoes of your dying friends' prayers.

"How much did we drink that day?" Rufus said.

"I don't recall."

"You recall every second, pardner. Just the same way I do. No matter how much I drink, I've never been able to forget." He looked up. "I should have done it your way, shouldn't I?"

"There's no need to talk about it."

"Yes there is. I want you to know that I still remember everything. And I know you do, too. That's why you ain't ever married that pretty Maria, isn't it? You're still punishing yourself."

"And if I take you back, you'll tell it all?"

"It's all I've got to make you leave me alone," Rufus said. "Look at me. What else can I do?" He stared up at Sam, his eyes wide and wet. "All I'm asking is for my old buddy to save my life just one more time."

Sam Penn walked away from the cabin that had been washed ashore intact by the Black River. Somewhere a small part of his mind still wondered at the miracle of how such a thing could have happened. Inside the cabin Rufus still sat on a good chair at a good table on good floorboards. There'd even been an oil lamp hanging on a hook on one wall. For all Sam knew, come the night, that lamp might still work. But the rest of his thoughts twisted and turned like a snake that had been speared to the ground with a pitchfork.

"All you gotta do is say you never found me," Rufus had said. It was easy to say. Hell, it was easy to do. But it was no more the right thing to do than living every day of your life like you weren't a murderer and a rapist. And that's what they were. A line ran through their lives linking every living moment back to that time in the hills of Tennessee. It was more than a line. It was something living, like an artery. It was a river of blood.

Roof had tried to blank it out with alcohol, but alcohol was the cause of it—that and the bloodlust that they'd had trained into them— so *he'd* simply never touched a drop again, letting the memories come at him with as much sharpness and pain as they could. He deserved nothing less.

They'd discovered the two wounded soldiers and the nurses in a small church house, back off the main trail a mile or so. He and Rufus and their hollow growling bellies had been out searching for rabbits and squirrels but what they'd found was a cave cut into the rocks, hidden behind piled up brush, and inside about a dozen crates of mountain whiskey.

They'd laughed and jigged around a little and then cracked open a bottle and drank and worked out how much the liquor might be worth if they could somehow get it back to camp. Then they drank some more and decided to head on a little further and see if they couldn't find a wagon they could commandeer. Then they could make their fortunes.

But the strong liquor and their empty stomachs soon started to blur such intentions. By the time they came across the Yankees, they were almost too drunk to walk or talk straight, and the only coherent thoughts they were having were about girls they'd left back home and men they'd left on the battlefield.

In any normal event they'd have been no match for anyone. But one of the Yankees had no legs and the other was blind.

At the time everything seemed to happen in a mist. It was almost as if it was someone else cursing and yelling at the injured soldiers and blaming them for every dead comrade and disfigured friend, as if it was someone else swearing at the Yankees, kicking the blind one and knocking the legless one from his cot to the floor, throwing the nurses against the wall when they protested, forcing them all to drink whiskey, and more whiskey, and more whiskey still.

And then, as the mist got darker and ever thicker, shooting close to the blind man's ears, the legless man's shoulders, hearing them beg and scream and loving it. Blood on one of the nurses' chins from somewhere. Tears on their cheeks. The fear in their eyes pumping the alcohol ever faster through veins full of anger and bravado. And almost in darkness, a darkness rimmed with red shadows and shrieking ghosts, reloading and this time aiming at flesh, again and again, this one's for Joe, and this one's for Connor, and this one's for Wark and what are you screaming for, there ain't no injustice here Yankee, Wark lost his legs, too, and then burned to death, so take that, and that, and that. And finally, in total blackness, taking everything from the nurses, and only afterwards, their lives.

It wasn't until later, when twisted bellies vomited and vomited until there was nothing but blood and bile and acid coming up, that the fog cleared.

And it had stayed clear every single day since. For Sam, at least. Rufus had gone in search of a different darkness, and for the most part, Sam thought, he seemed to have succeeded. But it was a darkness that took everything he had to give—honor and health and sanity and money and friends and . . .

Honor.

The word cut like a rebel knife. Everything he had ever fought for, killed for, tried to live up to, had been about honor.

And now, to ride away, to leave a man free who shouldn't be free just because he had once been a friend who had saved your life, or because he threatened to tell things about you that you never wished anyone to know, was not the honorable thing to do. It was merely the easy thing.

So he stopped, cast his eyes heavenward, but found nothing there except some clouds brown with rain, and he turned back to the cabin.

This time Rufus, he knew, would be ready for him. This time the whiskey might be on the floor and the gun in his hands. This time Rufus would know Sam meant business. The man was in no state to put up a fight so he might simply raise that gun and fire.

Sam circled around the back of the cabin, one eye on the shack, one eye on the ground. Sure enough, there was another wire, more cans. His partner might have firewater for blood, and his teeth and muscles may have wasted away, and his sense of right and wrong was lost, but his brain was still sharp when it came to self-preservation.

Sam stepped over the wire, climbed across a few river boulders, and peered into the cabin through the gap between two broken rear boards.

Rufus held his Colt .44 in his hand facing the door. Every few seconds he twisted his head and looked behind at the rear window of the shack.

We know each other so well, Sam thought.

And then came another thought: I have to take him alive. It was nothing to do with honor or old friendships or even proving to oneself that, whatever Rufus might say in the coming days, Sam would have the character to stand up and face the repercussions. It was purely that killing Roof would be too easy. It would be like shooting a lame and starving horse. He hadn't turned around back there, hadn't come to this point in his life, just to shoot a cursed animal.

He looked about, seeking inspiration, trying to conjure up a plan. The wetness seeping through his boots gave him the answer. At the rear of the cabin the river swirled around the base timbers. It may actually have been rising as if a whole new melt had suddenly joined the torrent upstream.

Sam studied the way the cabin rested against the boulders. There was a single leg-strut wedged in between two rocks, bending slightly under the cabin's weight, but acting like a keystone, holding everything in place. He glanced back at the river and he recalled how his buddy couldn't swim too well, then he eased himself away from the cabin, and moved carefully and silently up into the tree line.

In the time it took him to get back to his horse and lead her in a wide arc to the rear of the cabin, the river had risen a few more inches. It wasn't raining here, but somewhere up in the mountains those brown clouds must have been delivering a hell of a spring storm.

He took his rope, crept back to the cabin, and tied it around the key strut. He ran the rope back to the horse, and secured it around his pommel.

Then he whispered for the horse to pull.

For a few moments nothing happened. He felt the muscles of the horse's neck, its flanks, its back straining. The saddle straps bit into the horse's belly. The saddle moved. The cabin didn't. He twisted around. Water was lapping at the back of the cabin. The strut looked to be bending more than it had but still nothing gave.

He pressed his heels gently against the horse's flanks.

Nothing.

Now he faced the cabin again and he hauled on the rope himself, his own arms and shoulders straining, his teeth gritted.

The first crack sounded like a gunshot; the rope went slack and the broken strut came flying through the air like shrapnel. The second crack was longer, like the sound of a cannonball ripping through wooden defenses. Then there was a groaning and the cabin started to tilt backwards, twisting a little, the river grabbing at it again now, reclaiming what it had once owned.

Sam was hauling the rope back in when Rufus burst out of the cabin door. Maybe the pressure of his feet on the porch was the only extra force that the river needed for no sooner was Rufus free of the cabin than it groaned again and moved into the flow like a gunboat easing out into deep water. For a second Rufus didn't appear to realize that Sam had been the catalyst behind the launch. He seemed confused over whether or not to hold tightest to his gun or his bottle. He plumped for the bottle, Sam noticed, holding that in his favored right hand, accuracy of liquid to lips seemingly his priority. As the cabin spun out into the middle of the river Rufus turned to watch his temporary home sail away and his eyes alighted on Sam.

"I knew you'd come back," he said, and he raised his hand as if expecting it to be full of Colt rather than whiskey.

Sam never said anything. He simply continued coiling his rope.

"I knew you would," Rufus said, a note of regret in his voice. He dropped the bottle then pointed his gun at Sam and started firing.

Rufus's aim was so wayward that Sam never even heard the whistle of bullets through the air. Six shots later he finished coiling the rope and edged the horse ever closer to his once partner. Now he opened up a loop at the free end. Briefly his eyes met those of Rufus. His partner had dead eyes now, eyes that had tried six times to kill him and failed. A sound that may have been a sob escaped from Rufus' mouth and then he turned and started scrambling over the rocks towards the trees and his horse and a world somewhere to the south full of whiskey.

Sam spun the lariat over his head three times, and with an accuracy borne not of practice, he said to Maria later, but of righteousness, he dropped the loop right around Roof's torso and arms.

Then he pulled the rope tight.

The day after they hanged Rufus Franklin, Sam Penn asked Maria Delgado to be his wife.

"I never thought you'd ask," she said. Her voice was neutral.

"I had a few things on my mind."

"For six years?"

"They were big things."

"Jackson Lloyd has been telling some folks that Rufus was shooting his mouth off in the jailhouse about something you and he did in the war."

"I heard."

"Most folks say that Rufus drank so much over the last twenty years that even when he had no liquor he was still drunk."

Sam looked at her, the big green eyes and soft curves, the sweet smile and the glisten of tears in those green eyes. She was going to turn him down. That thing he and Roof had done was too dark, too bad, and too damn evil. With this knowledge came a tidal wave of despair. Yet somewhere behind that wave there was, at least, the fact that he'd finally acknowledged what he'd done, allowed it to be told, allowed the truth to breathe. And, whatever else happened, he was a free man.

She saw it in his eyes and reached out and touched his hand.

"It's okay," she said. "Whether it's true or whether it's not, it doesn't matter. The Sam Penn I know is the best man I know."

He couldn't speak.

She looked at him. "You brought him back, Sam. No one else could have done that. You didn't have to. Yet you did."

He nodded.

She smiled.

"The answer is yes, Sam," she said.

CRAZY SHE CALLED HIM
Roy Carlton

Daniel Stephensen, writing as Roy Carlton, lives in Melbourne, Australia. His favorite Western writers include Glenn Lockwood, Ben Bridges (David Whitehead), and Matt Chisholm (Peter Watts). And he'll always make time for Zane Grey or a Cleveland Western.

They lay sprawled on the floor in the sawdust and rat droppings of an abandoned saloon in a half-built Nebraska way station called Six Mile Creek. She wouldn't move her knife from his throat, so he kept his hand tight around hers. Fair trade.

She said, "You're a crazy sonuvabitch. Why'd you kill him? We still don't know where the goddamn gold is."

He smiled at her with admiration, thinking maybe he'd like to marry a woman who talked like that. A woman who called him a sonuvabitch. "It's all right," he said. "Dalton will tell us."

She bared her teeth. "You are crazy."

"Ah, quit acting so sour. Don't look at me that way. Everything'll be just fine, you'll see."

She chewed thoughtfully, but the knife stayed where it was. At last she said, "You're an idiot. You don't have the faintest goddamn clue what you're doing."

"Yeah? Yeah? Well you look like a cow!" He mocked her: chew chew chew. She calmly moved the knife away and spat a line of black juice in his eyes.

"Ah! Damn you woman, damn you to hell! I can't see!"

He rubbed his eyes and cried for a while in the dark, worn out and lost. She said nothing, showed no remorse; never was one to admit a wrong, Miss Barlow. After a while he gave in and pulled her close anyway, and they curled up listening to the rats dig out the walls.

The corpse lay near the batwings, throat deeply cut.

"Huh. I do recollect."

Miss Barlow eyed him narrowly. "Tell me, then."

"Well . . . that's not what I meant. This is Dalton Reed, that's all. Doctor Judah's boy."

With his knife he slit Dalton's left shirt sleeve to the armpit. On the inside of his upper arm was a small tattoo, an outline of Nebraska. An X marked the spot.

"That's it, I recall the tattoo." He pointed at the X. "Where do you reckon this is?"

Miss Barlow turned his face to hers and pushed back his hair, her eyes briefly caring. He thought she might kiss him. He pursed his lips in hope.

She said, "Do you know me, Charles?"

"Well, sure I do, Miss Barlow. I couldn't forget your pretty face." He nuzzled her hand like a puppy, but she pushed him away.

"We don't have time for that. Don't you remember where they hid it?"

"Well, you know, I think this is where we are. That looks like the creek, don't it?" He traced a thin tattooed line that curved past the X. Miss Barlow moved her shoulders in reply.

"I think that's it," Charles said. "Must be it." He rolled Dalton Reed onto his back and stripped him, searching for more tattoos. But there were only skin rashes and old scabs, and much too much hair. Miss Barlow turned away; she couldn't stand the smell.

Three empty graves in the town cemetery yawned like baby birds waiting for grubs. Charles dragged Dalton into one and buried him using a rusty shovel he found in the roofless stable. Job done, he leaned on the shovel and wiped sweat from his eyes with a gingham rag. Good old rag, a constant friend. He folded it carefully, and after several attempts returned it to his pocket. He could not keep his hands from shaking.

"What happened in this town?" Miss Barlow said. "So many graves."

Charles thought about it. "I don't know."

"Did Judah kill them?"

He shook his head. "Something else. The water maybe. The pox. Who knows."

Miss Barlow shaded her eyes and looked out across the prairie. The sky was a brilliant deep orange, the tall grass golden and rippled by the warm wind.

He admired her profile, her pretty face.

"Marry me, Miss Barlow."

"What's that?"

"I said, 'Marry me'."

She laughed. "Not without a dowry I won't. Where'd they bury that gold, huh?"

He thought about it, snapped his fingers. "I do remember. I was here before, with Dr. Judah."

"I know," Miss Barlow said. "But where did they hide the gold?"

He hesitated. "What gold?"

"What do you mean 'what gold?' Judah's gold."

He stared. "Who's Judah?"

"Ah, hell. . . . "

Charles took her hand apologetically, but she snatched it away. "Judah Reed. Dr. Judah." She knocked her knuckles on his head.

"Hey, get out of there! I was just playing. I recognize the name now, for sure."

"Did you kill him already, Charles?"

"Kill who?"

"Dr. Judah."

"Oh. No, not him. Why won't you marry me, Miss Barlow? I can give you a good life. I'm a good man, folks'd tell you that."

She snorted. "Folks like who?"

"Well . . . anyone. Anyone I know. They'd all tell you what a good man I am, for sure."

Miss Barlow turned away. Charles caught her around the waist, sliding his hands up her belly without any real intent but fun, but she spun away and slapped him hard in the face. The noise was like a firecracker in his head.

He stood alone then, watching the darkness gather. He counted sixteen older graves arranged four-by-four up the slope of the cemetery. The long grass slumped across them, beaten by the endless wind.

Miss Barlow was the type to take matters into her own hands as a last resort.

"I've surveyed this so-called town," she said. "Did you know there are seven rooms in this saloon?"

"No, I did not. Seven, huh?"

"Seven. And not one has a bed. They built seven rooms without a bed. And those houses out there are made of iron sheeting and broken up shipping crates."

Charles raised a finger. His eyes shone. "I remember this. Dr. Judah had them brought down from Canada." He hesitated. "Where's Dalton? We could ask him."

"You killed him, Charles. Why did you kill him? Where's the goddamn gold?" Miss Barlow stood, hands on hips, eyes burning, pretty as a dance-hall girl.

Charles took her hand and sat her down at the cleanest table. "Marry me, Miss Barlow. I love you, I'm sure of it."

"Not without a dowry I won't."

"Well, like what?"

"Like a case of Confederate gold. And some diamonds would be nice."

"Confederate diamonds?"

"Any diamonds. I'm not fussy."

"Confederate gold and plain old diamonds. Well, I don't know where I'm going to get those, Miss Barlow." He steepled his fingers. "There's a war on, you know."

She looked at him for a long time before her eyes softened. "You're drifting, Charles. The war was a long time ago."

"Oh. Did we win?"

"Yes and no. Where did they hide the gold?"

He frowned, nodding slowly, lips pursed to give the impression of serious thought.

The whiskey he found in Dalton's pack was terrible, but Miss Barlow needed something to calm her nerves. She lay her head on the table and gazed at their lantern through the bottle, adoring the way the glass warped the flame.

"Where's the gold, Charles?"

He took a deep breath, blew it out slowly. "Six Mile Creek."

Miss Barlow pushed their map across the table.

"Heck, that's Dr. Judah's treasure map," Charles said. "Where'd you get that?"

"I picked your pocket."

The prominent feature of the map, titled JUDAH REX MAPA ORO in a shaky uppercase script, was a creek marked SIX MILE. Charles had the distinct impression he had seen a similar curve elsewhere. Near the creek certain trees had been roughly sketched, and two detailed rock formations were labeled STONE CROW and LEFT FOOT. Connecting the trees and the rock formations, the mapmaker had drawn a five-pointed star, inverted. An arrow, pointing to a drawing of a house, was labeled '1,000,000 gold.'

Miss Barlow indicated the house. "That's us. There we are. Where's the gold?"

Charles pointed. "There?"

"Goddammit, where? Where is it, Charles? What did they write here?"

She turned the map over and stabbed at a sentence written in the same shaky script as the title: WITHOUT ME YOU IS ALONE.

"What does it mean? Is it some kind of riddle?"

Charles shook his head. He couldn't recall.

"Goddammit, I followed you from Louisiana to here looking for this damn gold," Miss Barlow said, "and I'm starting to think you don't even know where it is." She stood up and paced. "What in hell did they do to you, anyway?"

Charles examined his surroundings again. The saloon looked familiar. He thought he had been here once, maybe before it was built. The smell of sawdust reminded him. Sawdust and warm wind.

He held up a finger, listening. The sound of a whistle. A train whistle.

"I was building a railroad."

But Miss Barlow shook her head. "You blew it up. The railroad was supposed to come here, but you and Dalton blew it up. Was that to keep folks from finding the gold? Why'd they even build the town then?"

Charles strained to see clearly. The whistle of the train, the grinding of brakes, the explosion. He saw railroad tracks snapping and springing back to reach for the sky. But had it happened?

"How do I know how to blow up a railroad?"

"From the war. You made bombs."

"What war?"

110

"The only damn war, idiot. The war with the North. Why'd they build this town?"

Charles shook his head. "I don't know. Why would anyone build a town? We wanted to live here."

Miss Barlow laughed, and stopped laughing. "You wanted to live here."

Charles moved his shoulders.

"Here."

"Aw, heck, I don't know. What do you think?"

"About what?"

"Where they buried the gold."

"How in hell should I know?"

Charles stared at her. She had such pretty eyes, a pretty nose, pretty lips.

"Marry me, Miss Barlow. I'll give you a good life. I'm not a bad man."

She sat down and lay her head on the table again. "I can't marry you."

"Why not?"

"I need a dowry."

"Oh." Charles considered the problem. He rubbed his hands where the palms hurt, but he could not stop them from shaking. He smiled at Miss Barlow with honest affection. "You've followed me close on a year now."

"Sixteen months."

"Well, ain't that the constancy of love?"

"Yeah, it is. Love for gold."

"Aw, don't hurt me, Miss Barlow. I don't want to go on alone. Marry me, won't you?"

She pushed the whiskey bottle across the table. "Drown your sorrows, Charles."

A memory of her cut the mist in his head. They were riding through fields of wildflowers, the air thick with pollen. Sunset shone through parting storm clouds and turned the pollen to gold dust. It coated his skin, turned him the color of a god, and he stood in the saddle and cried out in triumph.

111

He woke sharply, lying on the bar, pulse hammering in his neck. Sunlight shone through the front windows, casting wavy heat shadows. Something cold and hard pressed at his cheekbone, and he swatted it. It came back again, and clicked.

"Settle, Charles."

He rolled, grabbed the barrel of the rifle as he fell and tried to jerk it away, but fell on his backside instead. The man holding the rifle pushed out foul breaths in something like laughter. His beard was not as neat as Charles recalled. He had a thug's crooked features and dark-ringed eyes shadowed by a thick brow. But as ever he wore a fine suit, if somewhat trail-worn.

"Dr. Judah."

"Charles, m'boy. You remember me."

He nodded. "I don't forget you."

The man shook his head in mock wonder. "You find my gold, boy?"

"Dalton's got it, suh." Charles sat up. Judah Reed raised his rifle a touch. "He's at the next marker," Charles said. "Told him I'd wait for you."

Dr. Reed nodded. "Smells like someone died here."

"Rats, suh."

He laughed, and stopped laughing. He put the rifle on the bar and lifted his hand away, fingers outstretched.

Charles moved faster than he recalled he could. He sprang up and seized the doctor's thin neck. Reed gagged and fumbled for his six-gun, but Charles lifted him off-balance and ran him clear across the room into a wall. He squeezed hard. Dr. Reed, grinning, lifted his gun to Charles' temple; but Charles had seen this in his dream. He opened his Barlow knife with a flick of the wrist and pressed the point to the doctor's throat.

"I can't hold steady, suh. I got the quakes."

The knife shivered. Its edge from tip to hilt had been honed razor sharp. Judah Reed tried to swallow, and the movement brought forth a trickle of blood that wove through his shaving rash.

The gun cocked at Charles' temple. "Where is my gold, boy?"

"I said I sent it on with Dalton." Charles breathed hard. His mind seethed with disassociated thoughts.

At last Dr. Reed relaxed the trigger and lowered his gun. Hesitating, Charles moved his knife away. He could not keep his hands from shaking. The six-gun came back around in the fist of Reed's haymaker.

Charles ate sawdust. He saw himself riding with Miss Barlow. The sawdust was gold and he was covered in it. His face a golden face, his black skin buried. He tried to move and retched, but there was no food in his stomach. Acid bile scorched his throat and jolted him back to life, and he tried to gain cover.

Judah Reed followed his fleeing asset and calmly kicked it in the ribs, lifting it off the floor. He enjoyed the smoothness of his kick, the precise positioning of his boot to cause maximum pain with minimum damage. No man likes his slaves to be broken.

"Get up, boy. Get up, I said!" He kicked Charles in the legs, kicked him in the head, the guts, the back. His hair fell into his eyes as he aimed again at the ribs and, briefly distracted, he misplaced his toe. Some say the power behind a kick is paramount, but Dr. Reed believed firmly in toe placement. If the toe is even a little off. . . .

There was a muffled crack, and Charles screamed. He balled up and clutched his side with clawed fingers.

Dr. Reed flinched at his error, but judged the damage to be minor and went on; he liked to work up a sweat. He stopped when he felt wetness seeping through a hole in his boot between toe and sole. What do the cobblers call that? Oh yes, he thought, a laughing sole.

He sat down and caught his breath, pulled off boot and sock and wiped blood from his toes.

"It's good to find you again, Charles," he panted. "I miss my boys. Where's that pretty wife of yours?"

Charles made gurgling noises.

"I'll patch you up, stop complaining. Goddamn peace has made you Negroes more dear than ever. And you can read, boy, you're worth a fortune to me. Where is that bitch of yours, anyhow?"

Judah Reed shook sand out of his boots. "Incidentally, due to the demands of our northerly kin I must pay you a salary upon our return. I reckon a dollar per annum should suffice." He laughed, shook his head. "A whole dollar. How about that, boy? You'll be the richest quadroon around." He laughed again.

"You and me," Charles rasped, "never. . . . "

113

His Barlow knife lay in the dusty gap between bar and floor, just within reach.

"You and I, Charles, for Christ's sake. You animals never learn, do you?"

But Charles could not make his hand move.

Memories bulged from the pre-dawn shadows, fighting for his attention against the pain of his illness and the pains in his body. He saw dead ancestors, old Congolese who had withstood their lives with dignity; but now instead of mouths they had duck bills, and their black skin was split and scarred with chancres and boils.

Then he was sitting by a campfire sharpening his knife, alone with the stars and Miss Barlow, sliding her across the whetstone. His uncle used to sing a song to various tunes he made up, but the words were constant:

I been livin' here all my life,
All I got is a Barlow knife.
Buck horn handle and a Barlow blade,
Best dang knife that ever was made!

Charles watched himself attempt to kill a jackrabbit with that Barlow knife. The rabbit had short horns, thick knotted protrusions growing out of its face. It was sick and slow, but still he couldn't catch it.

Skin and bones, he went without supper again. He sharpened Miss Barlow by the fire and sang his uncle's song to help ignore the hunger. That night he dreamed of a golden bowl with a golden spoon and a golden tub full of jackrabbit stew, the best dang stew that ever was made.

He opened his eyes and saw rays of sunlight cutting through the windows. They caught the dust in the air and turned it into golden snow.

The saloon was silent. He hurt all over, and the pain doubled when he breathed. But it also brought focus, and he rose away from the mud inside his head and unfolded himself to the floor.

The pains fought each other as he moved, but his favorite was the throbbing in his mouth. The ache of missing teeth was a pleasant one, by comparison. He moved his head and vertebrae cracked, and back the other way, more cracks, and back and forth until he could move it relatively freely. The pain in his back eased, and relief spread across his damaged ribs. He sucked in a sharp breath and winced. Not broken, he thought, but badly bruised.

It was only when he saw his trousers hanging over a chair that he realized he was naked. His ribs had been strapped with a filthy bandage, which made him laugh. Surely Dr. Judah had not nursed his own slave; though it would be a Christ-like thing to do, Charles thought bitterly. Dr. Judah loved to think himself a Christ among men.

Charles pulled on his trousers, filthy and worn at the seat. With difficulty he crouched and looked under the bar.

"Best dang knife that ever was made," he muttered. "Come here, Miss Barlow. Let me hold you."

Her blade was sharper than a barber's favorite, and the alterations Charles' uncle had made to the folding knife's mechanism made it stronger when extended. Charles had taken pains not to forget how to use her, even if his mind lost everything else. Press the button, and a catch released the blade. A single wrist-flick had it out. Release the button and there the blade stuck, firm as an Arkansas toothpick.

The pain he had held back bore hard on his guts. He panted against it, folded and pocketed Miss Barlow and slumped against a table, heart racing.

He noticed on the table the map he had taken from Dalton Reed, its riddle taunting him:

WITHOUT ME YOU IS ALONE.

Without expecting to, Charles recalled. His split lips parted in a half smile, and from the lower, deeper cut, a trickle of blood ran into his mouth. The sour metallic taste jolted his mind into focus. He had known the answer all along, he thought; it just slipped his mind. He fingered the knife in his pocket.

Behind him the batwings banged open.

"Charles, m'boy! How do you feel this morning? Let me medicate you again."

Charles slumped to the floor. The fear was too much; the pains rushed back to their rightful owners, and he gasped and ground his teeth to make his gums hurt. He needed that dull ache, the one he could manage.

115

Judah Reed's hands hooked under his arms and lifted him into a chair. Charles leaned on the table, brought his breathing under control.

"You know, you're a filthy bastard," Reed said merrily. "You've got syphilis, quite advanced. It's a wonder you aren't out singing sea shanties to my horse."

Dr. Reed opened his medical bag and readied supplies for a tonic: a smoked glass bottle labeled 'KI,' a small tin cup, and a leather pouch tied around the middle. He pulled out the bow and unfolded the pouch, revealing a dozen tiny glass vials filled with cloudy liquid. He measured a small dose from the KI bottle into the tin cup.

"And incidentally, she is my horse, Charles. I do have some sympathy, but you'll have to be punished for the theft." He hesitated. "I noticed a fresh burial up on the hill that I assume is your wife's." He looked into the black man's bloodshot eyes. "I am sorry, boy. She was a fine woman."

Dr. Reed broke the neck off one of the glass vials and tipped the liquid into the tin cup. He smelled the tonic.

"This is why you people need white men. First sniff of freedom and you're off whoring in New Orleans, isn't that right? From the look of your chancre scar you've been ill for several years, Charles. I'd favor it'll go to your mind soon, if not already. But I can treat you. My iodide tonic is the best I've seen—laudanum aside." He laughed, and held the cup to Charles' lips. "Whoops. Steady hand, Dr. Reed. This doesn't come cheaply."

Charles avoided his eyes. He drank the liquid, coughed at the bitter taste. "Thank you, suh."

Dr. Reed nodded and turned to pack up his medicines. Charles stood quickly, and from his side came a soft mechanical click. He wrapped one hand around Judah's eyes, pulled back his head and buried Miss Barlow in the side of his neck. She made a soft thump. Judah's legs buckled and he gave a choked scream, but Charles would not let him fall. Grimacing with bloody teeth, he tried to drive the knife clear through Judah's neck, but the blade was too short for that kind of violence and he had gouged crookedly. He corrected the angle as best he could, and Miss Barlow found an artery.

Blood gurgled from Dr. Reed's mouth, but Charles held steady. Blood ran down his arm along the lines of his straining muscles. Of the many ways he had imagined to kill Dr. Judah with the little knife, this

116

was the hardest, the cruelest, the most certain. It was taking longer than he expected, but he did not relent. He held Judah Reed's head back with desperate strength, watching the life drain from his lone good eye. Soon it was as vacant as its glass companion.

Cleaning Miss Barlow in the dirt outside, the answer came to him again.

WITHOUT ME YOU IS ALONE.

'You and I'. Without 'I', you is alone.

The eye.

Four days passed before Charles felt well enough to travel. Miss Barlow watched him prepare a dose of tonic for the road. He had taken the medicine and Judah Reed's three Winchester rifles, one of them a Yellow Boy carbine in rare condition.

Miss Barlow said, "You know what you're doing there?"

He shrugged. "Makes me feel better, that's the important thing."

"Well, I love you even if you never get well. Look at these, I'd marry Mr. Winchester in a heartbeat."

"You love me?"

"What?"

"You said you love me, Miss Barlow."

"No I didn't. I love this gun, that's what I said."

"That's a rifle."

"Well, we're happy just so. Aren't you going to take one?"

"No, they're all for you."

"Oh, Charles!"

"I got you, anyhow."

"Did you remember where they hid the gold?"

"I did at that." He picked up Judah Reed's glass eye and tossed it in his hand. His shaking had subsided.

"Well that's funny looking gold." Miss Barlow pouted. "You're teasing me."

"Oh no, I wouldn't do that, Miss Barlow. Look here." He held the glass eye up to the light and looked through its pupil. Etched in tiny script on the back of the eyeball, magnified by a lens set inside it, were directions to Judah Reed's gold.

"Oh, I see now," Miss Barlow said. "Aren't you a clever feller."

"Well, it's not where I first recalled, but it's close. A day or two west is all, where the creek branches."

Miss Barlow threw herself around his neck and kissed him on the mouth, hard and with some discomfort given the firearms between them, but they managed.

"Goddammit, I do love you, Charles. You're handsome and brave and you bring me gold."

"Oh I will, Miss Barlow. I will do that." She had the prettiest lips, he thought, and the prettiest eyes, and the prettiest face, just like Ada's. His heart swelled with love and pride.

"And after that," she said, "let's go on west and find a peaceful spot by the seaside for a home." She smiled at him like Ada always had, full of hope and caring. "You sure you feel good now, Charles?"

"I do, Miss Barlow. I'm a whole new man, I promise."

He folded the knife and put it in his pocket, and went outside to his horse, watered and waiting. The sun, still rising, beat down hard already, but Charles didn't mind. If all the day gave him was a mean wind blowing hot and dusty right in his eyes, he'd take it with the brightest smile anyone ever wore. Heart pounding, he swung up into the saddle and turned his horse to the west.

STRETCH-HEMP STATION
Ben Bridges

Under his own name and a fistful of pseudonyms, David Whitehead (Ben Bridges) has been writing Black Horse Westerns for more than twenty years. He founded a fan club dedicated to the celebrated "Piccadilly Cowboys" in 1976 and at the age of 21 became consultant for IPC's Western Magazine. *For more information check out www.benbridges.co.uk.*

Walt Bevan came to with a low, drawn-out moan, awakened—as usual, these past few mornings—by a bad dream he'd sooner forget. He rolled over, saw by her absence that Nellie was already up and doing, and told himself blearily, Well, that figures. Nellie hadn't been sleeping much better'n him, just lately.

He lay there a moment longer, feeling old, addle-brained, and more than a mite desperate. Then, damned if he'd feel any sorrier for himself than he had to, he tossed back the rumpled sheet and threw his bowed legs over the edge of the tick mattress.

Finger-brushing the fine white hair back off his sun-darkened forehead, he stepped into a pair of gray wool pants and thumbed wide brown suspenders up over his sloped shoulders. His boots came next, a sorry-looking pair of scuffed old stovepipes, and after that he went in search of his wife.

He knew he wouldn't find her indoors, so he didn't waste time searching the station. He just shuffled straight through the common room and out into the gloomy, pre-dawn yard beyond.

His home, Stretch-Hemp Station, straddled a rutted wagon-road set amid sandy flats and screwbean mesquite. The station itself, a single-story structure split in two by a covered dog-trot, was built from logs chinked with mud, and the stable and sheds on the far side of the trail were constructed in like fashion.

As Walt appeared in the station doorway, a scrawny collie called Sam slunk over with his head held low. The dog, white through the chest and forelegs and black everywhere else, had sharp-pointed ears and inquisitive, black-patch hazel eyes. No longer sure how to take his previously amiable master, however, the animal halted a few feet

119

away, offered a couple of wary tail-wags and then waited hopefully for a response that never came.

Nellie, Walt saw, was standing about thirty yards to his right, her work-worn fingers knitting absently as she contemplated the rim of a gentle slope that lifted skyward behind the station. The slope itself had been cleared of timber about twenty years earlier, partly to provide cheap, but by no means entirely suitable, material with which to build the place and partly to deny Indians—Comanches mostly, but every so often a few fractious Kiowa, Cheyenne, and Arapaho as well—the cover they needed to sneak up on it.

Now only one tree remained up there to crown a slope otherwise choked with cholla and greasewood, one single, gnarled post oak that stood thirty feet high. No one had ever told them why it had been spared when the construction team first set to work, and neither had they ever thought to ask. It just had.

Walt studied his wife pensively as the rising sun continued to sketch her in shades of red, ochre, and amethyst. In her late fifties now, and thus of an age with him, she had big hips and a generous bosom that her thin cotton dress was finding increasingly difficult to contain. A short woman, she wore her longish, iron-gray hair fixed in a knot at the back of her head.

Clearing his throat to let her know he was there, Walt went to join her with Sam trotting cautiously at his side. "You all right?" he asked when he was close enough.

"Just thinkin'," she replied vaguely.

"Well, don't," he advised. "All the thinkin' in the world won't change things."

"No," she agreed. "But. . . . " Breaking off, she studied him closely through troubled brown eyes, then half-whispered, "How long you suppose we can go on like this, Walt?"

He knew exactly what she meant, of course, but some belligerent streak made him demand, "Like what?"

"How long can we keep goin' 'til we break?"

"Long as we have to, I guess," he replied stubbornly.

He was about to say more when he realized that Sam had started up the hill, headed for the post oak, and all at once his fists clenched and he yelled, "Sam!" with such force that Nellie flinched and Sam spun around fast and immediately slunk back down to join them, his brushy tail tucking beneath his body.

"Goddamn you, dog!" Walt snarled.

Watching him, and seeing only a stranger where her husband used to be, Nellie said quietly, "I'll start breakfast."

As she walked past him, he felt an urge to reach out and tell her he was sorry, that he loved her, that nothing was ever going to come between them, he promised. There were a thousand-and-one things he wanted to say in that one brief moment, but then she was gone, and it was too late to say any of them.

While Nellie got the place cleaned up and ready for the noonday halt, Walt went over to the stable and turned the horses out into the corral. He swept out the stalls and topped up the troughs, then found some shade and, as the morning progressed, tried to concentrate on mending harness.

But his mind just wasn't on it. As the sun tried its best to bake the little home station he'd managed these past fifteen years, his eyes returned time and again to the lone post oak. As the day wore on, its shadow would crawl down the slope like a restless stain until it almost touched the station itself, and he would see it, as he had seen it for days now, more like the shadow of an accusing finger.

'Course, back when they'd first moved out here, the place had been named for that very tree. Post Oak Station. Forty miles from the swing station at High Point and closer to sixty from Coperas.

Upwards of twenty coaches a week had passed through here back then, going from Coperas to Fort Stockton and back again. But then the railroads had linked up and the stage lines, especially the smaller ones, had found it almost impossible to compete.

So economies had been made. The less-profitable routes were axed. Stock tenders quit and never got replaced. And many of the more isolated swing stations were abandoned altogether.

But Post Oak Station, standing as it did midway between the start and the end of the line, had always stayed open for business.

Not that they called it Post Oak Station anymore. They hadn't called it that in twelve years. Nowadays it was known as Stretch-Hemp Station, and with good reason.

It had all started with the arrival of the afternoon stage from Canfield: better'n two thousand pounds of bright red Concord weighed down with baggage, mail and passengers, running twenty minutes late and leaving a rising plume of back-lit yellow dust in its wake.

While Walt set to work unhitching the lathered team, the passengers had climbed down to stretch their legs and then disappear into the station for a cup or two of Nellie's strong coffee and a bite to eat. There was a merchant, he remembered, a couple of chamber pot and pin drummers, two women, a soldier whose single bar identified him as a lieutenant, and a stocky cowboy in need of a shave.

As always, Walt's son, Luke—a tall, slim boy with unruly sand-colored hair and his old man's long, pared-down features—had been there to walk the sweating horses 'til their breathing calmed, leaving Walt himself to back their replacements into the traces and set to work drawing the cinches firm.

He'd been doing that when the posse rode in.

There were seven of them sitting saddle behind the eighth—townsmen mostly, saloon workers, a blacksmith's apprentice, and a couple or three cowboys, each one hot, dusty, and somber-looking. Without taking his green eyes off the station, the rail-thin fifty-year-old at their head indicated the star pinned to the front of his leather vest and said, "Amos Drake, Sheriff of Canfield."

Walt had frowned. "Help you, Sheriff?"

Drake dismounted and the men behind him did likewise, a few hitching expectantly at their hurriedly-donned belt guns. Without bothering to reply, the lawman pushed past Walt and strode toward the station with the posse-men following eagerly at his heels, and Walt fell into step beside him, ducking as they went through the low doorway and into the common room beyond.

The driver, messenger, and passengers were seated on benches either side of a long sawbuck table. They'd been working their way through corned beef, carrots, and mashed potatoes when the posse arrived. Now the meal lay forgotten and all heads had turned enquiringly.

"Charlie Altman," said Drake, pulling to a halt. "Best you come quietly, now. You're under arrest."

A fleeting moment of shock followed the announcement. Then one of the two drummers climbed to his feet and said, "What? What am I supposed to've done?"

"You killed a woman named Annie Redhead," snapped Drake.

The drummer's dark eyes suddenly bulged. "She's dead?" he murmured before he could stop himself. Then, defensively, "I didn't kill anyone! The damned cocotte tried to steal my wallet, so I slapped her, that's all!"

"You beat her to death when she refused to give you your money back," Drake countered grimly. "That's the story she told as she lay dyin', an' be she sportin' girl or no, we don't stand to see our women treated that way!"

Sensing the strength of feeling among the men who'd come to arrest him, Altman hurriedly reached into the folds of his black coat and tore out a gun. "Stay back, the lot of you!" he cried. "I mean it!"

Nellie, framed in the kitchen doorway, put a fist to her mouth.

"These men at my back are mad enough at you as it is," growled Drake. "Put up that smoke-wheel before you make things worse."

Good as it was, however, Altman ignored the advice. "Stay back, I said! And you, station-keeper! Go saddle me a horse! Now!"

"Nope," said Drake, before Walt could move. "You're comin' with us, Altman, so you just put up that pistol, or so help me I'll come over there and take it away from you myself."

"It'll be the last thing you ever try!" warned Altman.

Undaunted, Drake started to advance on him, one hand outstretched. "I'll take the gun," he said softly.

"You'll take one end of it!" screamed the drummer.

And then, from a distance of no more than three feet, he shot Drake twice in the chest.

The bullets folded Drake in half and flung him to the dirt floor. One of the women screamed, there was a sudden ripple of movement that ceased almost as soon as it started, and then there was only silence, save for the sheriff's soft moans as the life seeped out of him.

Altman himself stumbled back a pace, apparently stunned by what he'd done. He seemed unable to take his eyes off the dying man—until the lieutenant suddenly sprang up and made a grab for him. He twisted then, brought the gun up and fired again, and the lieutenant cried out and went down clutching his hip.

One of the posse-men yelled, "Get him!" and after that all hell broke loose. Women screamed, men yelled, Walt started shouting for them to wait, to stop, and Altman, sending a warning shot into the ceiling, bawled at them to get back or else.

His words fell on deaf ears, though, and within seconds they were upon him and tearing the gun from his fist.

Squealing now, Altman lashed out blindly, broke one man's nose, kicked another between the legs, and knocked some teeth out for a third. But then they had him by the arms and were dragging him through the door, leaving Nellie to tend the wounded soldier and Walt to close the dead sheriff's staring eyes.

By the time Walt joined them outside, one of the posse-men had produced a length of good, strong hemp and was jabbing a finger at the post oak from which the station had taken its name.

Oh Lord, Walt remembered thinking. They're gonna hang him.

And in a way, who could blame them? This man had killed a woman in their town. He'd just killed the man to whom they'd entrusted their law and order. He'd injured three of their number and he'd damn-near killed the soldier-boy. So these hot, dusty, saddle-sore men were fired-up and hungry for vengeance, and what was right and what was wrong never came into it.

Still, even as they slammed a crude noose down over Altman's head, Walt begged them to reconsider. This wouldn't be justice, he argued, it'd be murder. Better to let the law take its course, surely?

But there was no reasoning with them, and shoving him aside, the posse-men drew the hemp collar tight and dragged Altman through Nellie's flower garden, trampling her yellow coneflowers and just-blooming horsemint underfoot, then on up the brushy slope toward the tree, and young Luke, still standing in the corral with the gunfire-spooked horses milling around him, saw and heard it all.

He heard Altman scream curses at his captors and then, just as quickly, start begging them for mercy. He saw them fling the rope over the stoutest branch and then take up the slack on the loose end. He saw Altman's legs leave the ground as he was jerked higher, higher, higher, and watched as Altman's fingers clawed desperately to keep the hemp from biting any deeper into his throat.

Luke saw, too, the change that came into Altman when he finally realized that this was it, that he was actually going to die and that this

124

was going to be the manner of his passing. He saw the last furious, frantic kicking of his legs, the gradual, inexorable darkening of his face from pink to plum and then to near-black, and finally he saw the drummer's hands flop to his sides, his legs stop their thrashing and settle to a weird, spastic quivering.

Luke saw and heard all that, and he was just twelve years old.

Walt sighed at the memory.

In the days, weeks, months, and years that followed, Nellie often woke up nights claiming to hear a sound drifting down from the post oak like stretched hemp creaking gently back and forth. Walt had always told her it was her imagination, and said pretty much the same thing whenever she talked about the station being cursed.

After all, things hadn't turned out so bad, had they? For a start, that soldier-boy had lived, was a captain now, last he'd heard, and he hadn't even been left with as much as a limp. Pretty darn' good for a man who'd been shot in the hip.

And comes to that, what about Luke?

Oh, the events of that day had quieted him down some, sure, but they'd shaped him as well, and though he never said much at the time, it soon became clear that he'd started seeing things differently somehow, less like a boy and more like a man.

A couple of weeks before his sixteenth birthday, he'd finally announced that he wanted to become a peace officer, and when Walt asked him why, he said it was because he figured justice ought to be dispensed by the law and not by a riled-up lynch mob, and there was certainly no arguing with that.

So about a year later he left home and got a job with the marshal of Grey Rock, feller name of Jim Cushing. Luke wasn't much more than a glorified errand boy who swept the floors and acted as turnkey whenever the need arose, but to him it was a start, and eighteen months later he became Cushing's junior deputy.

Deputy Marshal of Bakersfield followed, and when old Harry Casey retired, he was elected Town Marshal. These days, Luke was a government man, a Deputy United States Marshal, no less.

But this, Walt suddenly reminded himself, was no time for idle reflection. Somehow the morning had slipped away and the noon stage from Fort Stockton was due in any time now.

It rocked to a dusty halt forty minutes later, and while the reinsman, George French, jumped down from his high seat and gestured that his passengers should head for the common room and a little refreshment, Walt went to work on harness and horseflesh. Almost immediately, however, he spotted Sam making his way back up the slope to the post oak.

Without thinking, he snatched up a fist-size clump of dry earth, shuffled clear of the coach and pitched it at the animal, bawling, "God damn you, Sam, get away from there!"

As Sam disappeared into the scrub with his tail between his legs, George and the passengers turned to give Walt a curious look. Frowning, George asked quietly, "You all right, *amigo*?"

Not trusting himself to speak, Walt only nodded and went back to work, anxious to get the stage the hell out of there as fast as he could.

Thirty minutes later he joined Nellie in the station doorway and watched as George gathered his lines, kicked off the brake, and got his four-horse team headed west again. George only glanced back once, to look at Walt as if he'd never seen him before.

Feeling Nellie's eyes on him too, Walt demanded irritably, "What is it now?"

"That question again," she replied, and turned away.

That question again, he thought. How long can we keep goin' 'til we break?

Lord, he really didn't know.

He was just about to head for the stable and fix a hay-and-grain mixture for the horses when something made him cut his gaze away to the west.

He didn't see anything at first. Then, barely visible through the heat-haze, he made out a rider coming in off the flats at a weary trot. A lone rider leading a single pack-horse. . . .

A moment later he called Nellie's name, and when she reappeared in the doorway he snapped, "Go fetch the Colt, an' stay out of sight!"

"What—?"

"Just do it!" he ordered.

Nellie turned her head then, looked away to the west, and saw the approaching rider. "Who . . . ?"

"How do I know?" he spat. "Jus' get the Colt!"

Standing her ground instead, she asked scornfully, "Again?"

The word slapped him like an open palm, but he let the accusation in it pass. "Again," he growled. "Or maybe you didn't see what that feller's fetchin' in with him?"

Nellie took another look, shielding her eyes to see clearer this time. A second later she whispered, "Oh, Lordy. Is it . . . is it a body, Walt?"

The rider was close enough now that there could be no doubt. A dead man rolled in a gray woolen blanket was hanging belly-down over the pack-horse, his legs sticking out one side, his bouncing, half-covered head dangling on the other.

Guts tight, Walt turned his attention back to the rider himself, a lean man with broad shoulders and what looked to be long legs, whose dark, wide-brimmed hat threw his face into shadow. As he came nearer, Walt saw that he carried a pistol at his waist and a badge pinned to the chest of his gray placket shirt, a shield into which had been cut a five-pointed star.

"Walt," said Nellie, her voice suddenly thickening with emotion. "Walt, it's Luke!"

Walt's face went slack again. Luke? Their Luke? But almost immediately his relief gave way to an even stronger sense of alarm. They hadn't seen Luke in more than a year. Why did he have to show up again now, of all times?

A few minutes later their boy entered the yard and tied his animals to the remains of an old rear wheel that was leaning against the stable wall. Sam came chasing out of nowhere to greet him, giving Walt a conspicuously wide berth as he did so, and Luke made a playful grab for him before crossing the yard at a jog and gathering Nellie into his arms.

"Ma!" he said warmly. "As pretty as ever, I see!"

Unable to speak for the moment, Nellie waved the compliment aside and dabbed at her eyes with a small lace handkerchief. While she struggled to compose herself, Luke turned to Walt and offered his right hand, and after the briefest hesitation, Walt took it. "Son," he said formally. "Good to see you again."

Luke had aged some beyond his four-and-twenty years, and exposure to sun and wind had darkened his skin and lightened his short, sandy hair. Whiskery and travel-marked though he was, however, he was still very much their Luke, with his mother's bright brown eyes and his old man's gaunt features.

"By God," he said. "You two are a sight for sore eyes."

But Walt's attention was fixed on the dead man. "Brought comp'ny with you, I see."

Luke grimaced. "Bank robber name of Tom Guffey," he replied. "I caught up with him this morning. I'd have sooner taken him alive, but he didn't give me the choice. I'll stow him out of sight in a minute."

"I'd appreciate it," said Nellie, throwing Walt a quick glance. "Then you'd, ah, better come in out of the sun. Reckon we got some catchin' up to do."

Luke nodded. "Reckon we have, at that."

But fifteen minutes later they were seated at the sawbuck table, sipping fresh-boiled coffee, and trying to think of things to say. Eventually Walt muttered half-heartedly, "Well, this sure is a turn-up. You, ah, stayin' long, son?"

"Figure I'll head on back to Kelton tomorrow. Doubt that Guffey'll keep much longer'n that."

"I'd best get to bakin', then," said Nellie, pushing up from the table. "I'll fix a special supper tonight an' it'll be like old times."

But old times had never been like this, filled with furtive looks and invisible barriers, and they all knew it.

As she headed for the kitchen, another uncomfortable silence settled over the common room. To break it, Luke asked how business was and Walt told him it was steady. With the subject thus exhausted, Luke excused himself and went outside with Sam at his heels. In the yard he fished out the makings and rolled himself a smoke.

Walt watched him through one of the station's small, smeared windows, feeling edgier than ever. Eventually, finding it impossible to sit still, he got up, wiped his palms on the seat of his pants, and went to join him.

Luke was squinting up at the post oak.

And Sam had already climbed the slope and was rooting around by the base of the tree.

Seeing that, Walt yelled, "Sam! Get away from there!"

The dog flinched at the anger in his voice and took off, vanishing over the far side of the ridge. Recovering himself, Walt made a loose gesture with his right hand and mumbled, "Damn dog. Always nosin' after somethin'."

Luke just carried on studying the tree.

"What, ah, what's on your mind, son?" Walt asked with careful indifference.

"Just thinkin'," Luke replied, drawing smoke. "'Bout bein' home again. That old tree an' what we saw happen up there all them years ago."

"It was a bad business, right enough," Walt allowed. "But it turned you into the man you are today, I reckon. Though sometimes I wonder if that was a good thing or a bad one."

Luke threw him a curious glance. "How so?"

"Yours is a risky business, son," said Walt. "Was you a clerk or a farmer, your ma 'n me, we wouldn't worry so much."

"I make out okay," Luke assured him.

They fell silent again until, at length, Luke said, "Is everything all right, Pa? With you and Ma, I mean?"

"Why shouldn't it be?"

Luke shrugged. "I get the feelin' you're frettin' over something. An' I don't think it's just over whether or not I'm goin' to stop lead someday."

"You're imaginin' things, son."

"I don't think so," Luke persisted with unnerving certainty. "You seem awful jumpy, Pa, an' Ma ain't much better. An' what about Sam, there? That dog admires you somethin' fierce as a rule, but today he won't go anywhere near you." He shook his head. "There's an atmosphere around here you can cut with a knife, an' I don't like it an' I can't ignore it. If there's anythin' wrong—"

"There isn't."

"But if there is, I'd want to help."

Losing patience, Walt heeled around to face him. "Listen to me, Luke," he growled. "If you really want to help, you can start by keepin' your nose out of my—"

"Oh, for God's sake, Walt, tell him!"

Nellie's voice, coming right out of the blue, made both men turn fast. She was standing in the station doorway, close to tears again if the expression on her face was anything to go by.

Staring at Walt, she half-sobbed, "Tell him an' be done with it!"

129

"Tell me what?" Luke asked tightly.

His parents continued to look at each other for a long, taut moment. Then Walt let go something that sounded more like a moan than the sigh it was meant to be, and whispered tremulously, "Oh, Lord, son! What's gonna become of us? We've done killed a man!"

He swayed then, and his legs would have buckled altogether if Luke hadn't reached out to catch him.

"Ma, you got any whiskey around the place?"

" 'M all right. . . . " protested Walt.

"The hell you are. Ma?"

"In . . . inside."

"Get it."

With Luke supporting him, Walt stumbled back into the dining room and flopped down at the table. Someone—he guessed it was Nellie—shoved a mug into his hands and he smelled strong spirits. He drank, choked, shivered, and then started to feel a mite stronger, and when his vision finally cleared some he saw Luke studying him soberly from the other side of the table, Nellie sitting beside him, weeping softly.

"What's going on here, Pa?" Luke asked gently.

It came in a rush, then, like poison draining from an open wound, and once he started talking, Walt couldn't have stopped the words even if he'd wanted to.

It had happened little under a week earlier. Nellie had been weeding the flower garden when she'd spotted a man coming in from the west, a man afoot, leading a horse that was moving slowly, carefully, not so much tired as injured.

Because you could never be too careful in these parts, she'd immediately fetched Walt, and together they watched the newcomer slowly close the distance between them. The horse, a bay with three white socks, was having a hard time of walking straight. Sand was stuck to his left flank and thigh, indicating that he'd taken a fall, a hard one, judging by the painful way he moved.

Reaching a decision, Walt said, "Go get the Colt. Chances are we won't need it, but you never can tell. Go fetch it, stay out of sight, an' keep it handy. An' watch that trigger. It's got a light touch."

Wiping her damp palms on her apron, Nellie turned and vanished inside.

A few minutes later the newcomer limped into the yard, as sore-footed as his mount. He was a thick-set man of an age with Luke, wearing a hickory shirt tucked into riveted jeans, and carrying a gun at his hip. "Mornin'," he called when he saw Walt.

Walt nodded back. "You look like you've come a fair piece."

"That I have," the man agreed. He had a round, pleasant face, clear blue eyes, and a dusting of light whiskers along his jaw. "An' the pace has told on poor old Chick, here."

"What happened?"

Before the newcomer could reply, Sam came over to brush against his legs, and the man bent at the waist to run his free hand along the dog's spine. "He stepped in a gopher hole, took a fall," he said after a while. "Was lucky not to break a leg, I reckon." Suddenly he thought to introduce himself. "Name's Johnny Moffat, by the way. Proud to know you."

Walt shook with him: He had a strong, firm grip. "Name's Bevan, station manager here. If you'd, ah, care to step inside, the wife'll coffee an' cake you while I take a look at your mount."

"I'd appreciate that," said Moffat. "Thing is, Mr. Bevan—"

And that was when it happened—when the gun in Nellie's hands went off with a roar like thunder, when Nellie herself screamed in a mixture of shock and surprise, when Sam disappeared with a frightened yelp, and when Johnny Moffat's hat was torn from his head and he fell to his knees with his eyes filled with horror, then hit the hardpan face first.

The area just above and behind his left ear was a red, glistening mess.

Walt watched him go down, his mouth working like that of a fish on a riverbank. His thoughts were scrambled, half-formed. Wha. . . . What did. . . . What happened? And then he heard himself saying it, his voice high, breathless, his tone baffled, confused. He dropped to his own knees, went to touch the dead man and drew back when he heard Nellie let go another long, awful wail.

He looked up, saw her standing in the station doorway, the Colt looking as big as a saddle-gun in her tiny, work-roughened hands, smoke still drifting lazily from the long barrel like the ghost of a snake making its getaway.

Pale as chalk, Nellie muttered, "Walt, it . . . the gun, it . . . it jus' went off. . . ."

He stared at her for a long, dumb moment. Of course it went off. That damn' smoke-belcher always had been unreliable, that's why he'd warned her about the hair trigger. But then he remembered Nellie wiping her palms on her apron. Maybe those damp, slippery fingers had made what happened even more inevitable.

"Is he . . . ?" she began.

Bracing himself, Walt checked the body. There was no heartbeat that he could detect.

"He's dead," he said in someone else's voice.

"Oh God," said Nellie. "I killed him, Walt. I killed him!"

"And then you buried him," guessed Luke. "Up there, 'neath the oak."

She eyed him bleakly. "We're not proud of it, son," she husked.

"Then why the heck didn't you just lay the poor sonofabuck out someplace cool and report what happened to the authorities?" he demanded.

Walt sat forward. "Because there was always the chance they might not've believed us!" he rasped. "An' even if they had, what would it have told them about us, Luke? That we're gettin' old, that's what. Too damn old to think straight an' too damn addled to act right."

He snorted. "You think the stage line'd keep us on out here after that? Oh, no. Even if they gave us the benefit of the doubt, we'd still end up losin' everythin', boy, everythin'. This place. Our jobs. Our pension." He shook his head. "An' if it went the other way, if they decided we'd killed that feller deliberate. . . . " His voice cracked. "Your ma'n me, how long you suppose we'd last in prison? How long you suppose we'd last without each other?"

Luke sighed, recognizing the truth of his words. "So you decided to bury the body and just keep quiet about it."

"I dragged him up there, to the tree," Walt confessed miserably. "Damn near killed me to do it. Then I dug a grave, a shallow one. I didn't have the strength to dig it deep, the ground was too hard. I rolled him in, covered him up, figured to go back, make a better job of it next day, but . . . I couldn't go up there again, son, I jus' couldn't."

Walt's eyes suddenly went large and desperate. "Aw, son," he said, "you can't know what it's been like, living with it. We've hardly slept, we've hardly spoke. It's been. . . . "

He broke off then and, unable to fight it any longer, he started sobbing.

Luke stood up and strode outside. After a moment Walt and Nellie went after him. He got a shovel from one of the storage sheds, the same shovel Walt had used five days earlier, then climbed the slope with Sam forging out ahead of him.

When he reached the base of the tree, he examined the ground for a while, then shook his head, slammed the shovel into the ground and came back down to rejoin them.

Walt, a smaller, deflated image of his former self, said quietly, "What are you gonna do, son? Turn us in?"

Luke said, "I ought to. But there's no one up there, Pa."

"What?"

"That grave you dug—it's empty."

Luke studied them both for a thoughtful moment then said, "I think you better come with me."

Still in shock, they followed him meekly back across the yard to the shed. The late Tom Guffey, still rolled in the blanket, was stretched out against the right-side wall, exactly where Luke had dumped him earlier. Now he knelt beside the dead man, threw back the blanket and said, "Look familiar?"

Nellie grabbed Walt's arm and Walt grabbed the doorframe. "That's him!" he breathed. "Johnny Moffat."

"It's Tom Guffey," corrected Luke.

Nellie shook her head. "I don't. . . . "

"This sonofabuck tried to rob the bank at Kelton about a week ago," said Luke. "But he didn't reckon on the manager telling him to go to hell. He went crazy, shot the manager dead, crippled the marshal, an' then lit out empty-handed, knocking down and killing a seven-year-old boy on his way out of town."

"Are you sure it's the same man?" asked Walt.

"Oh, it's Guffey, right enough," Luke replied. "Anyway, this is how I read it—Guffey lit out of Kelton and rode like the devil 'til his horse took a fall, then came here looking to buy or steal a replacement.

133

But before he could do any such thing, Ma killed him. Or thought she did."

"I shot him in the head!" said Nellie.

An old neckerchief was knotted around the dead man's head. Luke slipped it off so that they could see the blood-encrusted gouge that scored Guffey's skull just above and behind the left ear. "You shot him, right enough, but you didn't kill him. You knocked him cold and when Pa couldn't find his heartbeat you naturally assumed you'd killed him."

"But I buried him!" Walt protested.

"In a shallow grave you didn't even fill in properly," Luke countered. "He likely regained consciousness later, feeling sick as hell and with his brain half-scrambled. He got out of that grave, staggered away and decided to hole up someplace 'til he was healed. That'd fit the facts."

"Why?"

"Because when I happened across him, he'd fixed himself a rough-and-ready camp down along Quitman Creek, and he was afoot, no sign of a horse anywhere. I rode in on him by accident, didn't even know he was there 'til he jumped up and started shooting at me. I fired back, got him with the first shot."

"Which means. . . . " murmured Walt, with a kind of wonder.

"Which means you didn't kill 'Johnny Moffat'," said Luke. "I did. You folks didn't kill anyone."

Walt rested his chin on his chest for a moment. The heady rush of relief and gratitude was almost too much to handle. He felt Nellie's hand on his arm and covered it with one of his own. "It's all right, now," he whispered. "Everythin's all right."

She nodded.

Allowing the blanket to drop back over the dead man's face, Luke straightened up. "Well," he sighed, "you folks got an ugly hole up on yonder rim needs filling in. Reckon I'll go up there and see to it."

Walt drew a deep breath, squared his shoulders, and cleared his throat. Reaching down to scrub Sam's head affectionately, he sniffed noisily and said, "Come on, you mangy critter. Let's go watch Luke do some work!"

DESERT SURRENDER
Kit Churchill

Although born in South Wales, United Kingdom, Andrea Hughes,
writing as Kit Churchill, has always been fascinated with America's
Old West. Indeed, her great-grandfather was a pioneer to North
America in the late 19th century. She has been an avid reader of
Westerns, particularly Black Horse Westerns, since her teens, and also
enjoys gardening, music, and talking on the telephone.

Jay Calvin took the ragged end of the cigar from her mouth and spat on the ground. She glanced back over the open, arid desert and saw, again, the dust cloud behind her. Damn that marshal, what was his problem? One card game, one crooked card game, and he had been after her for five whole days. After pulling a bandana from around her neck, she mopped the sweat from her face. Well, he was going to have one hell of a fight to get her behind bars. She'd done that once; she didn't intend doing it again.

Jamming her hat back on her head, she spurred her horse forward. His breathing was labored and shallow, and she realized he couldn't keep up this pace much longer. She would have to think of something soon. The horse was the one thing she still had left from her parents, and there was no way she was going to kill him over a dispute from some damn card game. This guy wasn't going to go away and she wasn't going to outride him on this horse. She had tried backtracking, riding in rivers, everything she learned in five years on her own, but nothing had thrown him. She scoured the sun-baked landscape ahead until she spotted another dust trail, closer than the one behind, and moving fast in her direction. Not being able to think of anything else, she prayed they were men and susceptible to the charms of a young woman. Right now, that was all she had left.

After some time she made out that the dust trail belonged to two riders. Two men. Well, they could be good or bad, but they couldn't be worse than the threat of a jail cell that was coming up behind her. Dismounting, she pulled off her hat, letting her long, dark hair tumble over her shoulders and casually she undid the next two buttons of her shirt. Her hand felt for her six-gun in case trouble was coming in front of her as well as behind.

Then she waited.

Both riders pulled up their horses a half-dozen paces in front of her. The older of the two tipped his hat in her direction. "Howdy, miss. You seem to be in some hurry. Can we be of assistance?"

"Well," she turned and looked back anxiously. "I sure hope you can, mister. You see that dust trail?" She motioned behind her, hoping she looked scared enough. "That belongs to one mean son of a bitch who I don't really want to get reacquainted with."

"Really?" The younger of the men got down from his horse. His thick blond hair flopped lazily over his eyes, and his smile was eager and friendly. "Nice to meet you, ma'am. I'm Luke Coley, and this here is my pa, Gus. We own a ranch pretty near. Maybe you could ride back with us, if you're in trouble. We'd look after you, wouldn't we, Pa?"

Gus Coley chuckled and dismounted. She could see where the boy got his dazzling blue eyes. "Well, I tell you what, lady. Let's just say we wait for this hombre, and see what he wants, huh? Then, if you're in the trouble you say you are, we'll stick by you and you can come back to the ranch with us."

Jay had no intention of waiting around for the marshal to turn up.

"Well, sir," she undid yet another button on her shirt and pulled it down, revealing dark, purple bruising covering a slim white shoulder. Pulling it down a bit further, she stopped just before she reached her breast. It was bruising from another fight, another man, but it could come in mighty handy now. "I can see why you might want to wait for him, but I'm not in too much of a hurry to meet him again. You see, don't you?" The tears that welled up had done the trick in the past.

"Pa!" The boy was horrified at the sight of the bruising.

But his pa would take some more work. "I'm sure sorry about that, miss," Gus said, shaking his head. "Whoever did that is one sorry swine, but I still say we'd better wait and see what this fella wants. If he is as mean as you say he is, maybe we can get him off your back for you."

She turned slowly to her horse, running her hand down his mane. From her viewpoint behind her horse, she could see the dust trail coming closer. This had better work. Hell, men normally believed her, didn't they? Decent men, anyway.

As the marshal drew closer, Jay turned her face away.

"That's far enough, mister," Gus Coley called out, pulling the rifle from its scabbard. "Let's say you just take your gun belt off there, while we work this thing out."

The marshal looked quickly over at the girl and smiled, shaking his head. "Look, I don't know what tale this woman has been telling you, but whatever it is, it isn't true."

Gus gestured with his hand. "Maybe and maybe not. Just take off that gun belt, and we'll talk about it."

The marshal unbuckled and threw his gun belt forward, then dismounted and walked towards the group. "I see Jay's already introduced herself. I'm Marshal Alan Bodie, by the way." Pulling his coat back, he revealed a shiny tin badge. "Let me fill you in some more," he said and then he drew a piece of paper out of his pocket that had the girl's likeness sketched underneath the word "Wanted".

"No!" Jay turned to the Coleys. "You see, that wanted poster ain't true. It's just not true."

"Let me take a look at that." Gus studied the poster and glanced at the girl. "Sure is a good likeness of you alright, miss."

"Please. . . . " She glanced down, contrite. "Okay, I admit, I'm no angel. I've done things wrong. But nothing that deserves that wanted poster, and nothing that deserves this." Pulling her shirt back, again she revealed the bruises.

"Yeah," the boy said, gesturing at the marshal. "How do you explain that, huh?"

Marshal Bodie shook his head. "Whoever did that, it sure wasn't me. The life this girl leads, it could have been one of a number of men. Now, if you don't mind, gentlemen, I have business to take care of."

"Oh, come on." Jay looked up at Gus Coley. "Who are you gonna believe, me or him?"

"Well, I'll tell you, miss." Gus strode over to his horse and remounted. "I reckon I'm gonna believe that wanted poster. Luke, get back on your horse. This is none of our business."

"Please. . . . " She rushed over to the Coley horses. "Don't leave me here with him. You only have his word he didn't hurt me. How do you know he didn't?" Grabbing the older man's reins, she lifted pleading eyes to his.

Bodie sighed. "Come on, Jay. Just admit that you're caught and come back and do your time."

She cast him a dark glare. "My horse is wore out. So's yours, I reckon. Where the hell do you think we're gonna go in a hurry?"

"Marshal," Gus Coley gestured at their horses, "whatever that kid has or hasn't done, she's right about them horses. Our ranch is about half an hour's ride due west. What say you come back with us and rest up? In the morning, you can get an early start, wherever it is you're going."

"Well, that's decent of you, sir." Bodie pushed his hat back on his head, revealing a mop of brown, curly hair. "I sure could use the rest. So could our mounts." He gently patted his horse's neck and considered his options. "Okay, we'll come with you. First things first, though." He strode over and pulled handcuffs from his back pocket and drew the girl's hands up in front of her.

"And just how am I gonna escape, marshal, with three men watching me?"

"Let's just say I'm not taking any chances."

It was nightfall before they reached the ranch. Hunger gnawed at Jay's stomach and it seemed like every muscle in her body throbbed from being in the saddle too long.

"One of our hands will take care of the horses." Luke smiled towards her and dismounted. "I'll show you around."

Inside the large ranch house was surprisingly feminine, decorative drapes on the walls and chairs signifying a woman's touch.

Gus sat on one of the overstuffed arm chairs and looked at the girl. "Luke can bunk in with me. You take his room and the marshal can sleep on the sofa there."

"Afraid not, Gus." Marshal Bodie shook his head. "That girl is not leaving my sight until I get her back in my jail. We're rooming together."

"I don't deserve to be treated like this," Jay retorted, resentment burning in her eyes. "It was just one crooked card game."

"One crooked card game, huh?" Bodie snorted. "Well, it so happens I wired a friend of mine in Wyoming. Seems there's a whole lot more to your story than one crooked card game, isn't there, Jay?"

"Nothing I deserve to get hung over. If you know as much as you say, you know that." Jay could feel the old, familiar anger welling up inside. She had survived alone, the best way she could, for five years. If that didn't correspond exactly with the way the law wanted her to live, well that was just too bad.

"No one said anything about getting hung," Bodie said. "Reckon a spell in a women's prison would do you no harm though. Might even shock you into getting back on the right road."

"Who the hell do you think you are to judge me? You know nothing about me."

"Hey, whoa there!" Gus held up his hands. "Let's just eat and save the war for afterwards, shall we?"

After they had eaten, they sat drinking coffee. Jay stared into the hearth, and watched as the shadows from the flames danced on the walls. For a while, Gus stood in front of the fire. After a long silence, he turned toward her.

"Why don't you tell me how you got into this fix in the first place?" He bent down and lit a smoke from the fire. "I had a daughter like you, some time ago. Luke's half sister. She died early, too early. Sure would hate that to happen to you."

Jay lowered her eyes, studying Gus. "Look, mister. You seem nice. But I'm not in the mood for talking, or for being preached at."

Gus pulled up a chair and sat in front of her. The crinkles around his eyes and the graying hair did nothing to mar a still-handsome face. He reminded her of her pa and for one brief moment she wished she could bury herself in his shoulder and just let go of everything.

"How old are you?" Gus asked, dragging on his smoke.

She didn't answer.

"About nineteen, I reckon," he surmised. "Where are your folks? Where's your pa? Don't seem right you riding out here on your own like this. You can tell me to mind my own business, but as I said you remind me some of my daughter."

Jay stood up quickly. "I appreciate you trying to help an' all, but I'd rather be left alone, thanks." And she walked away, across the room. He was getting too close and if there was one thing she didn't need right now it was people getting close, opening up old wounds.

Gus sighed. "Okay, have it your way, lass. Seems a shame, though."

Marshal Bodie unfolded from his chair and stretched. "If you don't mind, Gus, I suggest we all hit the hay. Me and that young lady over there have an early start in the morning."

"Alright, you two sleep in here. You need anything, just give us a shout."

"How about my rifle and six-gun?" the girl said, turning her back on the marshal and slumping down on the sofa.

The first thing she felt the next morning was a strong grip on her shoulder, shaking her awake.

"Come on, young lady. You've got about five minutes to wash and eat breakfast and then we're out of here." Groaning, she noticed that the marshal obviously had been up some time. His face was clean shaven, and his thick dark curls were slicked back.

"Gosh, you're all heart, marshal. Are you married? I doubt it, if this is how you treat ladies."

"You're not a lady."

She threw a sour smile his way and picked up one of her saddlebags from the floor by the sofa.

"I'm just gonna get a brush out of here, marshal. Don't worry, it's not a gun I've got stashed away."

"I know. I searched your bags last night."

"Figures." Standing before the mirror, she pulled the brush through her long, dark hair. Five years spent on the trail, living rough, had done nothing to harm the splendor of her shining curls, and this was the one nod to femininity she allowed herself. Her clear, almost translucent skin and deep brown eyes were "gifts" from her mother's side of the family.

Luke stumbled out of his bedroom, tucking in his shirt. "Hi, Jay."

"Hi there, Luke." She gave him a smile and he blushed.

"Pa said you might be leaving early. Mick, our cook, won't be up yet, so I thought I'd fix you something."

"Thanks, Luke. At least someone knows how to be a gentleman around here."

Breakfast was soon over and they were saddled, ready to leave. Gus walked up to Jay's horse and took her hand.

"Bye, Jay. You behave, lass. Do the time you've got to do and then stay clear of trouble. You've got a lot of life ahead of you and you don't want to waste it running from the law."

Jay gave him a smile, knowing he meant well. "Thanks, Gus."

After everyone had said their goodbyes, Jay and Marshal Bodie rode out under the blistering sun. Jay's wrists were cuffed, and the marshal led her horse. She had no intention of following Gus' advice, and already she was planning on taking the best chance she would have to escape.

It seemed like they had been riding all day, but from the position of the sun Jay could see it had only been a few hours. Her head throbbed, and the sun felt like it was trying to burn through her shirt.

"Marshal, is there actually a human being inside that iron shell of yours? It's too hot, we need to rest and get some shade."

"You'll get plenty of that in my jail."

"Alright then, if you don't care about me, then care about my horse. He needs a drink."

Getting no reply, she groaned and pulled her hat down further over her eyes. "I have known some mean sons of guns in my time, but you just about beat the lot of them hands down."

"I doubt that."

After another hour's ride, the marshal headed the horses beside a clump of cottonwoods.

"Okay, we'll stop here, rest a while."

"Gee thanks, marshal. You sure you're not going soft?"

He reined in his horse in the shade of one of the trees and dismounted. "If I were you, I'd worry about getting rest, not smart talking."

"I can do both." After dismounting, she removed her horse's saddle and blanket and wiped him down with a cloth from her saddle bag. Then, pouring water from her canteen into her hat, she let the horse drink his fill.

"You sure take care of that horse, that's one thing I'll say for you."

"Belonged to my pa. Not in a hurry to lose him."

They made camp without speaking.

Afterwards, as they sat drinking and eating the food Gus Coley had provided, Jay noticed the marshal watching her.

"What you lookin' at?"

141

"I was wondering, like Gus last night, how you came to get into this fix."

"I don't have to explain myself to you." She shifted position, uncomfortable on the hard ground.

"No, you don't. But you owe it to yourself to live better than you're doing. And you know you do, otherwise you wouldn't be so hell-fired touchy about it."

She stood up defiantly. "I told Gus, I'll tell you. It's none of your business. I'll do what I want." With that, she turned and headed off into the bushes.

"Hey, where do you think you're going?"

Laughing shortly, she threw the answer back over her shoulder, "I'm not escaping . . . yet. Where do you think I'm going? Or do you want to come and watch me powder my nose, as well?"

"Keep close to the camp."

"Wouldn't dream of it," she called back sarcastically. Walking some distance away, she turned, checking if she could see the marshal. She had gone too far from the camp, but there was no one around here anyway, so she figured it didn't matter. For a moment, she just reveled in being alone, until the faintest noise made her turn. It had sounded like a twig snapping, but scanning the area, she could see nothing. Shrugging, she dismissed the sound, and began to undo her jeans. Another louder noise sent a chill running down her spine, and she whirled around in time to see five men emerging from the bushes, guns drawn. Instinctively she reached down for her six-gun, but stopped herself in mid-movement because her gun belt wasn't there. She was just set on warning the marshal, when a vile-smelling hand closed over her mouth, making her gag.

One of the men pushed through the boxwood to stand inches from her face. A long, vivid weal ran down his cheek and his black eyes held more hatred than she had ever seen.

"Shhh," he whispered. "We wouldn't want to alert your friend over there now, would we? You really should have been more careful, you know." He held up a knife to her face, running the blade down her cheek, increasing the pressure when the blade reached underneath her chin. Warm blood ran down her neck, as her skin was pierced by the jagged edge. He stood back, glancing down her body. "Hey, you're

142

even better close up! This is our lucky day. We didn't expect a prize like you to just fall into our laps."

She struggled, but the man behind her twisted her arm back until she thought the bone would snap. The man with the knife motioned for them to head to the camp. As they pushed through the bushes, the marshal leapt up, drawing his gun.

"Now that would be stupid." The leader walked into the clearing. Four guns pointed at the marshal's chest. "Drop your iron before both of you die."

Cursing, Marshal Bodie hesitated, and the girl berated herself for her stupidity. She had been planning how to escape from him and she'd walked into much, much worse.

Jay's captor barked, "I'd drop it, mister, if I was you. Nate Calhoun's a man of his word. If you don't do as he says, your friend here dies."

Reluctantly, Bodie threw down his gun, and Jay saw the anger burn in his face. But she wasn't ready to give up yet. The man holding the gun to her head wore double gun-belts, as befitted an ornery gunslinger, but she intended to make full use of them. As her captor's attention was drawn toward the marshal, she snaked her arm slowly down her side. Her mouth was still covered by her assailant's hand, and opening it as wide as she could, she brought her teeth down into his fingers, biting into hard bone and tasting blood. The man lurched back and bent over, yelling. Jay lunged and grabbed his spare gun from its holster, pointing it at his forehead before he could straighten up. "Drop your guns or your friend gets it, square and center," she ordered the desperadoes.

Without wasting a second, Calhoun, the leader, raised his rifle and fired into his companion's face. Blood spattered over Jay, and she gazed in horror as her captor fell to the ground, a neat round hole in his forehead. Before she could recover, the butt of Calhoun's rifle smashed into her face, spurting blood from her nose, and she could feel her eye swelling.

"Leave her alone!" Bodie stepped forward, but the three guns trained in his direction halted him.

"Be careful, bitch." Calhoun grabbed a handful of her hair and yanked her head up. He thrust the muzzle of the rifle against her face.

"Be careful before I forget you're worth more to us with your face in one piece."

Pushing her to the ground, Calhoun turned to his companions. "Let's get this cleared up and on our way. We haven't got all day."

Staring at their partner slumped on the ground, none of the other outlaws moved.

Calhoun glared at them. "I said get moving." He added in a deep growl, "Zack was careless. I don't work with careless men. She can ride on Zack's horse."

"What will we do with this fella, boss?"

"What we normally do. Strip him down to the waist and tie him out. Few hours in this sun will see him off."

There was nothing she could do now, and she knew it. After they had tied her hands, they shoved her over to the dead man's horse. She mounted clumsily, pain pounding through her head.

"Hey, *chiquita*!" One of the outlaws, a Mexican, had begun tying her feet to the saddle, but he stopped in his work to run his hand slowly up her leg. "We're going to have some fun later, eh?" He grinned, revealing a set of rotting, blackened teeth. "You wait."

As they rode away, Jay turned and looked at the marshal. One man was stripping the shirt from his back as another pointed a rifle at his chest.

"Jay, I'm sorry!" Bodie called amidst laughter from the men.

She said nothing, not sure whether she was more annoyed at him or herself. The day wore on, and the sun was as merciless as her captors, the heat adding to the nausea that clutched at her stomach. Ahead of them was the open desert, shimmering heat waves, and a vast barren landscape. She lifted her bound hands and gently examined her swollen cheek and eye that was nearly shut. As the endless heat and the pain from her bruised face began to take its toll, Jay feared they were never going to stop. Right now, all she wanted was to get down from this horse, just lie on the ground. That was all.

As night fell they came to a series of deep arroyos and the leader turned his horse into one of them and rode into a camp that looked as if it had been in existence for some time. A group of men called out greetings as they entered. Riding further into camp Jay gasped in horror as she saw a collection of women all huddled together away from the men. Some of their faces were as bruised and blackened as her face felt. Coming to a halt in front of the group, one of the men came up to her, slashing with a knife at the rawhide that bound her feet to the stirrups. He reached up and grabbed her shirt, pulling her off the horse, unconcerned with how roughly she fell to the ground.

"Get over there with the others!" Someone kicked her from behind and she stumbled, almost crashing into one of the women.

"Sorry," she mumbled, as she righted herself.

Staring at the woman beside her, Jay noticed that her eyes were blackened and her dress was torn away down the front, revealing bruised breasts. She glanced down the line of women. Some were rocking, staring into space, hopelessness in their eyes. Others just sat, looking at the ground, their faces empty of expression.

"Hasn't anyone ever tried to escape?" she whispered to the woman beside her.

"Escape," the woman snorted, not turning her head. "Yes, one woman tried to escape. We've been here about two weeks, more coming all the time. One woman tried to run about a week ago. They tied her out, right there in front of us. . . . " She pointed, staring at the ground as if seeing the whole scene again in her mind. "After each of the men had their turn, they used her for target practice. And left her there until she died. I can still hear her begging for us to help her die." At last the woman turned and looked Jay full in the face, her eyes expressionless. "You still want to escape?"

Giving in to the nausea that had gripped her stomach all day, Jay turned and retched. Rage washed over her at what had been done to these women, and the intensity of the feeling made her head throb even more. For now she was too sick and weak to do anything, but she sure as hell wasn't going to let these bastards get away with this.

She closed her eyes and forced herself to breathe slowly, calming her mind. She had to think. These women looked as if they had all but given up hope. The marshal was probably dead by now, so she was the only one who could save them. She studied the camp. Flickering firelight danced over the men. It was an oddly cozy scene for one that held such horror, she thought. Funny how firelight did that. Her mind went back to last night, at the Coley house. If only the Coleys were here now. If only Marshal Bodie was here now.

Finally, the men settled down, stretching out around the campfire—all, that is, except the Mexican. She watched as he got to

145

his feet and walked toward them. Her breath came in short gasps and her heart pounded.

"The other men are going to sleep now before they enjoy themselves." He bent down to cut the bonds on her feet. "They say they need rest after today's hot ride. Me, I can't wait."

"Leave me alone, you son of a bitch," she yelled at him, fear making her voice louder than she intended.

One of the dozing men lifted his head off his saddle. "Hey, *mano*, you going to pleasure yourself with her, you keep her quiet, huh?"

"*Sí*, good idea!" The Mexican unfastened a filthy bandanna from his neck and thrust it into Jay's mouth, tying it behind her head. He grabbed her shirt, pulled her to her feet, and dragged her to the side of the clearing. She saw his fist come at her again and she fell to the ground, darkness closing in on her. Perhaps it would be better this way. To be half conscious, to not feel anything. Then, from the depths of the blackness an idea dawned, slowly and faintly, but it was there and she forced her way back.

His hands tore at her belt and the buttons of her jeans. She should have struggled, but she had decided to be compliant as he yanked her pants down, along with her unmentionables. A sharp pain shot through her backside as stones cut into her bare skin. The Mexican unbuckled his gun belt, tossing it nearby, his eyes blazing with lust, eyeing her, one hand groping at her breasts as the other struggled with his pants.

She had one chance and took it. Before he'd exposed himself she pulled him down on top of her with her left arm while her free hand grabbed at the pistol in his holster. She used the butt with all her hate, all her force, and hit him hard behind the ear, repeatedly, until he lay still on top of her. Breathing with difficulty under his heavy, stinking body, she slid from under him. Hurriedly, Jay pulled up her pants and fastened her shirt as best she could.

Crouched low, she moved to the other women and before any could express surprise Jay signed for silence.

The snores from the rest of the camp confirmed most of the men were asleep. They had posted a guard at the opening of the arroyo, but his attention was directed outside the camp.

They probably didn't believe a bunch of beaten, tied women would prove any trouble. Moving quickly she cut the rawhide from the legs of one woman and moved up to her hands. With her head bent, concentrating on her work, she didn't hear the man behind her until it was too late. A fist smashed down against her temple and the world around her suddenly caved inward.

The next sensation Jay Calvin felt was an ache behind her eyes as the sunlight filtered through the trees and down onto her prostrate form. She groaned. Her head seemed to be bursting from inside and pain stabbed at her jaw. Quickly she shut her eyes again, not wanting to face what would greet her when she looked around. Better just to lie here, feign sleep. After an all-too-brief period, a boot smashed into her ribs and she groaned again from the intense pain. Her hands and feet had been retied, this time tighter, and she was back with the other women.

"Wake up." Slowly she struggled to her knees, trying to cradle her aching side with her arm. All she could see was a pair of worn boots, the leather cracking around the sides, and the frayed ends of a pair of blue denims. The man's legs were placed wide apart, in an arrogant stance of supremacy. The boots belonged to Calhoun and he bent down and pulled her up from the ground, forcing her head level with his.

"Listen, bitch." She closed her eyes, unwilling to gaze at him. "You listen good. That stunt you pulled last night was stupid. Very stupid. You've cost me two men already!"

Curious, Jay opened her eyes. Behind Calhoun was the spread-eagled body of the Mexican. Her legs felt weak and her heart hammered. They'd used knives on him and he must have taken a long, painful time to die.

"You're getting too expensive, no matter how good a body you have. You ain't worth the hassle, honey!" He spat on the ground. "So I'm going to make an example of you."

Her heart lurched. Next to the body of the Mexican were four posts that had been knocked into the ground, about six feet apart. A cold horror filled the pit of her stomach. A line of men stood beside the posts, lustful grins on their faces.

They dragged her over and forced her onto the ground. They cut the rawhide that bound her hands and feet and, despite the agony of her bruised, battered ribs, she struggled. But it was to no avail. They were too strong, too powerful, and she was outnumbered.

Calhoun barked, "Stop pussy-footin' around and tie her!"

Rough hands clawed again at her jeans, pulling them off her. Her hands and feet were tied to the four poles. Spread-eagled, offered up to them, she clenched her eyes tight. Her chest heaved and she wanted to vomit but her stomach was empty. She heard men murmuring and sniggering and then the sound of a man's belt buckle clattered on the ground. "I'll show you guys how it's done!" snarled Calhoun. A second later, she felt the weight of his body descend on hers and the stink of him turned her stomach. Tears of impotent rage filled her tight-closed eyes as she realized there was nothing she could do to stop this. She forced her mind away, trying to retreat somewhere safer, kinder, and was so successful that she barely heard the sound of the gunshot booming through the camp.

"Get off her!" a man barked.

Jay opened her eyes with a start but the desperado on top of her obscured her view. The line of lusting men was backing away, their mouths mere slits, fear in their eyes as they scanned left and right.

"You're not moving quick enough, mister. I said get the hell off her!"

The man hurriedly scrambled from atop Jay, fumbling with his trousers, and joined his companions.

Their guns were drawn, but they had no idea where the voice, or the gunshot, came from.

"Drop your guns and toss them in a pile. Then move over to the east side of the gully, away from the women." For a moment no one moved and the sound of another gun shot rang through the camp. "Now, you bastards, or these bullets will start finding targets."

Soon, a pile of gun belts lay on the ground.

The voice called out again. "Okay, we're coming in. In case you think of trying anything funny, we're leaving guards up here with their guns trained on you. Anyone who wants to try anything, please do. It would be our pleasure to put bullets in you bastards."

A group of ten riders came into the camp. A wonderful, warm sense of relief flooded through her as she recognized Gus and Luke Coley at the head of them.

"Luke, you and the boys see to those bastards. Tie them up good, and don't be too easy on them." Gus stepped quickly from his horse and ran over to Jay, picking up her clothes. He knelt beside her.

148

"Oh, Gus," she sobbed, her body shaking despite the bonds. "I'm mighty glad you came!"

"Yeah, me too, honey," he said, hastily placing his hat on her to recover some of her modesty. He cut the rawhide that bound her.

With his back to her, Gus did his best to shield curious eyes from her, while Jay pulled on her jeans and shirt.

"I guess I'm as decent as I'll ever be, Gus," she said.

Gus turned and took her into his arms. She buried her face in his shoulder, feeling safe at last. As she lifted her head, she saw Luke coming toward them, hat in his hands, and after she had hugged Gus, she pulled him to her.

"Luke, thank you. I can't say. . . . "

"Jay, I'm so sorry." He studied her, wincing as he examined her battered face. "My God . . . look at you."

"It's okay. At least you and Gus are here now. The rest doesn't matter." They stood for a moment, reveling in each other's company, until Gus' voice broke the spell.

"Come on, honey. We're going back to the ranch. You need some rest and a doctor, and there's one lawman back there who's sick with worry about you."

"Marshal Bodie's alive?" Jay whirled around to stare at Gus, disbelief in her eyes.

"Well, more dead than alive, honey. . . . "

"But how did you find us?"

"You were both darn lucky. Two of my boys were coming back from a trip east and they found the marshal strung out, cooking in the sun. After he recovered enough to talk, first thing he talked about was you. He wanted to join us but he weren't in no fit state. Just a matter of trailing you after that."

"And what about the poor women?" Jay turned to see they had been set free and were hugging each other, tears streaming down their faces. Gus motioned to Luke.

"Luke and the boys are going to take the women and these bastards back to Fort Worth. The women will be safe there."

Jay nodded. Everything seemed to have been put right. She glanced sadly at the horses at the rear of the camp. Everything except the one thing she loved more than anything in the world; the horse she had been determined to look after . . . and that she had lost.

Gus saw her glance and smiled at Luke. She caught the wink they exchanged and stared at them, not daring to hope.

"Oh, yes. Didn't I tell you? There is one more surprise for you." He smiled and nodded and said, "He's back at the ranch. My boys found him tied up where they came across the marshal. These bastards were probably too consumed with lust to worry about horse flesh. Damn careless to leave a horse of that quality behind."

Jay turned to Gus, unable to express the feelings that seemed to burst from inside her.

"It's okay." Gus stroked the hair away from her bruised and bloodied cheek.

"Gus, I don't know how I'm ever going to thank you." Glancing up, she gave a half smile. "You've saved my life."

The ride passed quickly, despite the stabs of pain shooting down her side. She rode cradled in Gus' arms, too weak from her ordeal and her bruised and battered body to manage a horse alone. It seemed an age since she had last been at the ranch yet Jay realized with a shock it had only been yesterday morning when she and Marshal Bodie left the place. Her thoughts turned to him and as they rode up to the front porch she tentatively eyed Gus.

"He's in there, honey. Go and put his mind at rest."

Climbing painfully off the horse she made her way to the front door. Marshal Alan Bodie lay on the couch in the front room, his eyes closed, his face sunburned, blistered, and barely recognizable. Slowly walking toward him, she picked up the handcuffs from the table beside him.

"Hello," Jay whispered.

Bodie's eyes opened slowly and creased in concern as he saw her.

"Jay, what did they do to you?"

"I might ask the same, but it doesn't matter now." Holding out the handcuffs, she grinned as much as her bruised face would allow. "Okay, Marshal Bodie. I give up. If you want me, I'm yours."

HECATE
P. McCormac

Philip McCormac always had a hankering to become a writer.
He claims blame for nine Black Horse Westerns under various
pseudonyms with another Western due later this year.

Gat him upon his mule.
—*2 Samuel 13:21*

Ben Foster sipped at his bourbon, staring into space. The batwings creaked and drew his attention. He watched indolently as the hairiest human he had ever seen barreled inside. With one sweeping glance the newcomer took in the almost empty saloon then walked over to the bar. He rested both hands on the top of the bar and affected to read the bottles lining the shelves behind Ben Foster's head.

Tangled iron-gray hair hung to below the man's shoulders. An equally unkempt beard sprouted from his face and hung to mid chest. To enhance the hairy effect the man wore animal skins. A coonskin cap complete with tail perched atop his head. The sleeveless sheepskin jacket had seen better days and appeared to be molting.

"Howdy, stranger," Ben Foster said. "Can I get you anything?"

"I'm looking for a drink that'll quench my thirst and still leave my tonsils in place."

Ben Foster smiled indulgently. "Red Nugget whiskey should do the trick. Smoothest drink this side of the Rockies."

He plucked a bottle from a shelf behind him and poured a measure of amber liquid into a glass.

"Try that."

The newcomer put the glass to a gap in the beard and drank noisily. When he put down the empty glass he sucked at the hair around his mouth then expelled his breath in a fierce gust.

"Umm. . . . I've drunk mule's piss and it tasted better'n that poison," he said speculatively. "Better try another just to make sure it is whiskey and not piss."

Ben Foster's hand tightened on the whiskey bottle.

"Mister, if you don't like our drinks you can always try somewhere else."

"I was told when I got to California Crossing to make sure to call in and sample Ben Foster's hospitality. You go and get Ben Foster down here. I want to make a complaint. I sure don't like your attitude."

"Son of a bitch, I am Ben Foster. You can have that first drink on the house. Now turn around and go crawl into whatever rat-hole you came outta."

A broad grin split the bearded face of the stranger. "Ben Foster, you're sure one mean son of a bitch. What way's that to greet an old friend?"

Ben Foster's eyes narrowed and he peered intently at the stranger. "Old friend! I sure as hell didn't know I had a monkey for a friend."

"Monkey, my ass. Kent—Tom Kent."

"Well I'll fart in a ten gallon hat. Tom Kent! You had me going there for a moment. Tom Kent! I was about to chuck you out in the street." Ben Foster slapped the bar. "I'll be danged." He poured from the bottle. "Here, have another glass of piss. What the hell brings you down here?"

The whiskey disappeared into the hairy mouth. "Just kidding about the whiskey." Kent smacked his lips. "It is good stuff. O'Leary sent me."

Ben Foster placed his hands on the bar top and stared earnestly at Kent. "Keane O'Leary," he said slowly. "How is that old reprobate?"

"He's doing okay. Wants to throw a jamboree and for you to organize it."

Keane O'Leary rode into California Crossing on a big, sturdy roan. Ten of his men had ridden in earlier to make sure the town was safe for his visit. O'Leary never left anything to chance. An outlaw town would attract bounty hunters. The price on his head was enough to set up a man for life.

Flags and bits of colored cloth were hung out in honor of his visit. The inhabitants of California Crossing lined the sidewalks and called out greetings to the famous bandit chief. He ignored the crowds, staring straight ahead as he rode in with his entourage.

Around O'Leary rode a bunch of hard-eyed gunmen. It was said the bandit leader never traveled anywhere without a bodyguard of at least twenty men. They rode straight to the dance hall where Ben Foster waited to greet him.

"Dang my hide, Ben Foster, you're getting nearly as old as myself. Let's get this party rolling. I'm dry as a buffalo chip."

While O'Leary pushed inside, Ben Foster courteously waited and escorted O'Leary's daughter, Sheila. The hall rapidly filled with excited men and women.

Ben Foster hurried to the bandstand and yelled for attention. "California Crossing welcomes old friends."

A cheer broke out and he had a job calming the crowd enough to be heard.

"There's plenty of food and drink—whiskey, wine, and beer. Should be enough to satisfy the most persnickety amongst you. Just eat and drink and have a good time."

Whatever else he wanted to say was lost, as the crowd charged rowdily to the bar. At a signal from Ben Foster the fiddlers and harmonica players struck up a lively tune. Soon the hall was abuzz with music, talk, laughter, and tobacco smoke.

When the celebrations were well under way, O'Leary sauntered up to the band. The music ceased as he held up his arms. As the mob of boisterous revelers noticed him, the noise fell away. All heads turned expectantly towards the top of the hall.

"Most of you are wondering what this celebration is all about," the bandit chief began. "Well, it's an engagement party. The man I have chosen to marry my daughter has been my right-hand man these last few years. That man is Sam Cornwell." O'Leary turned and extended his arm towards a man in the crowd. "Stand up, Sam."

Cornwell, a handsome man with jet-black hair and a dark, bushy moustache grinned sheepishly as he stepped up beside the bandit chief. He was tall with the broad shoulders of an athlete. Cheering broke out as O'Leary motioned his daughter forward. He smiled benignly at his offspring.

"What say you, Sheila? How does this set with you?"

Her open, attractive face was unsmiling as she stood before him. A .44 was thrust into the waistband of her cord trousers. A red, silk blouse completed her attire, matching the warm glow on her flushed cheeks.

"No, Father, I am not going along with this."

153

The old eyes lost a little of their warmth. "Come, come, is this some sort of joke?"

"I want to live my own life. I want to live a normal life and not have to pack up and run every time a lawman rides by. Frank McQueen has asked me to go with him. We want to buy a horse ranch up in Nevada. All we ask is a stake to get us started."

A silence fell across the hall. The only sounds were boots shuffling on the boards.

"Sheila, of all my possessions you are the most precious. Now think carefully. What say you to your pa? Make an old man happy and reconsider."

"Pa, I have considered long and hard. I want a life of my own. Can't you understand that?"

The leathery face lost some of its color. O'Leary's mouth twitched. "Ungrateful child!" he snapped. "From now on I have no daughter. Get out of my sight! I never want to see you again."

The blazing eyes suddenly focused on the tall good-looking young man standing slightly behind his daughter.

"Frank!" The name was spit out like a curse. A gun appeared in the old man's hand.

"No!" Sheila flung herself between her father and Frank. "Pa, no!"

The Colt trembled as the anger grew. Suddenly a shabby, hirsute figure stood before O'Leary.

"For God's sake, Keane, this is your daughter! Put the gun up. This is no cause for gunplay."

The anger was transferred to the speaker.

"Kent, get outta my way! This is my family and I'll settle my own disputes."

"No, Keane, I'll not stand by and let this happen. No way can this be settled by a killing spree."

"You intend to brace me, Kent? You want to go out in the street and face me, man to man, gun against gun?"

"Keane, you know I'd go to hell and back for you, but this is madness. Your own daughter! Give her what she asks. You can afford to stake her and her man. They deserve better than this."

"Nothing, nothing! I'll give them nothing! I have no daughter to give to. Get outta my sight. All of you! And you, Kent—if you're here come sundown, I'll come gunning for you."

154

The mule had a serene look about it that belied its nature. Tom Kent was not to know that. Having ridden horses most of his life he knew nothing about mules. In his newly reduced circumstances it was all he could afford. The stable hand that sold it to him lauded the animal's ability to go for days without food or water.

"That beast saved my life once. I was stranded out in the Sierras. Injuns had raided and taken everything. All I had 'tween me an' survival was that there mule. She took me outta that wilderness. Wouldn't be here today to tell the story but for that there old gal."

It hadn't occurred to Kent to query why the hostler wanted to part with such a valuable beast at the knockdown price he was asking. He had paid the few dollars from his dwindling resources, purchased a dilapidated saddle, and prepared to ride out.

The Kent that negotiated the purchase of the mule was unrecognizable as the same man who had argued with Keane O'Leary over his treatment of his daughter. Gone were the masses of hair from face and head. The smooth face of a middle-aged man now looked out at the world. Baggy overalls and plaid shirt had replaced the skins that had been his trademark from his trapping days.

Kent's first inkling that he may have been hoodwinked over the properties of the mule came when he began to saddle the beast. Casually the large gray head came around and two mean eyes regarded his efforts. Too quick for him to avoid entirely, large yellow teeth snapped shut on his hip.

"Goddamn bitch," he swore, and tried to prise himself loose.

Fortunately the overalls were too big for him and the mule's teeth closed over what was mostly a wad of fabric. Nevertheless, the skin of his hip was nipped painfully. To make the mule loosen its grip Kent had to batter the animal on the nose with a fist. When finally released, he hopped about rubbing his hip and swearing long and luridly. The mule bared its teeth in a wicked grin.

"Goddamn animal, I'd sell you to the slaughter house for meat only you'd probably poison anyone as ate you."

The mule made a strange whickering sound and Kent could have sworn the animal was laughing at him. He now approached the beast with extreme caution. So busy was he watching for those snapping

155

teeth he was unaware as he tightened the girth that the mule was busily inflating its stomach.

His next task was to get the bit in position. Having considered the problem, Kent edged around toward the rear of the animal. He had his knife in one hand and the bit in the other. Quickly he stabbed the blade into the animal's rear end. The mule jumped, kicked out, and at the same time opened its mouth to bray its displeasure. By this time Kent was at the head and he jammed the bit in position, though not without some risk to his fingers.

"Got you that time, you nasty little beastie," he gloated, but his heart sank at the thought of having to go through all this every time he had to saddle up. If he hadn't been in a hurry to vacate California Crossing he might have considered confronting the man who had sold him this beast from hell.

From then on, everything to do with the mule was performed while giving the wicked teeth and hooves a wide berth. In spite of these precautions, the animal at one stage managed to stand on his foot.

"Hell's bells, if you ain't Satan's sister come to haunt me!" Kent swore, hopping about in agony for the second time. "Hecate, that's what I name you. Hecate! It was said of Hecate that even the wolves cringed when she came near."

About two miles out of California Crossing, Hecate allowed her stomach to deflate. She did this to the accompaniment of a loud, sustained fart. Kent was just starting to chuckle at this indiscretion when the mule changed direction. The saddle tilted and Kent, arms flailing as he tried to keep his balance, fell heavily onto the road. Hecate continued blithely onward as if unaware of the catastrophe that had befallen her new master.

"Goddammit, maybe I should've faced down O'Leary. At least it would have been quick instead of this slow death by attrition."

Kent picked himself up and hobbled painfully after the mule.

"Come back here, you harlot of Hades."

The mule let him almost catch her for a mile or more before she tired of the game and set about grazing placidly on sage growing by the side of the road. Footsore and somewhat irked, Kent warily approached the beast. He took out his revolver and placed the muzzle in the mule's ear.

"If you ever do that to me again I'm gonna blow out your goddamn brains."

The mule regarded him calmly out of one jaundiced eye then pursed its lips and snickered. Kent instinctively knew the mule was calling his bluff. The animal had set the limits of its master's dominance. He realized he was in a no-win situation. Wearily he set about the arduous task of tightening up the saddle girth and remounting.

"Hecate, only one of us'll walk away from this relationship and I ain't sure I'm gonna be the one still standing."

So depressed was Kent that he did not realize the mule had turned about face and was retracing its steps back to California Crossing. When Kent realized what had happened he resigned himself to spending another night in the town. He made his way to the livery and off-saddled, all the while wary of snapping teeth and stomping hooves.

"Hecate, I don't know whether to shoot you or just abandon you here."

A rider pulled up outside leading a second saddle horse. "You there, take care of these horses."

"Take care of them yourself, you fat oaf. Or maybe you're so dumb you don't know how."

"Fella, you don't know who I am. I work for O'Leary. Now do as you're told. I'm late as it is."

"Huh! Work for O'Leary!"

Kent was well aware of the identity of the traveler. The man's name was Oscar Brennan and had taken over from Kent as scout for the gang.

"What do you do? Clean the shit house for them?"

"You son of a bitch, I'm gonna whip your ass."

"You'll wipe my ass you mean."

As the bandit went to dismount Kent reached out and gripped his boot.

"Let me help you down."

A quick heave and the man tumbled out of the saddle and landed heavily in the dirt.

"Son of a bitch!" Oscar was scrambling to his feet as Kent kicked him savagely in the shoulder. "You wanted to wipe my ass so stay down on your knees."

The bandit tried to rise again and this time Kent's kick caught him in the rear end. He stumbled outside. Again and again Kent kicked the man, driving him along the street. Kent gave the man no time to go for a weapon even if he had been so inclined. Each time Oscar tried to rise, Kent kicked him. The pair progressed along the street with the bandit cursing and yelling at his attacker and Kent calling him whatever offensive names he could dredge up.

The hubbub brought people into the street. Ben Foster and a cluster of men came out to see the fun.

"Hold on there, fella," Ben Foster called. "What's all the kicking for?"

Kent paused, his chest heaving from the effort of kicking his enemy all the way from the livery.

"This dog threatened to kick my ass. I'm giving him lessons on how it's done."

The bandit looked up hopefully at the crowd and as he did so noticed Sam Cornwell, the man he was seeking.

"I have a message from O'Leary," he called in desperation. "I was on my way to see you when this animal attacked me. You're to bring in Frank McQueen."

Kent's boot on the side of the man's head silenced anything else he might have said.

"He's a liar as well as a coward," raged Kent aiming another kick.

"Stop! For God's sake stop!"

Cornwell stepped forward and pushed Kent back from the cowering Oscar. He stared down at the battered man.

"Get up," he commanded and turned to Kent. "You're in trouble, fella. You picked the wrong man to kick. No one messes with the O'Leary people." Cornwell nodded to the men with him. "Take him."

"What the . . . ?"

Kent stood no chance as Cornwell's henchmen quickly grabbed him.

"Oscar," Cornwell called. "Now's your chance to get even."

Oscar came over with a smirk on his chubby face. He backhanded Kent, who immediately retaliated and kicked Oscar in the kneecap. As the bandit hopped back cursing, Cornwell yelled at the men holding Kent, "Get him down!"

Without more urging they clubbed and kicked their captive to his knees. Seeing his tormentor helpless, Oscar booted Kent in the midriff. Kent grunted and hung gasping for breath.

Then the burly man set to work on him. With undisguised malice the bandit rained down vicious punches and kicks. As the beating progressed, no one was sure if the victim was conscious or not. Each time a blow landed blood sprayed from cuts on Kent's ruptured face and nose.

In the end it was Ben Foster who stepped in to end the brutal beating. "That's enough. You don't want to end up killing the fella."

The bloodied man was dragged back to the livery stables and slung inside.

"Next time our paths cross, I'll kill you," Oscar snarled as he planted a parting kick on the semi-conscious Kent.

Painfully, the battered man dragged himself inside the stables, slipping in and out of a black void. He wasn't sure, but it seemed that through the mists of pain, something soft and moist was caressing his face. Barely able to open pain-dazed eyes he peered up at his benefactor. For a horrible moment he thought it was the face of the mule, then he passed into oblivion.

He was barely able to move when he regained consciousness. The inside of the barn was dim. Standing over him was the mule. It turned a baleful eye toward the man as it sensed him stirring. He climbed painfully to his feet. As he tried to shuffle forward he stumbled and would have fallen only he flung his arm round the neck of the mule. It stood patiently while he clung desperately, waiting for the stables to steady.

Man and mule moved slowly forward into the light. Kent was unrecognizable. His features were swollen to grotesque proportions. Though his face was clear of gore, dark bruises and cuts disfigured his skin. His shirt was caked with dried blood.

"Sweet Jesus, man, you bin sparring with that there damn mule?"

Kent blinked and stared at the man and woman who were holding two saddled horses. He recognized Sheila O'Leary and Frank McQueen, her chosen beau.

"Damnedest thing." Kent stared at the big, gray beast standing docilely behind him. "I bin fighting this mule for most of yesterday. It tried to bite and stomp me and then when I crawled in here to curl up and die it must've licked my face clean and been watching over me all night." He shook his head. "Damnedest thing."

"Who did this to you?"

"Sam Cornwell and his sidekicks." Kent looked somberly at the couple. "Cornwell's looking for you two."

"Cornwell!" Sheila exclaimed. She turned and stared at her companion. "Pa must have put him on to us. We'd better hurry."

"Take me with you. I reckon that Cornwell might just be on the prod and if he finds me he might kill me next time."

"Can you ride?"

"Just let me get this beast saddled up and I'll be ready to ride."

"We'll meet you outside but do hurry."

Kent still exercized extreme care as he saddled and bridled the beast. He was somewhat bemused for his mount stood quietly and failed to take advantage of his weakened state.

"I can't figure you, Hecate. I guess you're plotting something dire. I only wish I knew what it was. And," he added wryly, "I sure as hell hope I'm not around when you try it."

They rode all day. Kent, still weak from his beating, found it hard to keep his eyes open. Time and again he jerked his head up after snoozing for a few moments in the saddle. He looked at his companions. They too drooped in the saddle, showing similar signs of weariness.

"We got to stop and have a rest soon," he ventured. "Otherwise I'll topple off this mule and break my neck. Mind you, with all these aches and pains I'd probably not notice."

"You're right, old man," Frank agreed. "We'll look for a suitable place to hole up for a while."

They rode about a mile further when they saw a giant cottonwood that had fallen during a recent storm.

"Should give us cover for a while," Frank muttered. "We'll rest here."

They dismounted and each found a place to settle among the foliage of the fallen tree. Kent groaned as he almost fell from the mule. He curled up on the ground and was asleep immediately.

Kent grunted as Hecate, with an evil leer on her face, stomped on him again and again. The pain was brutal and real.

160

"Goddamn you, I'll kill you this time, you son of a bitch," Kent swore.

"Wake up, you mad fool," a voice insisted.

Pain seared through his side as a boot crunched into his damaged ribs. Kent groaned and opened his eyes. Cornwell and Oscar Brennan stood gazing down at him. Groggily he shook his head and looked around. Sheila O'Leary and her companion Frank were sitting on the ground with their hands tied behind them. Nearby was the mule. It seemed intent on munching its way through the downed cottonwood tree. Another kick and another agonizing bolt of pain.

"For God's sake, stop kicking me. I don't want no trouble. I'm heading for the gold diggings. I've had enough of the O'Learys to last me a lifetime. I'm getting out."

Oscar kicked Kent again. He tried to roll with the kick but was too slow and the boot caught him in the spine. He arched his back in agony.

"Oh, God, this hurts too much."

A gun barrel slashed him across the back of the head and he saw stars. When the lights had settled in his head, the men were still there, patiently waiting and grinning at his discomfort.

"Mister, we can beat you to death. It'll take time but we'll enjoy doing it. We were to bring these two in alive but we got no instructions about you. I guess we'll leave you here for buzzard meat."

In spite of the odds Kent went for his gun and slapped an empty holster.

"Is this what you're looking for, you sad bastard?" Cornwell held up Kent's revolver.

"You know something, fella?" Kent groaned. "Things started going wrong when I had that haircut. I guess I should'a heeded that fella, Samson, in the bible. His story went something similar. Only instead of Delilah I drew the short straw and got Hecate."

"Cut the crap, lughead. I want you to beg for your life."

"Believe me, fellas, I don't wish to die. Ouch!" He grunted as Oscar booted him in the face. Kent moaned. Warm blood trickled from a pulpy nose. He buried his face in his hands and tensed himself.

Oscar squatted down beside him. "Look, make this easy on yourself. Just beg for your life and I'll put a slug in your head. It'll be a

161

nice, clean death. We got what we came for so now we wanna hightail it back to California Crossing with this pair."

Kent peered up at his tormentor. The man was toying with his gun—spinning it on his forefinger. At intervals the barrel would be pointing at the man on the ground. Kent winced every time that happened, expecting each time an explosion.

"Please, fellas, believe me, I didn't even know who this O'Leary fella was. I ain't got no beef against him. I just want out with a whole skin."

There was a click as the gun was aimed at Kent's midriff.

"I guess you're hankering after a gut shot."

Kent slowly sat up with a frightened look on his face wondering if he could snatch Oscar's gun and turn it on himself and end his suffering.

"What you say, Cornwell?" Oscar grinned up at the gunman standing behind him and watching his companion torment his victim.

Cornwell screamed. His face turned white and he arched up on his toes and began to flail his hands helplessly in the air. Oscar gawked up at his boss. He made to rise and Kent kicked him between the legs and made a grab for the six-shooter.

While Cornwell screamed for his friend to help him Kent and Oscar wrestled on the ground for possession of the gun. The gunman head-butted Kent and he almost lost consciousness. Only a desperate desire to stay alive kept him fighting. The gun went off and Cornwell gave a strangled, gurgling sound as the bullet took him full in the chest. Slowly he keeled over on top of the men wrestling for the gun that had just cut short his life.

"Goddamn it, Cornwell! What the hell . . . ?"

Kent sunk his teeth into Oscar's hand. With a yelp the bully let go the gun. He was struggling to get out from under the collapsed Cornwell. While Kent fumbled to get a grip on the disputed revolver, Oscar grabbed for Cornwell's gun and turned it on Kent. Kent went still.

"Drop it, you bastard. I'll blow your head apart."

Kent allowed the weapon to fall from his slack fingers. He stared helplessly at the muzzle of the gun just a few feet from his face. The gunman scrambled to his feet.

"Get away from Cornwell," he ordered Kent as he prodded his boss with his foot.

"Cornwell, what the hell's the matter?"

Oscar's hand was shaking so much he had to use both hands to hold his gun steady. When Cornwell did not answer, the man screamed obscenities at Kent.

"You killed my partner, you bastard."

Kent might have pointed out the gun that killed Cornwell was in Oscar's hand when it went off but thought now was not the time to dispute the point. He sat on the ground waiting for the shot that would finish him. "Let it be clean," he prayed.

"Bastard," screamed the gunman as he cocked the weapon.

He never got to fire it. Large, yellow teeth closed over his wrist. Jaws that had been shredding branches of cottonwood crunched down on bone and gristle. Oscar screamed as his arm was reduced to minced flesh and splintered bones. He dropped to his knees, still screaming. The gun fell from fingers suddenly deprived of nerves and blood. Only then did the mule release the mangled arm and step back. Blood pumped in scarlet streams onto the ominously still Cornwell.

Kent stood up with a gun in his hand. He did not aim it for neither of his attackers posed a threat. The mule had backed away and now stood facing him. That wicked grin was on her face.

"Hecate," Kent whispered, "I . . . I. . . . " he paused, lost for words.

There was a moan from the injured man. "Help me."

Oscar was staring pathetically at Kent. Blood was still pumping with slightly less vigor from his mangled arm. There was blood on his companion, blood on the leaves of the cottonwood, and blood on the injured man's clothing. "Help me," he said again in a faint voice.

Kent looked critically at the blood-soaked surroundings.

"That's a terrible mess you're making. I hope you're gonna clean up after. You know how hard it is to get blood out of clothing. Your friend Cornwell's just soaked in the stuff."

The wounded man did not answer. He had keeled over and now lay in a dead faint, his arm still pumping blood into the earth. It was only then that Kent noticed the huge rip in the backside of Cornwell's pants. Blood and feces had run in streams down the man's legs. He turned and looked at the mule. Hesitantly he walked over to the beast. Slowly he reached out and placed his hand on the broad forehead. The mule

163

ignored him and carried on munching leaves. Kent stroked the rough gray head.

"I'll be a hunchbacked packrat! If you ain't something, Hecate."

The mule turned its head and gazed up at Kent. The man stared into big violet eyes, poised to leap out of range of those deadly teeth. The mule snickered then went back to champing leaves. Shaking his head Kent turned and walked over to the two bound captives. "I guess now that we've rested, we can continue on our journey."

SNOWS OF MONTANA
Matthew P. Mayo

Matthew P. Mayo is a magazine and book editor and author of two Black Horse Westerns: Winters' War *and* Wrong Town. *He lives in an old farmhouse in downeast Maine, USA, with his wife, Jennifer, and two dogs. When he's not editing or writing, he's kayaking, shoveling snow, or mowing the lawn. Visit him at www.matthewmayo.com.*

Pap was right. You never know in life from one minute to the next just what's coming at you. Take that morning a month back. I don't believe in fences and there I was, on my worn-through knees in that Texas dirt, scratching around in a hole that if it got any deeper my cheek would have been grazing ground level, when I heard that far-off dog bark.

I stood, slower than I would have liked. Farming will kill a man, maybe not as fast as a bullet or a noose or a snakebite but it will do the job just as thoroughly in the end. I raised a hand to try to keep the sun from intruding on whatever it was I hoped to see. Which, it turned out, was nothing. Yet.

I shucked my hat and wiped my sweltering head with the soaked kerchief wadded up inside the sagged crown. To my right those flopped posts were laid out like men who've given up after a long time of not wanting to, each one needing a hole and a man to dig it. And that's where it comes back to me.

I'm Ernie Palchik, Pal to my friends and a cowpuncher by trade, though before I set out on my grand adventure in early June it had been months since I rode old Plug more than twenty minutes at a stretch. When punching gigs came too few and far between I took what I could get. I'm proud as the next man but as my Pap always used to say, "Put you some pride in one hand and a beefsteak in the other, see which hand fills up faster."

When a man's got to eat and his coin purse is hollow and the growling animal in his gut is gnawing its way out, then his convictions get stuffed to the bottom of his war bag. I've been down that road many a time, though that was not exactly what drove me to work for the old couple, whose name, near as I could figure, was Schnelling. They spoke German and I don't.

The day I chanced on their place the old man showed me around. I expect he was never a tall fellow but he sure had turned those big hands of his to a fair amount of work. If I read him right he built the farm himself. And a prettier place you'd be hard-pressed to find. That house was a picture—all upright boards painted white and that roof shingled, not scrap-tinned like so many little farms are, with a pretty little shade porch and three rockers on it.

I looked past the flower beds—pinks and some purples—I never learned my flowers, other than sage, but I guess that doesn't really count, and there just beyond the vegetable patch, all fenced in with white picket like you'd see in a town, was a girl pinning washing to a line. She had her hair up just like the old woman's but this girl's was dark. I guessed her to be younger than me, but beyond being a girl by a few years. I put her at eighteen or twenty.

The old German's clean-shaven face scowled up at me like he'd caught me dosing his coffee with cinders. I tried a smile. "Your daughter?" Same look. Then he held a hand out like a plate in front of him and scooped up an imaginary version of what was drifting over from the little house—the most heavenly food smells that have ever entered a man's nose.

My Pap raised me and the other six and he was a good man but he was no cook. So when good food is on the stove, I am the first to walk toward it like I've been caught up in the mumbo-jumbo from one of them roving preachers. My eyes go wide and my nostrils flex of their own accord and it won't do but I have to eat right then and there. And I'll promise anything for a plateful of good, home-cooked food. The smells from that old woman's kitchen got me at the perfect time— perfectly wrong for me, dead-on right for the old folks and that girl.

That first night the only English out of them I heard was "Work" and "Eat". I reckoned those were two things I knew quite a bit about. There seemed no shortage of food to come out of that old woman's stove. Soon as my plate looked half empty, she'd come up behind me with her chunky arm brushing my head and ladle more stew and dumplings and pan-fry chicken onto my plate.

She was stern and had a mannish face under that knob of tight gray hair with two short sticks poking from it. And she had long lines coming down either side of her mouth like a talking doll I'd seen in a stage show once a few years back in El Paso.

But Lord could that old woman cook.

I was just tucking into my second glass of buttermilk—they kept a milk cow, thank God—and I noticed I'd missed scratching out all the dirt from under a couple of my fingers with my picket knife—the old lady insisted on a superior scrubbing before she'd let me into her kitchen to eat—when the girl walked through the room with a sewing basket. Her face didn't quite match the earlier promise of the back of her neck. I wouldn't go so far as to say ugly, but she was on the hard side. She had a pretty figure though. Filled out in all the right places and that dress looked to be almost painted on.

There was a line of little pearl buttons running from just under her throat right down the front of her and they all looked to be doing their job and then some in keeping things in order. Still, it was good to see someone closer to my own age. She smiled at me so shy and it helped her face. I set the glass down and nodded. If she was their child I doubt she knew any amount of English but I said, "Hello," and her mouth opened.

All I heard was a tapping sound and her eyes hardened like a cat's. Her whole face tightened and then she looked away. The old man was rapping a hard old claw finger on the oilcloth to get my attention. It worked. I heard the girl leave the room, that dressy swish you only ever hear when a woman's around.

I was about to toss my napkin on the plate and say, "Thanks for a fine meal," when the old lady set down in front of me a steaming wedge of apple pie with a thick crust browned just right. She didn't smile. He didn't change his look. His old claw hand was still resting on the table top where he'd been tapping it. Then that pie reached up and touched my nostrils and I sat back down. I would be gone soon anyway. Let them think what they needed to. And truly, the pie was worth it. God, but that old woman could cook. I've probably said that already.

After the pie I crossed the dark yard to a spot in the barn where there was a cot with a corn-shuck mattress that had more memory-of-shuck than shuck to it. I lay there in the dark, smoking a quirley—

167

nothing like a slow smoke after a good meal—and I thought of what brought me there.

Twelve years of bumping skins from one hot spot to another and next to nothing to show for it but my horse, Plug, and a few scraps of clothes; it finally wore me down. I decided to head north. It was an itch I'd wanted to scratch since I was a kid down along the border when we got that first snow of my life. I was twelve and I'll never forget it.

A passing friend of Pap's, some old-timer from all over, called what we got a dusting. Then he'd gone on to tell ol' wet me just how much snow places like Montana actually got. That decided me right there and then.

All them years later and I was finally ready to go, but I couldn't get any takers to join me. Not even my good friend, another saddle tramp name of Snapper. He'd been there and said it was nothing but "damn green hills". 'Course, he was there in the summer, but I knew I could probably handle whatever snow Montana had to offer me.

I didn't take a pack horse. I wanted the freedom of self reliance. Also I didn't own one. I reasoned I had enough money in my pocket to get there without working too hard—if I shied away from towns. That's about where I made my big mistake. I took what I thought would be a short cut away from all manner of civilized temptations. And that led me right off the path altogether.

I drifted to sleep that first night at the Germans' place thinking of a fine big snowstorm and me holed up in a warm line shack looking out a window at more snow than I ever could have dreamed of. I guess no one really wanted a line rider's job, but I did. Curse my thoughts, because they kept returning to that girl whose face was not one a man would call to mind in quiet moments. Though the rest of her made a fine memory.

On the morning of the eighth day the old man ranted at me in German. I expect the gist of it had to do with that girl because he kept wagging a finger at me and pointing to his eyes and then wagging some more as if to say he saw me. And then he'd say her name, "Marta," getting redder in the face all the while. I reckoned she was kept on a snug lead all her life.

Sad as it was, it wasn't any of my concern. I planned then and there to pull up stakes. They could find someone else willing to put up with their crazy ways.

That day the sun really put its shoulder to the wheel and I couldn't think of much else except how, if I ever lived through this job, I would never leave the back of my horse again. It was then, just as I pictured me and Plug working our way through chest-deep snowdrifts and not caring a lick, that I heard the German couple's old dog barking. I listened to it for a full minute and it almost sounded like it was getting closer.

And then I heard a snapping sound like someone sizing down old branches across a knee for a campfire. Or like back bacon crackling in a pan. Or gun shots. Then I saw something low and small, the dog maybe, in the heat waving up from the ground. I walked forward, craning my head and squinting as if that might help. Then it dawned on me I wasn't hearing the dog any more.

I pulled down the last of the water from the canteen and headed for whatever it was I saw. A few hundred yards from it I knew the dark spot I'd seen was the dog. It was laying there in the stubbly grass by the side of the cart track.

I knelt down, saying, "Hey, old girl. What's the problem here?" Her tail gave a weak wag and her front legs trembled and I saw in the dirt and grass beneath her old black and brown ribcage the earth was moist and dark. And a spot on her top side was wet, too.

Someone had shot that old dog. I patted her head and her bloodied tongue just lay there in the dust. She was gone. I stood and looked around me.

Because of the long, gentle roll of the land I could not see the house and barns from where I stood. Those snapping sounds had been gunfire. The dog looked to be hit once, maybe twice. But I'd heard a dozen or so snaps. What were the other shots for? I sucked in a deep breath and took off cross-fields at a slow run toward the ranch buildings. After ten or fifteen minutes I came to the brow of the second rise and made out the tops of the buildings in the distance.

Before I got there I guessed I would find an unfortunate scene. As I drew closer to the dooryard I saw no smoke from the kitchen chimney. And then I saw the old man. He lay on his side, the black boiled-wool suit bedeviled with dust. The shirt was still white around the neck and cuff with that big old claw of a hand angled upward like he was pointing. His hat had blown off across the yard and his eyes stared up at me. The white V of his shirtfront was the deepest red I had ever seen, darker around the four bullet holes between his chin and the top of the vest.

I cut my eyes toward the house. The front door was open but I couldn't see inside. The old woman and the girl would surely be holed up in there if they protected themselves from whoever did this.

I low-walked, half crawling on my knees right up to that damned white picket fence and pushed my way through the little gate. I scrambled through as fast as I could and rolled right into the little flowerbed before the porch, keeping as low as possible. There wasn't a sound to be heard from the house.

"In for a penny," I said in a low whisper, echoing what Snap usually said right before we crossed a river with a green herd. He was from England. A more confident or amusing bunch of people I have never found. Except maybe for the Irish. But it was a German family I was more concerned with at the moment.

I sort of rolled and dragged my way across the porch, intending to make it to the right of the door but upended the near rocker onto myself before flopping like a landed fish against the door. It opened wide and there on the kitchen floor not two feet from me was the old lady.

I lay still and heard a bubbling sound and looked to the stove, though I knew nothing was cooking. I leaned over toward the old lady.

She lay chest down but her back was a mess of wounds, the dress and apron all punched in and smoked around the holes. Shot from behind. Blood pooled beneath her.

Her eyelid fluttered like a moth wing and the bubbling noise came again. It was her breath. I leaned close to her and said, "It's going to be alright, ma'am. You'll be fine. I'm going to get you fixed up and fetch a doc." I said a lot of things and in truth I'm sure I promised to rope her the sun if it would help keep her from dying on me.

But she raised her head and fixed that eye on my face. She said, "Marta. . . . " in little more than a whisper. Then her head dropped to the floor and that eye glassed over.

I just nodded and said, "Yes, ma'am. I'll find her."

Three for three, so far. It didn't bode well for the girl. I backed away on my knees and it was then as I looked into the room that I noticed the long slick of blood that led from what I took to be the formal sitting room at the back corner of the house. The old lady was shot there and had dragged herself into the kitchen before losing the fight.

The place was a mess. Dishes were broken and one glass pane was shattered. Probably by a bullet. I found spent shells on the floor. I'd never been in any of the rooms but the kitchen, so it was all a guessing game. Looked to me like someone had robbed them. What I couldn't find was the girl.

I scrambled up the stairs, my little pocket knife open and ready to throw. Fat lot of good it would have done me. The blade's duller than my teeth. I only use it to saw through chaw and pick at my fingernails.

I whisper-shouted, "Marta! Marta!" but there was no response. There looked to be nothing amiss up there. Whoever had done this didn't bother to head up the stairs. I made my way back down the stairs and into the kitchen, careful not to step in the blood trail. It was a gruesome sight.

I'd seen men shot before, but never a woman, even if she was old and didn't look like she'd ever been pretty in all her days. Time will do that to a person, I reckon.

On my way out of the kitchen, between the table and the porch wall, I saw a scrap of cloth and what looked like a hundred little white pebbles scattered on the floor. I bent closer. The pebbles were the little pearl buttons I'd admired on Marta's dress front. The scrap of cloth had a button still attached, hanging limp from its thread like the head on a little dolly that's been loved too much. That scrap, little flowers on a sky-blue background, was the opposite of the dark blue of the old woman's dress. "Marta," I said aloud and stuffed the scrap into my back pocket. Then I noticed the old woman's blood seeping wide, slowly surrounding those buttons.

The nag still stood at the corral where the old man reined up after dropping me off that morning in the field. In the barn I found my gear unmolested and grabbed my gun belt, skinning knife, and cartridges from my war bag and gave one last look around. "Plug?" Nothing. And that horse is quick to respond if he thinks there's the chance of extra feed in it for him. In that respect the horse and I don't differ all that much.

I unhooked the nag from the buggy traces and slashed through several other straps that got in my way. I cut the reins short and jumped on bareback. No time for a saddle. That girl had been abducted and I knew it was up to me to find out who was behind this mess.

The trail was plain enough, right toward that great knob of rock in the distance. The same one that I should have stayed on the far side of more than a week before.

By the time I got to the base of the rocky knob the sun was drooping down dead ahead of me, lowering and growing more orange as it dipped. I rode part way around the base, enough to afford me a good long look in the direction opposite the rocks and away west, but I saw no one. As we picked our way among the rocks I found a decent spot to climb on up. It was almost a trail.

The old nag was in no condition to go anywhere but to sleep. So I slipped down off her. I swear I heard her sigh in relief. I patted her neck and let the reins trail. Whoever had the girl had probably come up this way. I'd start with the little mountain of rock and try to explore the likely hides of its upper reaches before the sun left me altogether.

I drew my Colt and climbed up the rocks as quietly as I knew how. I saw hoofprints pushed here and there into the gravel that made up stretches of the trail. And within a few minutes from the base I peered around a house-size boulder and saw Marta.

Her back was to me. She was kneeling on the ground with her shoulders exposed, the top half of her dress torn apart and hanging. Her dark hair fell down her back and over her shoulders. Beyond her I saw Plug's white blaze facing me. He nickered and Marta looked over her shoulder at me. Her eyes went wide and she put her hands in front of her chest.

"Are you alone?" I whispered. She stared at me for a few seconds. She nodded.

"Are you sure? Where did they go?"

She said, "He has gone."

They were the first words I heard her speak. There was an accent but it was English I heard.

"He?"

172

"It was the one man."

"Are you sure? I mean that he's gone?" I looked around, expecting to be jumped any second, and felt a fool for not bringing my Winchester. Haste will kill me one day, I remember thinking.

She nodded and made to stand. "Did he hurt you?" I holstered my pistol and held her by the shoulders. A trail of dried blood marked her bottom lip and chin and one side of her face was bright red as if slapped. Her eyes had the puffed look of someone who spent a good while crying.

"Are you hurt?"

She shook her head.

"Can you ride?"

She peered up at me and wiped at her eyes. "Why?"

"I need you to go back to the farm. I'm not sure if it's the best idea but I have to go after that killer. This won't stand, Marta."

Her eyes grew big again and she said, "No no. I cannot go back alone." She looked around and said, "It will be dark soon and you will be gone."

"It takes forever for the sun to set itself proper. I can at least figure out if he's gone off yet or not."

She came at me then, her dress top hanging half down, and she hit me pretty hard with her fists on my chest and arms. I grabbed her hands and said, "Whoa. Okay, okay. I'll figure out something else. Whoa there."

She calmed and sort of leaned against me. Pretty soon she started shivering so I let her sink back to the ground and I stripped off my work shirt, which was a dirty long underwear shirt with holes and frayed edges. But it was better than her tattered dress. I handed it to her but instead of putting it on she just held it in front of her and sat there. I sat next to her. Then she leaned against me and so I sort of patted her head a bit while she cried.

I don't know how long we were there like that but I guess we both fell asleep leaning against that boulder. It had been a long day in every way possible. It was coming on dark, too, by the time I woke up. It took a few seconds before it all came back to me.

"Marta."

No response. She was laid right on my chest, hugging me tight, her head just under my chin. I could feel that she didn't have my shirt on. And of course neither did I. "Marta, are you awake?"

"Yes."

"We need to get off this rock. We need to get going."

"Why." It wasn't a question. And at that moment I didn't know what to do.

She did, though. She started in patting me on the chest and before I knew it we were what you might call in a full embrace and from there, well I truly don't know how to explain it. Things just plain happened. And all the while I'm thinking it's the most wrong thing I've ever done. But there wasn't a thing I could do about it neither. One minute I'm shushing her, telling her I'd help her figure it all out, next minute . . . well, I guess I've covered that.

The biggest surprise came later when I was feeling around in the near-dark for my boots and such. Her voice cut through the quiet, closer to me than I thought she was.

"You have saved me. And now that we are married we must work the farm together."

I swear an arrow to the back wouldn't have stopped me faster. I had a handful of boot and a handful of gravel and I just sat there in the dark with her off to my left, still too close, and I said in a whisper that sounded a lot like Pap and not much like Pal, "Whoa, whoa, girl. What do you mean 'married'?" I swallowed and dropped the gravel but kept the boot. "We had us a time, for sure. Things just got out of hand. There's a world of hurt waiting on us back there and we need to tend to that right quick."

She didn't say anything so I kept on talking. "Far as I know marriage is a whole lot more'n what we did here." I jammed the boot on my foot and yarned on it.

"What do you mean?" she said.

"Well," I said, "like a piece of official paper, stamped and signed and all. That's for one."

She reached out across my legs, still naked, and handed me that other boot. Then she leaned near my face and gave me that smallest of smiles like that one time in the kitchen.

You know the gulping sound a stone makes in a still pool when you drop it from way up? Like the water was waiting for that particular rock all its life and now it's satisfied? I heard that sound in my head.

We sat there, quiet for a few minutes. It didn't occur to me until a long time after, that it takes an awful lot of stones to fill up a pool.

Well, sir, we made it back late that night and as soon as we got there she was a tearful wreck. She wouldn't come out of her room upstairs all that night and most of the next day. And I guess I couldn't blame her. I took care of all the necessary cleaning up. Though some of it I wished I had a little help from her or someone, I can tell you. Arranging the bodies and all. Certain things a man's just not suited for.

I can still see their faces. It's not so easy as you'd think, trying to close eyes and mouths that death has sneaked up on and left open, caught in a moment like that with nothing or no one telling them what to do any more. But I got used to it and did what I had to do. Then I went and got the dog. The old dear was where I'd left her. I did my best for her as well.

Dug three graves and laid them out. Then I got Marta. She brought along the family Bible and read over them in German. I didn't grasp a lick except the Amen. I got that part. I said it twice, figuring I'd need it before too long.

After I filled the graves in, I walked back to the house and made some coffee. She'd not laid out food or fired up the stove. So I tended to that. Carved some bread off an old loaf and fried up some bacon. I didn't have the strength for much else. She ate some, and while I poured more coffee I cleared my throat.

"Marta, I know it's a rough patch for you. But we need to report this to the law. A bad thing has happened here. Bad as it gets and somebody needs to know. I figure on saddling Plug and riding back to that town, what was it called, Irasburg? Isn't that the closest?"

She put her cup down and stared at me hard. I'd seen that look somewhere. She finally spoke. "We have too much to do to waste on such a journey. Who will feed the animals?" Then her face sort of softened and she said, "I cannot stay here alone." She covered her head with her arms and rocked back and forth in her seat. "What if he comes back?"

I set the pot on the stove and tried to comfort her. She calmed down after a bit and I figured I'd bring it up again in a few days.

It wasn't until later that I placed where I'd seen that hard look she gave me. It was on her mother's face every time I sat down at the table.

I spent my evenings in the barn and that suited me right down to the ground. I was doing my best to forget just what it was I had done up there on that damned rocky knob. Truth be told, I didn't think once about Montana all that week. I was too tired.

What with milking that little scoop-face Jersey, tending the chickens, feeding the beeves, two hogs, and the young cattle, trying to figure out the crop situation, tending the garden, plus cooking, even the laundry, why I was dog-tired all the time. I never even made it back out to setting posts, which was just dandy with me.

It was about a week later—I can't be dead sure because as I say I was worn to half a frazzle—the sheriff rode up. I was between the barn and house, a pail of warm milk in one hand, a basket of eggs in the other, and he was already in the yard. Surprised me.

"Howdy," I said, seeing the faint reflection off his badge. I felt relief. He would solve all my problems. And I was grateful for the distraction from the chores.

"Howdy," he said. He was a shortish man, on the young side of old. Big moustaches like Pap favored. I never could get one to grow so it looked decent. It's my ginger hair. Too fair for a full set of whiskers.

"Step on down," I said. I set the pail and the basket on the ground and walked over to meet him. He sat a black horse, big with a white blaze on his forehead. Handsome animal.

"I'm Ernie Palchik. Friends call me Pal." I offered my hand and we shook.

"Muncey. Sheriff Muncey. Olga and Otto here?"

"Who?" I said, then it occurred to me. The old folks. "If you mean the old German couple, well, there's been some mighty misfortune here, sheriff. We can have some coffee and I'll explain it all."

He didn't move, except to put his hands on his hips. Then he scowled and said, "I guess you'll tell me whatever it is I need to know and right here. I know the Schnellings well. Olga and Otto and their daughter, Marta. Where are they?"

176

His tone served to open up the sky a bit for me and odd as it sounds I looked at the situation for the first time from a point of view that wasn't mine. And I didn't like what I was looking at.

Then Marta stepped from the kitchen into the shade of the porch. Sheriff Muncey said, "Marta, there you are. Mr. Peel at the bank sent me. Your father didn't meet his payment. We guessed something was wrong." He looked at me, then back to her.

She stepped down from the porch into the sunlight. I hardly knew her. Her face was red along one side, her lip bleeding, hair a mess, and her dress front torn open. She ran out, sobbing, right past me to the sheriff. I swore I smelled onions. Hell, I smelled a rat.

In between sobs we got her whole story. "He . . . he keeps me here." She pointed at me. "He shot my parents. And my dog, Lela. . . . "

The sheriff patted her shoulders and offered her his coat. I just stood there with my mouth wide, catching Texas flies.

"What's he done to you, Marta? You tell me now." Muncey spoke to her in a stern voice. I could see his jaw muscles working and he looked at me like he'd just caught me with a trick deck up my sleeve.

"This just ain't the truth, sheriff!" I tried but he wasn't having any of it.

"He raped me and told me to keep quiet or he would kill me, too."

"That's a lie, sheriff! Someone did those things, but I never! She's confused. Heck, I been doing all the work here, trying to convince her to go for the law all along. She worked her womanly ways on me. I had nothing to do with it."

The sheriff was pretty quiet and so was Marta. She'd stopped crying and was hugging his coat tight. It didn't take me long to realize I should shut my trap and right quick.

Finally Muncey spoke. "Mister, I've known this girl all her life and I've never met you. What makes you think I might believe a single word you have to say?"

Well, he put handcuffs on me and hooked me to the corral rail. Plug nudged me for feed. Sheriff came out of the barn with my Winchester and a little scrap of blue cloth with a button attached. He sniffed at the Winchester and noted how it had been fired hard in the not-too-distant past and not cleaned. He just held up the cloth and shook his head.

177

My Winchester. I'd not so much as touched it since I arrived at the little damn farm. But someone had. He stared at me a minute then went to the house.

There's not much to tell about the rest of that day or the next. Muncey stuck me, still handcuffed, on that old nag, though I swore to blue heaven Plug was my horse and there'd be hell to pay if I wasn't allowed my own horse to ride. Marta just stood there and shook her head no when the sheriff asked her if I was telling the truth.

So I rode to Irasburg with the sheriff. I tried for the first few hours to explain my situation to him. Finally he drew on me and told me to keep my mouth shut and save it for the district judge. Which is what I did. And now here I am at the federal penitentiary at Fort Barr counting on less than two full hands the days left to me before I swing.

In the end I got nothing out of my big adventure north but a full belly, a flat bed, and a hollow heart. Whatever it was that happened at that little ranch happened more or less right under my own nose. But I guess I chose not to see it. And now here I am, the clock on this life of mine ticking down.

I will say this cot ain't half as hard as the one at the farm. At least here I find I can close my eyes and think of Montana. Me and Plug riding through snow so white it's almost blue and pretty soon that snow's up over Plug's head and he doesn't mind one bit. He's still running through it, heading toward mountains that never get any closer but always look so majestic.

And the snow keeps rising and I let go the reins and reach out to sort of swim my way through it and find it's not snow at all. It's millions of tiny pearl buttons. And pretty soon they're over my head and I can't see or feel a thing save for those buttons all around me and they're filling my throat and mouth and I can't wake up.

HARD TIMES FOR THE PECOS KID
Lee Pierce

Born and raised in Texas, Lee Pierce grew up on small farms and ranches where he learned to appreciate the land. He has held numerous jobs but writing is his passion. His first Western novel, Armstrong's War, *was published in 2005 by Robert Hale Publishing. He lives in Dos Caballos, New Mexico, USA.*

"Son of a bitch," said the startled man looking down at the two tiny holes in his bright red Saturday-night-on-the-town shirt. He raised his head to look at who had ruined his new shirt. The hombre stood a few feet away, a six-shooter smoking in his hand.

"Son of a bitch," he said again and fell back against the bar. His knees buckled and he slid to the floor.

The shooter, a slender young man around five and a half feet tall, ejected two spent cartridges from his revolver and replaced them with fresh loads. His dark eyes roamed the silent barroom, staring hard at any man who dared make eye contact.

"My name is Billy Shortridge," he announced. "I just shot the famous shootist, Curley Bassham, to doll rags. That makes me the fastest gun in Pecos County, Texas, so I reckon you boys can call me The Pecos Kid."

Billy paused a moment to let that sink in, and then he continued. "Is there anybody in this saloon that don't agree with anything I just said?"

The place was quiet as a whorehouse on Sunday morning.

Billy strode over to the dead man's body. He reached down and fumbled through his victim's pockets. What money he found he placed on top of the bar. He unbuckled the worn gun belt and jerked it from around the dead man's waist. A bone handled .36 Navy revolver still rested in the holster. Billy wrapped the gun belt around itself and placed it next to the money on the bar.

"Bartender," said Billy, "how much money will you give me for this here shootin' rig?"

The barkeep gave the rig a once over. "I could give you, maybe, $20 for it," he said. "That'd be about it."

"I'll take it." Billy turned to face the dozen or so patrons of the saloon. "That twenty, along with the twenty-seven bucks Curley don't need anymore, will buy a right smart passel of drinks for anybody who wants to have a snort with The Pecos Kid."

A few men spoke up in the affirmative. One man, who was about the kid's height but fifty pounds heavier with a round red face, stepped out of the crowd and ambled up to Billy. He stuck out his right hand.

Billy hesitated, not moving his gun hand away from his six-shooter. The fat man lowered his right hand and stuck out his left. Billy took the offered hand and gave it a brief shake.

"I'd be right proud to drink with anyone who can sling iron like you," said the fat man, smiling. "Come on boys. What do you say? Are y'all gonna join us at the bar or not?"

The crowd immediately relaxed and began to buzz like bees in a hive about the gunfight as they bellied up to the bar. Some of them patted Billy on the back and mumbled their congratulations.

The small bar quickly filled up with freeloaders jostling each other for a free drink. Amos Quisenberry, the fat man, stayed right next to Billy. The body of the recently deceased was dragged into a corner to make more room at the bar. Ol' Nichols, the saloon swamper, settled in at the feet of the dead man. He commenced to pry off the corpse's boots, hoping to God they would fit him. His were so holey they barely qualified as footwear. With a little luck the shirt and pants would fit him too. The blood would wash out and a needle and some red thread could make the shirt look good as new.

Billy beamed at the adulation being heaped upon him. He'd always wanted to be a known gunfighter. Hell, fast as he was, it was his destiny.

As the whiskey and beer flowed freely, Amos kept it up at the kid's ear, going on about what a fine privilege it was to be in the presence of such a soon-to-be-famous man. All the while he was drinking more than his share of free liquor and watching the bartender out of the corner of his eye. When it looked like the drink money was dwindling down, Amos cleared his throat.

" 'Scuse me there, Jim," he said to the bartender in a loud voice. "About how much of that blood money is left? Us fellers appreciate the Pecos Kid's hospitality and we don't want to drink up any more than there is money to pay for it."

A chorus of agreement rippled through the room.

"Mr. Kid," Amos said looking as serious as he could with that ripe tomato face of his. "We all are surely obliged to you for sponsoring this here fandango and there ain't a soul in here who wouldn't be honored to buy you a drink tonight."

Billy nodded his head and smiled his most benevolent smile.

"Only thing is, Mr. Kid, most of us ain't worked in a mighty long spell. With the mines closed down and the ranches around here havin' more hands than they know what to do with, well, dang it, sir, there just ain't no jobs to be had and we got no money."

Billy got a puzzled look on his face but remained silent. He had no idea where this great glob of an idiot was going with his gibberish. It was time to hit the trail, anyway. He had a reputation to uphold.

Looking like he was about to retch and cry at the same time, Amos ignored the kid's befuddlement and blabbered on.

"Just so's you know, we all been quite some time down on our luck and we want you to understand how much this little drinkfest has meant to us."

The smile reappeared on Billy's face. What a sorry bunch of whiners he had shared his money with. He decided it was time to blow this one-horse town and prepared to say *adios* when the full-winded Amos started up again.

Amos motioned for Billy to lower his head. In a voice barely above a whisper, he spoke into Billy's right ear. "Mr. Kid, you been so good to us I hate to have to tell you this, but you deserve to know the truth."

"What truth?"

Amos cleared his throat.

"Now, most of these ol' boys in here are okay fellers, but they ain't real bright. They done spent most of their time underground diggin' whatever there was to dig. They work, spend their money on whiskey and whores, and work some more. It's a sad thing but it's all they know. Myself, I've been a sight more fortunate than these men. I've traveled some and seen the elephant more'n once."

Amos paused, took a deep breath, and let it out in one long, drawn-out sigh.

"What are you getting at, old timer?" said Billy, impatience filling his voice.

"Well, Mr. Kid, the fact is the man you killed ain't Curley Bassham."

Billy dropped the mug he was holding in his left hand. It hit the bar, bounced once and shot beer into the air. Ignoring the mess he stared at Amos.

"Naw, that ain't right," he said. "I seen him before. I killed Curley Bassham."

"You killed his little brother, Punt. They look nearly alike but poor old dead Punt wasn't right in the head. He tried to act like his big brother, but he weren't no gunman. Hell, I never even seen him pull his iron on another man. Truth is, I don't think he could."

Billy's mind began to jump around like a turpentined cat. "No, that can't be right," he said in a quiet tone. "The man I killed was Curley Bassham, the fastest gun in this part of Texas."

"Son," said Amos, sounding real fatherly, "you killed Punt Bassham who never harmed a livin' soul. And the worst of it is you done shot him down in cold blood. You murdered him."

A wild-eyed look came over Billy's face and he began to squirm like a beaver in a trap. Sweat dripped off his nose and puddled on the bar.

"There's two other things you need to know, Mr. Kid." Amos's round, red face softened to a rosy pink. "The first thing is that ol' Punt was Curley's favorite brother. The second thing is I've seen the real Curley handle a six-shooter and you ain't a flyspeck on a horse's ass compared to the man. Yes, sir, I 'spect when he finds out about what you done he's gonna hunt you down like a hydrophoby dog."

"I ain't afraid of him," said Billy looking none too sincere.

"Oh, I know you ain't," said Amos. "We all seen with our own eyes that you're just about fearless."

The fear in Billy's eyes contradicted Amos's last statement. He was scared silly. What the crowd in the saloon didn't know was that he almost didn't go through with the gunfight. Once he had called Bassham out, he wanted desperately to turn and run out of the saloon. All those days practicing shooting at cans and tree limbs hadn't prepared him to face a man who could shoot back. If he could find a way out of this fix, he would do it in a heartbeat.

Amos must have been reading the kid's mind. "Say, there, young'un, you sure are sweatin' a barrelful. Are you alright?"

"Uh, yeah, I'm okay," mumbled Billy. "It's just a little hot in here and, besides that, I just killed a man."

"You sure done that, *amigo*," bellowed Amos, slapping Billy on the back. "Well, Mr. Kid, I reckon we best be gettin' over to the hotel and findin' you a room."

"A room! What for?"

"Curley will be gunnin' for you and you won't get no rest 'til you face him and shoot it out. Might as well wait for him here and when he shows up get it over with."

"But, I was plannin' to move on today." Billy was trembling now. It took what little nerve he had left to keep him from running out the door and riding away.

Once again it seemed Amos was one step ahead of him.

"Of course," said Amos scratching his face with fat stubby fingers, "there might be another way, but I doubt a man like you would want to take it."

"What way?"

"You could skedaddle out of here right now and us fellers, bein' grateful for your generosity and all, could make up a big ol' whopper. We could tell Curley some big, ugly, scar-face varmint shot Punt, and then forked his bronc and rode west, hell for leather."

Billy stood silent for a moment. "I don't think I can do that," he said somberly. "I shot the man's brother and I reckon I have to take my medicine."

"Suit yourself," said Amos. "You won't have long to wait. Curley's due in town in about an hour. He's supposed to meet his brother here."

"In about an hour?" Billy said, owl-eyed.

"Uh huh, maybe less."

All at once, the thought of toiling away on his daddy's farm didn't sound too bad. Billy made a snap decision. "Mr. Quisenberry," he said, "I'm taking your advice and I'm going back home, but you have to give me your word not to tell Curley Bassham I killed his brother."

An odd twinkle flashed across Amos's eyes and his round face broke out into a broad grin. "Mr. Kid. I give you my word Curley Bassham will never hear your name."

"I'm obliged to you," said Billy.

"It's the least I can do for the Pecos Kid." Amos slapped Billy's back again.

"There ain't no more Pecos Kid," said Billy. "From now on I'm just plain Billy Shortridge, brown dirt farmer."

"Farmers don't wear no gunfighter's rigs," said Amos, winking at the bartender. "You best leave that outfit with me for safe keepin'."

"But I saved up a year to buy this six-gun and holster," Billy protested.

"All right," said Amos frowning, "but I can't guarantee somebody won't see you leavin' town with that rig on and squeal to Curley. He's a pretty smart feller. Might put two and two together and come up with who really shot Punt."

Billy rubbed his sweating hands together. "Okay, I reckon you're right. But how am I gonna get my money back for my rig?"

"We'll keep it here in the saloon until the trouble blows over. Then you can ride back and claim it."

"I don't know about that." Billy began to waver on his decision to run away before the real Curley Bassham rode into town. He wasn't sure he would ride this way again and the gun rig had set him back a pretty penny.

All of a sudden, Amos Quisenberry hollered. "Dang it! I thought I just heard somebody whisper they saw Curley ridin' into town from the west."

Billy jumped like he'd been blasted with double-ought buckshot. He shucked his gun belt and disappeared out the saloon doors in a dead run. In a moment, hoofbeats clattered on the hardscrabble street, rapidly fading into the east.

"Whoo-ee," spouted Amos, "that boy can flat out run when he has to. I don't recollect ever seein' nobody move that fast before."

"Somethin' else, too," said Jim the bartender drawing a fresh beer and setting it in front of Amos. "I never saw anybody pull iron any faster than that boy, either."

Amos nodded his head. "Say, Jim, how many drinks can we get for this here gunfightin' rig?" He laid the six-gun and holster on the bar.

"Now, Amos," said Jim. "I already traded for one outfit today. I ain't sure I can afford another one."

"Look at it this way, Jim. You'll own both gun rigs. Shucks, I bet you can charge folks two bits a piece to get a look at 'em."

"You think so?"

"Why sure. Just think of it. You'll have two gunfighters' rigs to show; one that belonged to Curley Bassham and the other that belonged to the mysterious stranger who plugged him. Shucks, Jim, it'll probably make this ol' saloon famous."

Amos smiled and handed the gun belt to Jim, who placed it under the bar next to the other one.

"Okay," said Jim, "two drinks for everybody, and remember I'll be countin'."

"I'll take a beer and a shot of whiskey," said Amos.

Leaning against the bar, he looked toward the corpse in the corner and watched Ol' Nichols clomping around in new boots. The dead man's shirt and pants dangled across his bony shoulders.

"Hey there," said Amos, "a couple of you boys help get rid of that stinkin' body. I swear, as bad as Curley Bassham smelled when he was alive, he smells a heap worse when he's dead."

CALLING ALL WESTERN FANS:

*If you like what you've read here, be sure to visit the following
Websites for more Old West action:*

The Official Home of Black Horse Westerns:
www.halebooks.com

*The Official Watering Hole of Black Horse Western Writers
on the Web*:
groups.yahoo.com/group/blackhorsewesterns

The Black Horse Express:
www.blackhorsewesterns.org

For more information on future EXPRESS WESTERNS publications:
www.expresswesterns.com

*And don't forget to request the best in Western storytelling
at your local libraries and book stores.*

*Keep a sharp eye on the horizon—
EXPRESS WESTERNS will be back in 2008!*